PRELUDE & OTHER STORIES

KATHERINE MANSFIELD

PRELUDE & OTHER STORIES

Edited and Introduced by
MEG JENSEN

MACMILLAN COLLECTOR'S LIBRARY

This collection first published 2021 by Macmillan Collector's Library
an imprint of Pan Macmillan
The Smithson, 6 Briset Street, London EC1M 5NR
EU representative: Macmillan Publishers Ireland Limited,
Mallard Lodge, Lansdowne Village, Dublin 4
Associated companies throughout the world
www.panmacmillan.com

ISBN 978-1-5290-4560-4

1 3 5 7 9 8 6 4 2

A CIP catalogue record for this book is available from the British Library.

Casing design and endpaper pattern by Andrew Davidson
Typeset by Jouve (UK), Milton Keynes
Printed and bound in China by Imago

Visit www.panmacmillan.com to read more
about all our books and to buy them.

Contents

Introduction

MEG JENSEN

'Don't lower your mask until you have another mask prepared beneath – as terrible as you like – but a mask.'

*Katherine Mansfield, letter to John
Middleton Murry, July 1917*

Writing should *seem* to reveal, but that *seeming* must itself be a carefully crafted mask. In this advice Katherine Mansfield once offered to her soon-to-be husband, we find the key rhetorical figure of Mansfield's own fiction: an ironic and yet deeply serious play between masking and unmasking, revelation and reticence, public and private. For Mansfield, the creation of such masks to disguise terrible truths is a central performative ritual, revelatory of human character. But today, more than one hundred summers after Mansfield wrote that letter to Murry, as I sit in the newly reopened London library, with one cloth mask across my face and a clean one in my bag, her warning takes on another, starker, meaning.

While I have researched, taught and published on Mansfield's works for decades, suddenly I find a new, heightened relevance for both her central trope of the mask, and for the figure of Katherine Mansfield herself: a writer both witty and wary, compassionate and cruel, a colonial immigrant with no fixed abode, a woman with chronic ill health and compromised immunity, forced into isolation during a global viral pandemic, a lonely figure longing for friendship and passion while needing to safeguard her fragile health and precarious income. Mansfield speaks startlingly and poignantly to us right now.

For Mansfield, as for contemporary society, a reliance on masks is more than a useful metaphor. Like the short story form itself, the mask articulates something vital about the way in which an individual navigates his or her role in a fractured, fractious and potentially deadly society. When worn, a mask is simultaneously a sign of safety and of disease, it shows one's sensitivity to others while also precluding intimacy and communication, both protecting and troubling the boundaries of public and private. Like the very best short stories, masks are a symbolic and literal expression of the solitude of every life. This collection includes those of Mansfield's stories that best exemplify the power of the short story form in a dangerous and isolating world to enlighten and confuse, to amuse and to break hearts, to lift one mask only to expose the other lying beneath. While such moments of unmasking correlate to some extent with what James Joyce called 'epiphanies' and Virginia Woolf 'moments of being', in Mansfield's short stories climactic events do not serve as revelatory encounters with difficult hidden truths, but rather as episodes that enable a character to develop other more complex and self-deluding narratives; in key moments in Mansfield's fiction, her characters turn away from difficult truths, forging new myths to justify their selfish and/or cowardly behaviour.

As critic Kate Fulbrook rightly observes, Mansfield's stories concern the 'terror at the clash between the self that exists in its masked and inauthentic form and the vulnerable, confused and unstructured self beneath the mask.' This terror is usually ethical in nature and was likely informed by her extensive reading of Anton Chekhov, who was in turn indebted to the works of Nikolai Gogol. In Gogol's *The Overcoat* (1842), we find not only an elegant rendering of the consequences of a moment of unmasking but also perhaps the origin of the ethical terror that haunts the works of Chekhov, Mansfield and the short story writers who followed them. Gogol's story concerns the poor clerk Akaky Akakievitch, who is cruelly mocked by his co-workers for his shabby, threadbare overcoat. Akakievitch struggles to buy a new one which is then stolen, bringing about a chain of events which end in his tragic death.

Near the end of the tale, however, Gogol tells us of one young man, 'new to the office', who joins in to jeer at Akakievitch until his 'compassion' is suddenly roused and the young man sees 'how much inhumanity there is in man.' Gogol notes that 'from that day forth everything was, as it were, changed, and appeared in a different light to him.' In that moment, it seems, some vital truth has been unmasked. And yet, the young man does nothing to help Akakievitch: the 'humble clerk' dies in ignominy. The mask of polite society is indeed lifted, but this revelation has no beneficent effect. It simply creates another, more terrible mask, one born not of ignorance but of wilful delusion, or what we might call 'virtue signalling'. Rather than take action, the young man simply 'hid his face in his hands'. And 'many times later in life', Gogol tells us, when the young man reflected on that day 'he shuddered', and in doing so wears a mask to hide his ethical terror, publicly signalling a 'woke' sympathy that consoles him for his private failure.

Interestingly, the figure of 'Katherine Mansfield' was

itself a kind of mask: she was born Kathleen Mansfield Beauchamp in Wellington, New Zealand on 14 October 1888, the third daughter of five surviving children of prosperous businessman Harold Beauchamp and his wife Anne Burrell. When Kathleen was five years old, the family moved to rural Karori, later the setting for many of her stories. In 1903, Kathleen and her elder sisters were sent to school in London and her travels in Europe introduced her, as Mansfield's biographer Claire Tomalin notes, to exciting glimpses of 'the *vie de bohème*'. Restless upon her return to New Zealand in 1906 and determined to get back to Europe, Mansfield created a bohemian life of her own, conducting dramatic affairs with both men and women and publishing short stories under the name *K. Mansfield*. In 1908, perhaps because of her flamboyant behaviour, Mansfield's parents allowed her to return to London, granting a small yearly allowance. She never went back to New Zealand, except in her fiction.

In London, she moved in with school friend Ida Baker, who became a lifelong devotee, nursemaid, companion and scapegoat. By early 1909, however, Mansfield's affair with musician Garnet Trowell had led to an unwanted pregnancy, heartbreak, a quickly arranged and immediately abandoned marriage to singing teacher George Bowden, the sudden arrival and intervention of Katherine's mother who whisked her pregnant daughter off to a spa in Bavaria and, finally, a painful miscarriage. It was while recovering in Bavaria that Mansfield first read Chekhov and by 1910, encouraged by Bowden with whom she remained on speaking terms, she began publishing her stories in the *New Age*. Soon her collection *In a German Pension* appeared, which included a story she plagiarized from Chekhov,

'The Child-who-was-Tired'. The plagiarism was recognized by relatively few contemporary readers (though Mansfield feared its discovery for the rest of her life) and the volume was widely read and well-received, bringing her to the attention of the young editor of a new literary magazine called *Rhythm*: John Middleton Murry.

Murry immediately became her collaborator, on-off lover and eventually her second husband. Mansfield and Murry befriended numerous London literary figures, most notably D. H. Lawrence, who would later include a Mansfield-like character in *Women in Love* (1920). Her friendship with Virginia Woolf has also been much written about and while Woolf's journals often voiced her envy of other writers' successes, she confessed in her diary that Mansfield's 'was the only *writing* I have ever been jealous of'. Indeed, Woolf's complex relations with Mansfield may have inspired the needy character Doris Kilman in *Mrs Dalloway* (1925), written shortly after Mansfield's death: at the end of Woolf's novel, Kilman pleads pathetically, 'Don't quite forget me'. This same unusual and beseeching phrase appeared in a letter to Woolf in June of 1917, which Mansfield signed, '& don't quite forget Katherine.'

Other literary contemporaries who admired Mansfield's work included Bertrand Russell, Lytton Strachey and Leonard Woolf, who championed her as 'an intense realist with a superb sense of ironic humour.' Soon, however, financial and physical calamities arose. In 1913, *Rhythm* collapsed and Mansfield became ill with what was finally diagnosed in 1917 as tuberculosis. She never fully regained her health and for the subsequent nine years of her life Mansfield travelled, often alone, other times with Ida Baker, Murry or other lovers, moving from flat to flat, seaside to mountain-top and country to country, searching for a cure that never materialized. Despite chronic physical, emotional and economic pressure, Mansfield kept writing, publishing reviews for the *Athenaeum* and the remarkable stories that formed her second collection *Bliss* (1920), further establishing her reputation. A third collection, *The Garden Party*, was published in 1922 and, though written in the face of debilitating symptoms and constant relocations, nevertheless contained some of her finest work, including 'The Daughters of the Late Colonel', which the novelist Thomas Hardy singled out for praise.

After a final desperate attempt at recovery at an experimental retreat near Fontainebleau, run by Russian-Armenian mystic George Gurdjieff, Mansfield died on 9 January 1923 at the age of thirty-four. She left behind a legacy of publications distinguished by clarity, economy, wit and compassion. She also left much unpublished and unfinished work, commanding Murry to 'publish as little as possible and to tear up and burn as much as possible.' As Tomalin notes, however, 'Murry edited and published almost all her remaining stories and fragments' including two additional volumes of short stories (*The Dove's Nest* in 1923 and *Something Childish* in 1924) and 'her journals, her poems, her reviews, and her letters', making a 'good income' and servicing a growing Mansfield fandom. Murry's selective editing of these, moreover, served to create yet another mask: a mythical, sanitized version of Mansfield that removed all evidence of her petty jealousies, mood swings and promiscuity.

But, in reshaping Mansfield as a tragic heroine, Murry singularly misrepresented the nature of her vision. As Frank O'Connor has noted, from Gogol to

Alice Munro, the short story form has 'never had a hero'. Instead, it concerns what he terms a 'submerged population group' from 'Turgenev's serfs' to 'Maupassant's prostitutes' all of whom dream in vain of escape. In her life as in her art, Mansfield was likewise concerned with the struggle of the 'submerged', those who, like her, had hope but little luck, and she regarded them through three distinct literary lenses.

The first of these is the lens of *Innocence and Corruption*. Mansfield's stories dramatize the collaboration between 'victim and victimizer who are caught in a cycle of self-falsification', according to Fulbrook. This same cycle continues today as widespread protests target monuments to victors that ignore the history of their victims, and the gig economy wrests economic and psychological control from the vulnerable and hands it to the powerful and prosperous. I begin this collection with 'The Doll's House', a story that is both a perfect encapsulation of innocence versus corruption, and, in my view, a perfect short story. The 'exquisite', 'too marvellous' and 'too much' doll's house of the title belongs to the wealthy Burnell family, who invite only the worthiest children in town to view it. This does not include the Kelvey girls, Lil and Else, who 'were shunned by everybody'. Many of Mansfield's short stories address just such poisonous social relations from the perspective of the innocent, whether the dreamily naive cafe worker Sabina in 'At Lehmann's', vulnerable to the predatory advances of a handsome customer, or the absurd yet sympathetic spinster sisters in 'The Daughters of the Late Colonel', who, raised to have no will of their own, struggle with their new responsibilities and freedom after the Colonel's death, fearing even to bury him without his permission.

The second group of stories in this collection gathers those of Mansfield's stories that dramatize key moments of disappointment, betrayal and bitter revelation in relation to love, romance, marriage and its aftermath. O'Connor observes that because the form requires 'a whole lifetime' to be 'crowded into a few minutes' the short story writer must accurately identify the single dramatic moment that will incorporate and represent, for example, 'the whole sordid story' of a 'romance and its tragic ending'. The stories in this section, *Love à la Mode*, do just that, and while this title hints at the irony suffusing many of these tales, it is also an acknowledgement of their contemporary relevance. In a world where carefully curated, if not blatantly false, digital selves lead to romantic encounters, these stories warn of the dangers of trusting one's heart to self-serving facades. In the unfinished story 'Mr. and Mrs. Williams', for example, a waspish narrator introduces a newly married couple who live 'at The Rowans, Wickenham, Surrey' and the necessities of their lives: 'golf, bridge, a summer holiday at the sea and an account at Harrods'. But dull Mr. and Mrs. Williams appear to have evolved into embittered, secretive spouses Isabel and William in Mansfield's later story 'Marriage à la Mode.' This couple are likewise ensconced in a comfortable suburban life, but while William longs for his busy wife's attention and 'exquisite freshness', Isabel is silently horrified by her husband's 'sentimentality', preferring the company of her sarcastic and urbane friends.

Further heartbreak, cruelty and secrecy are dramatized in other stories; a betrayed wife's misreading of her own feelings in 'Bliss', a single woman's furtive conversations with a doctor in 'This Flower' and the seedy relations between the odious Frenchman Raoul

Duquette, feckless English tourist Dick Harmon and his naive girlfriend, Mouse, who sums up her vulnerability by confessing 'Je ne parle Pas Français'.

In our current climate of self-isolation and social distancing, Mansfield's representations of alienation are both painfully contemporary and heartrendingly accurate. But they also speak to a wider social phenomenon of disenfranchisement, displacement, migration, ageing populations and shrinking marriage rates. The final group of stories here, gathered under the title *The Lonely Voice*, are those which best exemplify what Frank O'Connor calls the emblematic concern of the short story form: 'an intense awareness of human loneliness'. In stories such as 'Germans at Meat' and 'The Baron', Mansfield illustrates the isolation of a stranger in a strange land: from the pressure of being the sole representative of one's culture to minor linguistic misunderstandings and the barriers these form to friendship. Loneliness is not only the lot of the foreigner in Mansfield's stories, however. In works such as 'Miss Brill', 'Mr. Reginald Peacock's Day' and 'The Fly', retired tutors, socially ambitious musicians and silently grieving businessmen alike are shown as essentially living in solitude with their dreams, delusions and suffering, like the figures Miss Brill watches in the Jardins Publiques: 'odd, silent, nearly all old', who look 'as though they'd just come from dark little rooms'.

'Prelude', the final story in this collection, is Mansfield's longest and arguably finest work. It weaves together her characteristic concerns and considerable gifts, encompassing representations of victors and victims, innocence and corruption, romance and bitterness, the absurd isolation of the human soul and the equally ridiculous but also poignant acrobatics used to hide from the truth of that solitude. Mansfield began writing this heavily autobiographical story, set in the colonial New Zealand of her childhood, soon after the death of her younger brother Leslie in 1915. Leslie was killed while conducting grenade training in France, shortly after visiting her in London. In a journal entry, written as if to her late brother, Mansfield noted, 'I want to write a kind of long elegy to you – perhaps not in poetry. No. Perhaps in Prose.' Between 1915 and 1917, that prose elegy developed from a commemoration of Leslie to a tale told mainly through the eyes of the Mansfield-like child Kezia, and ends shortly before the birth of the baby who will grow up to be Leslie – forming a *prelude* to her lost brother's life. The inevitability of forthcoming tragedy, however, is hinted at in 'Prelude''s final scene in which the young Kezia faces a mirror but refuses to look at her reflection. Instead, feeling 'hot all over', Kezia steps down from the dressing table and 'tiptoed away, far too quickly and airily . . .', defiantly avoiding a tragic ending by leaving the final sentence unreconciled and incomplete.

'Prelude' was to become the first work published by the Woolfs' new Hogarth Press, its type set by Virginia herself, and appeared in July 1918 at the start of the Spanish flu pandemic and not long after Mansfield's diagnosis of tuberculosis. Like all of Mansfield's work, therefore, it takes tragic private and public concerns and shapes them into something wondrous, accurate, painful and beautiful. Here, as elsewhere, Katherine Mansfield offers her readers a generous act of artistic unmasking and also of self-preservation, deftly dramatizing a moment when everything could potentially change, before cleverly tiptoeing away, 'far too quickly and airily . . .'

INNOCENCE AND CORRUPTION

THE DOLL'S HOUSE

When dear old Mrs. Hay went back to town after staying with the Burnells she sent the children a doll's house. It was so big that the carter and Pat carried it into the courtyard, and there it stayed, propped up on two wooden boxes beside the feed-room door. No harm could come to it; it was summer. And perhaps the smell of paint would have gone off by the time it had to be taken in. For, really, the smell of paint coming from that doll's house ("Sweet of old Mrs. Hay, of course; most sweet and generous!")—but the smell of paint was quite enough to make anyone seriously ill, in Aunt Beryl's opinion. Even before the sacking was taken off. And when it was . . .

There stood the doll's house, a dark, oily, spinach green, picked out with bright yellow. Its two solid little chimneys, glued on to the roof, were painted red and white, and the door, gleaming with yellow varnish, was like a little slab of toffee. Four windows, real windows, were divided into panes by a broad streak of green. There was actually a tiny porch, too, painted yellow, with big lumps of congealed paint hanging along the edge.

But perfect, perfect little house! Who could possibly mind the smell. It was part of the joy, part of the newness.

"Open it quickly, someone!"

The hook at the side was stuck fast. Pat prised it open

3

with his penknife, and the whole house front swung back, and—there you were, gazing at one and the same moment into the drawing-room and dining-room, the kitchen and two bedrooms. That is the way for a house to open! Why don't all houses open like that? How much more exciting than peering through the slit of a door into a mean little hall with a hat-stand and two umbrellas! That is—isn't it?—what you long to know about a house when you put your hand on the knocker. Perhaps it is the way God opens houses at the dead of night when He is taking a quiet turn with an angel . . .

"Oh-oh!" The Burnell children sounded as though they were in despair. It was too marvellous; it was too much for them. They had never seen anything like it in their lives. All the rooms were papered. There were pictures on the walls, painted on the paper, with gold frames complete. Red carpet covered all the floors except the kitchen; red plush chairs in the drawing-room, green in the dining-room; tables, beds with real bed-clothes, a cradle, a stove, a dresser with tiny plates and one big jug. But what Kezia liked more than anything, what she liked frightfully, was the lamp. It stood in the middle of the dining-room table, an exquisite little amber lamp with a white globe. It was even filled all ready for lighting, though, of course, you couldn't light it. But there was something inside that looked like oil and moved when you shook it.

The father and mother dolls, who sprawled very stiff as though they had fainted in the drawing-room, and their two little children asleep upstairs, were really too big for the doll's house. They didn't look as though they belonged. But the lamp was perfect. It seemed to smile at Kezia, to say, "I live here." The lamp was real.

★

The Burnell children could hardly walk to school fast enough the next morning. They burned to tell everybody, to describe, to—well—to boast about their doll's house before the school-bell rang.

"I'm to tell," said Isabel, "because I'm the eldest. And you two can join in after. But I'm to tell first."

There was nothing to answer. Isabel was bossy, but she was always right, and Lottie and Kezia knew too well the powers that went with being eldest. They brushed through the thick buttercups at the road edge and said nothing.

"And I'm to choose who's to come and see it first. Mother said I might."

For it had been arranged that while the doll's house stood in the courtyard they might ask the girls at school, two at a time, to come and look. Not to stay to tea, of course, or to come traipsing through the house. But just to stand quietly in the courtyard while Isabel pointed out the beauties, and Lottie and Kezia looked pleased . . .

But hurry as they might, by the time they had reached the tarred palings of the boys' playground the bell had begun to jangle. They only just had time to whip off their hats and fall into line before the roll was called. Never mind. Isabel tried to make up for it by looking very important and mysterious and by whispering behind her hand to the girls near her, "Got something to tell you at playtime."

Playtime came and Isabel was surrounded. The girls of her class nearly fought to put their arms round her, to walk away with her, to beam flatteringly, to be her special friend. She held quite a court under the huge pine trees at the side of the playground. Nudging, giggling together, the little girls pressed up close. And the only two who stayed outside the ring were the two who were always outside, the little Kelveys. They knew better than to come anywhere near the Burnells.

For the fact was, the school the Burnell children went to was not at all the kind of place their parents would have chosen if there had been any choice. But there was none. It was the only school for miles. And the consequence was all the children of the neighbourhood, the Judge's little girls, the doctor's daughters, the storekeeper's children, the milkman's, were forced to mix together. Not to speak of there being an equal number of rude, rough little boys as well. But the line had to be drawn somewhere. It was drawn at the Kelveys. Many of the children, including the Burnells, were not allowed even to speak to them. They walked past the Kelveys with their heads in the air, and as they set the fashion in all matters of behaviour, the Kelveys were shunned by everybody. Even the teacher had a special voice for them, and a special smile for the other children when Lil Kelvey came up to her desk with a bunch of dreadfully common-looking flowers.

They were the daughters of a spry, hard-working little washerwoman, who went about from house to house by the day. This was awful enough. But where was Mr. Kelvey? Nobody knew for certain. But everybody said he was in prison. So they were the daughters of a washerwoman and a gaolbird. Very nice company for other people's children! And they looked it. Why Mrs. Kelvey made them so conspicuous was hard to understand. The truth was they were dressed in "bits" given to her by the people for whom she worked. Lil, for instance, who was a stout, plain child, with big freckles, came to school in a dress made from a green art-serge tablecloth of the Burnells', with red plush sleeves from the Logans' curtains. Her hat, perched on top of her high forehead, was a grown-up woman's hat, once the property of Miss Lecky, the postmistress. It was turned up at the back and trimmed with a large scarlet quill. What a little guy she looked! It was impossible not to laugh. And her little sister, our Else, wore a long white dress, rather like a nightgown, and a pair of little boy's boots. But whatever our Else wore she would have looked strange. She was a tiny wishbone of a child, with cropped hair and enormous solemn eyes—a little white owl. Nobody had ever seen her smile; she scarcely ever spoke. She went through life holding on to Lil, with a piece of Lil's skirt screwed up in her hand. Where Lil went, our Else followed. In the playground, on the road going to and from school, there was Lil marching in front and our Else holding on behind. Only when she wanted anything, or when she was out of breath, our Else gave Lil a tug, a twitch, and Lil stopped and turned round. The Kelveys never failed to understand each other.

Now they hovered at the edge; you couldn't stop them listening. When the little girls turned round and sneered, Lil, as usual, gave her silly, shamefaced smile, but our Else only looked.

And Isabel's voice, so very proud, went on telling. The carpet made a great sensation, but so did the beds with real bedclothes, and the stove with an oven door.

When she finished Kezia broke in. "You've forgotten the lamp, Isabel."

"Oh yes," said Isabel, "and there's a teeny little lamp, all made of yellow glass, with a white globe that stands on the dining-room table. You couldn't tell it from a real one."

"The lamp's best of all," cried Kezia. She thought

Isabel wasn't making half enough of the little lamp. But nobody paid any attention. Isabel was choosing the two who were to come back with them that afternoon and see it. She chose Emmie Cole and Lena Logan. But when the others knew they were all to have a chance, they couldn't be nice enough to Isabel. One by one they put their arms round Isabel's waist and walked her off. They had something to whisper to her, a secret. "Isabel's *my* friend."

Only the little Kelveys moved away forgotten; there was nothing more for them to hear.

Days passed, and as more children saw the doll's house, the fame of it spread. It became the one subject, the rage. The one question was, "Have you seen Burnells' doll's house? Oh, ain't it lovely!" "Haven't you seen it? Oh, I say!"

Even the dinner hour was given up to talking about it. The little girls sat under the pines eating their thick mutton sandwiches and big slabs of johnny cake spread with butter. While always, as near as they could get, sat the Kelveys, our Else holding on to Lil, listening too, while they chewed their jam sandwiches out of a newspaper soaked with large red blobs.

"Mother," said Kezia, "can't I ask the Kelveys just once?"

"Certainly not, Kezia."

"But why not?"

"Run away, Kezia; you know quite well why not."

At last everybody had seen it except them. On that day the subject rather flagged. It was the dinner hour. The children stood together under the pine trees, and suddenly, as they looked at the Kelveys eating out of their paper, always by themselves, always listening, they wanted to be horrid to them. Emmie Cole started the whisper.

"Lil Kelvey's going to be a servant when she grows up."

"O-oh, how awful!" said Isabel Burnell, and she made eyes at Emmie.

Emmie swallowed in a very meaning way and nodded to Isabel as she'd seen her mother do on those occasions.

"It's true—it's true—it's true," she said.

Then Lena Logan's little eyes snapped. "Shall I ask her?" she whispered.

"Bet you don't," said Jessie May.

"Pooh, I'm not frightened," said Lena. Suddenly she gave a little squeal and danced in front of the other girls. "Watch! Watch me! Watch me now!" said Lena. And sliding, gliding, dragging one foot, giggling behind her hand, Lena went over to the Kelveys.

Lil looked up from her dinner. She wrapped the rest quickly away. Our Else stopped chewing. What was coming now?

"Is it true you're going to be a servant when you grow up, Lil Kelvey?" shrilled Lena.

Dead silence. But instead of answering, Lil only gave her silly, shamefaced smile. She didn't seem to mind the question at all. What a sell for Lena! The girls began to titter.

Lena couldn't stand that. She put her hands on her hips; she shot forward. "Yah, yer father's in prison!" she hissed spitefully.

This was such a marvellous thing to have said that the little girls rushed away in a body, deeply, deeply excited, wild with joy. Someone found a long rope, and they began skipping. And never did they skip so high,

9

run in and out so fast, or do such daring things as on that morning.

In the afternoon Pat called for the Burnell children with the buggy and they drove home. There were visitors. Isabel and Lottie, who liked visitors, went upstairs to change their pinafores. But Kezia thieved out at the back. Nobody was about; she began to swing on the big white gates of the courtyard. Presently, looking along the road, she saw two little dots. They grew bigger, they were coming towards her. Now she could see that one was in front and one close behind. Now she could see that they were the Kelveys. Kezia stopped swinging. She slipped off the gate as if she was going to run away. Then she hesitated. The Kelveys came nearer, and beside them walked their shadows, very long, stretching right across the road with their heads in the buttercups. Kezia clambered back on the gate; she had made up her mind; she swung out.

"Hullo," she said to the passing Kelveys.

They were so astounded that they stopped. Lil gave her silly smile. Our Else stared.

"You can come and see our doll's house if you want to," said Kezia, and she dragged one toe on the ground. But at that Lil turned red and shook her head quickly.

"Why not?" asked Kezia.

Lil gasped, then she said, "Your ma told our ma you wasn't to speak to us."

"Oh, well," said Kezia. She didn't know what to reply. "It doesn't matter. You can come and see our doll's house all the same. Come on. Nobody's looking."

But Lil shook her head still harder.

"Don't you want to?" asked Kezia.

Suddenly there was a twitch, a tug at Lil's skirt. She turned round. Our Else was looking at her with big, imploring eyes; she was frowning; she wanted to go. For a moment Lil looked at our Else very doubtfully. But then our Else twitched her skirt again. She started forward. Kezia led the way. Like two little stray cats they followed across the courtyard to where the doll's house stood.

"There it is," said Kezia.

There was a pause. Lil breathed loudly, almost snorted; our Else was still as stone.

"I'll open it for you," said Kezia kindly. She undid the hook and they looked inside.

"There's the drawing-room and the dining-room, and that's the—"

"Kezia!"

Oh, what a start they gave!

"Kezia!"

It was Aunt Beryl's voice. They turned round. At the back door stood Aunt Beryl, staring as if she couldn't believe what she saw.

"How dare you ask the little Kelveys into the courtyard!" said her cold, furious voice. "You know as well as I do, you're not allowed to talk to them. Run away, children, run away at once. And don't come back again," said Aunt Beryl. And she stepped into the yard and shooed them out as if they were chickens.

"Off you go immediately!" she called, cold and proud.

They did not need telling twice. Burning with shame, shrinking together, Lil huddling along like her mother, our Else dazed, somehow they crossed the big courtyard and squeezed through the white gate.

"Wicked, disobedient little girl!" said Aunt Beryl bitterly to Kezia, and she slammed the doll's house to.

The afternoon had been awful. A letter had come

from Willie Brent, a terrifying, threatening letter, saying if she did not meet him that evening in Pulman's Bush, he'd come to the front door and ask the reason why! But now that she had frightened those little rats of Kelveys and given Kezia a good scolding, her heart felt lighter. That ghastly pressure was gone. She went back to the house humming.

When the Kelveys were well out of sight of Burnells', they sat down to rest on a big red drainpipe by the side of the road. Lil's cheeks were still burning; she took off the hat with the quill and held it on her knee. Dreamily they looked over the hay paddocks, past the creek, to the group of wattles where Logan's cows stood waiting to be milked. What were their thoughts?

Presently our Else nudged up close to her sister. But now she had forgotten the cross lady. She put out a finger and stroked her sister's quill; she smiled her rare smile.

"I seen the little lamp," she said softly.

Then both were silent once more.

THE GARDEN-PARTY

And after all the weather was ideal. They could not have had a more perfect day for a garden-party if they had ordered it. Windless, warm, the sky without a cloud. Only the blue was veiled with a haze of light gold, as it is sometimes in early summer. The gardener had been up since dawn, mowing the lawns and sweeping them, until the grass and the dark flat rosettes where the daisy plants had been seemed to shine. As for the roses, you could not help feeling they understood that roses are the only flowers that impress people at garden-parties; the only flowers that everybody is certain of knowing. Hundreds, yes, literally hundreds, had come out in a single night; the green bushes bowed down as though they had been visited by archangels.

Breakfast was not yet over before the men came to put up the marquee.

"Where do you want the marquee put, mother?"

"My dear child, it's no use asking me. I'm determined to leave everything to you children this year. Forget I am your mother. Treat me as an honoured guest."

But Meg could not possibly go and supervise the men. She had washed her hair before breakfast, and she sat drinking her coffee in a green turban, with a dark wet curl stamped on each cheek. Jose, the butterfly, always came down in a silk petticoat and a kimono jacket.

"You'll have to go, Laura; you're the artistic one."

Away Laura flew, still holding her piece of bread-and-butter. It's so delicious to have an excuse for eating out of doors and, besides, she loved having to arrange things; she always felt she could do it so much better than anybody else.

Four men in their shirt-sleeves stood grouped together on the garden path. They carried staves covered with rolls of canvas and they had big tool-bags slung on their backs. They looked impressive. Laura wished now that she was not holding that piece of bread-and-butter, but there was nowhere to put it and she couldn't possibly throw it away. She blushed and tried to look severe and even a little bit short-sighted as she came up to them.

"Good morning," she said, copying her mother's voice. But that sounded so fearfully affected that she was ashamed, and stammered like a little girl, "Oh—er—have you come—is it about the marquee?"

"That's right, miss," said the tallest of the men, a lanky, freckled fellow, and he shifted his tool-bag, knocked back his straw hat and smiled down at her. "That's about it."

His smile was so easy, so friendly, that Laura recovered. What nice eyes he had, small, but such a dark blue! And now she looked at the others, they were smiling too. "Cheer up, we won't bite," their smile seemed to say. How very nice workmen were! And what a beautiful morning! She mustn't mention the morning; she must be business-like. The marquee.

"Well, what about the lily-lawn? Would that do?"

And she pointed to the lily-lawn with the hand that didn't hold the bread-and-butter. They turned, they stared in the direction. A little fat chap thrust out his underlip and the tall fellow frowned.

"I don't fancy it," said he. "Not conspicuous enough. You see, with a thing like a marquee"—and he turned

to Laura in his easy way—"you want to put it somewhere where it'll give you a bang slap in the eye, if you
follow me."

Laura's upbringing made her wonder for a moment
whether it was quite respectful of a workman to talk to
her of bangs slap in the eye. But she did quite follow
him.

"A corner of the tennis-court," she suggested. "But
the band's going to be in one corner."

"H'm, going to have a band, are you?" said another
of the workmen. He was pale. He had a haggard look
as his dark eyes scanned the tennis-court. What was he
thinking?

"Only a very small band," said Laura gently. Perhaps
he wouldn't mind so much if the band was quite small.
But the tall fellow interrupted.

"Look here, miss, that's the place. Against those
trees. Over there. That'll do fine."

Against the karakas. Then the karaka trees would be
hidden. And they were so lovely, with their broad,
gleaming leaves, and their clusters of yellow fruit. They
were like trees you imagined growing on a desert island,
proud, solitary, lifting their leaves and fruits to the sun
in a kind of silent splendour. Must they be hidden by a
marquee?

They must. Already the men had shouldered their
staves and were making for the place. Only the tall
fellow was left. He bent down, pinched a sprig of lavender, put his thumb and forefinger to his nose and
snuffed up the smell. When Laura saw that gesture she
forgot all about the karakas in her wonder at him caring
for things like that—caring for the smell of lavender.
How many men that she knew would have done such a
thing. Oh, how extraordinarily nice workmen were, she

thought. Why couldn't she have workmen for friends rather than the silly boys she danced with and who came to Sunday night supper? She would get on much better with men like these.

It's all the fault, she decided, as the tall fellow drew something on the back of an envelope, something that was to be looped up or left to hang, of these absurd class distinctions. Well, for her part, she didn't feel them. Not a bit, not an atom . . . And now there came the chock-chock of wooden hammers. Someone whistled, someone sang out, "Are you right there, matey?" "Matey!" The friendliness of it, the—the—Just to prove how happy she was, just to show the tall fellow how at home she felt, and how she despised stupid conventions, Laura took a big bite of her bread-and-butter as she stared at the little drawing. She felt just like a work-girl.

"Laura, Laura, where are you? Telephone, Laura!" a voice cried from the house.

"Coming!" Away she skimmed, over the lawn, up the path, up the steps, across the veranda and into the porch. In the hall her father and Laurie were brushing their hats ready to go to the office.

"I say, Laura," said Laurie very fast, "you might just give a squiz at my coat before this afternoon. See if it wants pressing."

"I will," said she. Suddenly she couldn't stop herself. She ran at Laurie and gave him a small, quick squeeze. "Oh, I do love parties, don't you?" gasped Laura.

"Ra-ther," said Laurie's warm, boyish voice, and he squeezed his sister too and gave her a gentle push. "Dash off to the telephone, old girl."

The telephone. "Yes, yes; oh yes. Kitty? Good morning, dear. Come to lunch? Do, dear. Delighted, of course. It will only be a very scratch meal—just the sandwich crusts and broken meringue-shells and what's left over. Yes, isn't it a perfect morning? Your white? Oh, I certainly should. One moment—hold the line. Mother's calling." And Laura sat back. "What, mother? Can't hear."

Mrs. Sheridan's voice floated down the stairs. "Tell her to wear that sweet hat she had on last Sunday."

"Mother says you're to wear that *sweet* hat you had on last Sunday. Good. One o'clock. Bye-bye."

Laura put back the receiver, flung her arms over her head, took a deep breath, stretched and let them fall. "Huh," she sighed, and the moment after the sigh she sat up quickly. She was still, listening. All the doors in the house seemed to be open. The house was alive with soft, quick steps and running voices. The green baize door that led to the kitchen regions swung open and shut with a muffled thud. And now there came a long, chuckling absurd sound. It was the heavy piano being moved on its stiff castors. But the air! If you stopped to notice, was the air always like this? Little faint winds were playing chase in at the tops of the windows, out at the doors. And there were two tiny spots of sun, one on the inkpot, one on a silver photograph frame, playing too. Darling little spots. Especially the one on the inkpot lid. It was quite warm. A warm little silver star. She could have kissed it.

The front door bell pealed and there sounded the rustle of Sadie's print skirt on the stairs. A man's voice murmured; Sadie answered, careless, "I'm sure I don't know. Wait. I'll ask Mrs. Sheridan."

"What is it, Sadie?" Laura came into the hall.

"It's the florist, Miss Laura."

It was, indeed. There, just inside the door, stood a

wide, shallow tray full of pots of pink lilies. No other kind. Nothing but lilies—canna lilies, big pink flowers, wide open, radiant, almost frighteningly alive on bright crimson stems.

"O-oh, Sadie!" said Laura, and the sound was like a little moan. She crouched down as if to warm herself at that blaze of lilies; she felt they were in her fingers, on her lips, growing in her breast.

"It's some mistake," she said faintly. "Nobody ever ordered so many. Sadie, go and find mother."

But at that moment Mrs. Sheridan joined them.

"It's quite right," she said calmly. "Yes, I ordered them. Aren't they lovely?" She pressed Laura's arm. "I was passing the shop yesterday, and I saw them in the window. And I suddenly thought for once in my life I shall have enough canna lilies. The garden-party will be a good excuse."

"But I thought you said you didn't mean to interfere," said Laura. Sadie had gone. The florist's man was still outside at his van. She put her arm round her mother's neck and gently, very gently, she bit her mother's ear.

"My darling child, you wouldn't like a logical mother, would you? Don't do that. Here's the man."

He carried more lilies still, another whole tray.

"Bank them up, just inside the door, on both sides of the porch, please," said Mrs. Sheridan. "Don't you agree, Laura?"

"Oh, I *do*, mother."

In the drawing-room Meg, Jose and good little Hans had at last succeeded in moving the piano.

"Now, if we put this chesterfield against the wall and move everything out of the room except the chairs, don't you think?"

"Quite."

"Hans, move these tables into the smoking-room, and bring a sweeper to take these marks off the carpet and—one moment, Hans—" Jose loved giving orders to the servants and they loved obeying her. She always made them feel they were taking part in some drama. "Tell mother and Miss Laura to come here at once."

"Very good, Miss Jose."

She turned to Meg. "I want to hear what the piano sounds like, just in case I'm asked to sing this afternoon. Let's try over 'This Life is Weary.'"

Pom! Ta-ta-ta *Tee-ta!* The piano burst out so passionately that Jose's face changed. She clasped her hands. She looked mournfully and enigmatically at her mother and Laura as they came in.

> This Life is *Wee*-ary,
> A Tear—a Sigh.
> A Love that *Chan*-ges,
> This Life is *Wee*-ary,
> A Tear—a Sigh.
> A Love that *Chan*-ges,
> And then . . . Good-bye!

But at the word "Good-bye," and although the piano sounded more desperate than ever, her face broke into a brilliant, dreadfully unsympathetic smile.

"Aren't I in good voice, mummy?" she beamed.

> This Life is *Wee*-ary,
> Hope comes to Die.
> A Dream—a *Wa*-kening.

But now Sadie interrupted them. "What is it, Sadie?"

"If you please, m'm, cook says have you got the flags for the sandwiches?"

"The flags for the sandwiches, Sadie?" echoed

Mrs. Sheridan dreamily. And the children knew by her face that she hadn't got them. "Let me see." And she said to Sadie firmly, "Tell cook I'll let her have them in ten minutes."

Sadie went.

"Now, Laura," said her mother quickly, "come with me into the smoking-room. I've got the names some-where on the back of an envelope. You'll have to write them out for me. Meg, go upstairs this minute and take that wet thing off your head. Jose, run and finish dressing this instant. Do you hear me, children, or shall I have to tell your father when he comes home to-night? And—and, Jose, pacify cook if you do go into the kitchen, will you? I'm terrified of her this morning."

The envelope was found at last behind the dining-room clock, though how it had got there Mrs. Sheridan could not imagine.

"One of you children must have stolen it out of my bag, because I remember vividly—cream-cheese and lemon-curd. Have you done that?"

"Yes."

"Egg and—" Mrs. Sheridan held the envelope away from her. "It looks like mice. It can't be mice, can it?"

"Olive, pet," said Laura, looking over her shoulder.

"Yes, of course, olive. What a horrible combination it sounds. Egg and olive."

They were finished at last, and Laura took them off to the kitchen. She found Jose there pacifying the cook, who did not look at all terrifying.

"I have never seen such exquisite sandwiches," said Jose's rapturous voice. "How many kinds did you say there were, cook? Fifteen?"

"Fifteen, Miss Jose."

"Well, cook, I congratulate you."

Cook swept up crusts with the long sandwich knife, and smiled broadly.

"Godber's has come," announced Sadie, issuing out of the pantry. She had seen the man pass the window.

That meant the cream puffs had come. Godber's were famous for their cream puffs. Nobody ever thought of making them at home.

"Bring them in and put them on the table, my girl," ordered cook.

Sadie brought them in and went back to the door. Of course Laura and Jose were far too grown-up to really care about such things. All the same, they couldn't help agreeing that the puffs looked very attractive. Very. Cook began arranging them, shaking off the extra icing sugar.

"Don't they carry one back to all one's parties?" said Laura.

"I suppose they do," said practical Jose, who never liked to be carried back. "They look beautifully light and feathery, I must say."

"Have one each, my dears," said cook in her comfortable voice. "Yer ma won't know."

Oh, impossible. Fancy cream puffs so soon after breakfast. The very idea made one shudder. All the same, two minutes later Jose and Laura were licking their fingers with that absorbed inward look that only comes from whipped cream.

"Let's go into the garden, out by the back way," suggested Laura. "I want to see how the men are getting on with the marquee. They're such awfully nice men."

But the back door was blocked by cook, Sadie, Godber's man and Hans.

Something had happened.

"Tuk-tuk-tuk," clucked cook like an agitated hen.

Sadie had her hand clapped to her cheek as though she had toothache. Han's face was screwed up in the effort to understand. Only Godber's man seemed to be enjoying himself; it was his story.

"What's the matter? What's happened?"

"There's been a horrible accident," said cook. "A man killed."

"A man killed! Where? How? When?"

But Godber's man wasn't going to have his story snatched from under his very nose.

"Know those little cottages just below here, miss?" Know them? Of course she knew them. "Well, there's a young chap living there, name of Scott, a carter. His horse shied at a traction-engine, corner of Hawke Street this morning, and he was thrown out on the back of his head. Killed."

"Dead!" Laura stared at Godber's man.

"Dead when they picked him up," said Godber's man with relish. "They were taking the body home as I come up here." And he said to the cook, "He's left a wife and five little ones."

"Jose, come here." Laura caught hold of her sister's sleeve and dragged her through the kitchen to the other side of the green baize door. There she paused and leaned against it. "Jose!" she said, horrified, "however are we going to stop everything?"

"Stop everything, Laura!" cried Jose in astonishment. "What do you mean?"

"Stop the garden-party, of course." Why did Jose pretend?

But Jose was still more amazed. "Stop the garden-party? My dear Laura, don't be so absurd. Of course we can't do anything of the kind. Nobody expects us to. Don't be so extravagant."

"But we can't possibly have a garden-party with a man dead just outside the front gate."

That really was extravagant, for the little cottages were in a lane to themselves at the very bottom of a steep rise that led up to the house. A broad road ran between. True, they were far too near. They were the greatest possible eyesore and they had no right to be in that neighbourhood at all. They were little mean dwellings painted a chocolate brown. In the garden patches there was nothing but cabbage stalks, sick hens and tomato cans. The very smoke coming out of their chimneys was poverty-stricken. Little rags and shreds of smoke, so unlike the great silvery plumes that uncurled from the Sheridans' chimneys. Washerwomen lived in the lane and sweeps and a cobbler and a man whose house-front was studded all over with minute bird-cages. Children swarmed. When the Sheridans were little they were forbidden to set foot there because of the revolting language and of what they might catch. But since they were grown up Laura and Laurie on their prowls sometimes walked through. It was disgusting and sordid. They came out with a shudder. But still one must go everywhere; one must see everything. So through they went.

"And just think of what the band would sound like to that poor woman," said Laura.

"Oh, Laura!" Jose began to be seriously annoyed. "If you're going to stop a band playing every time someone has an accident, you'll lead a very strenuous life. I'm every bit as sorry about it as you. I feel just as sympathetic." Her eyes hardened. She looked at her sister just as she used to when they were little and fighting together. "You won't bring a drunken workman back to life by being sentimental," she said softly.

"Drunk! Who said he was drunk?" Laura turned furiously on Jose. She said just as they had used to say on those occasions, "I'm going straight up to tell mother."

"Do, dear," cooed Jose.

"Mother, can I come into your room?" Laura turned the big glass door-knob.

"Of course, child. Why, what's the matter? What's given you such a colour?" And Mrs. Sheridan turned round from her dressing-table. She was trying on a new hat.

"Mother, a man's been killed," began Laura.

"*Not* in the garden?" interrupted her mother.

"No, no!"

"Oh, what a fright you gave me!" Mrs. Sheridan sighed with relief and took off the big hat and held it on her knees.

"But listen, mother," said Laura. Breathless, half choking, she told the dreadful story. "Of course, we can't have our party, can we?" she pleaded. "The band and everybody arriving. They'd hear us, mother; they're nearly neighbours!"

To Laura's astonishment her mother behaved just like Jose; it was harder to bear because she seemed amused. She refused to take Laura seriously.

"But, my dear child, use your common sense. It's only by accident we've heard of it. If someone had died there normally—and I can't understand how they keep alive in those poky little holes—we should still be having our party, shouldn't we?"

Laura had to say "yes" to that, but she felt it was all wrong. She sat down on her mother's sofa and pinched the cushion frill.

"Mother, isn't it really terribly heartless of us?" she asked.

"Darling!" Mrs. Sheridan got up and came over to her, carrying the hat. Before Laura could stop her she had popped it on. "My child!" said her mother, "the hat is yours. It's made for you. It's much too young for me. I have never seen you look such a picture. Look at yourself!" And she held up her hand-mirror.

"But, mother," Laura began again. She couldn't look at herself; she turned aside.

This time Mrs. Sheridan lost patience just as Jose had done.

"You are being very absurd, Laura," she said coldly. "People like that don't expect sacrifices from us. And it's not very sympathetic to spoil everybody's enjoyment as you're doing now."

"I don't understand," said Laura, and she walked quickly out of the room into her own bedroom. There, quite by chance, the first thing she saw was this charming girl in the mirror, in her black hat trimmed with gold daisies and a long black velvet ribbon. Never had she imagined she could look like that. Is mother right? she thought. And now she hoped her mother was right. Am I being extravagant? Perhaps it was extravagant. Just for a moment she had another glimpse of that poor woman and those little children and the body being carried into the house. But it all seemed blurred, unreal, like a picture in the newspaper. I'll remember it again after the party's over, she decided. And somehow that seemed quite the best plan . . .

Lunch was over by half-past one. By half-past two they were all ready for the fray. The green-coated band had arrived and was established in a corner of the tennis-court.

"My dear!" trilled Kitty Maitland, "aren't they too like frogs for words? You ought to have arranged them round the pond with the conductor in the middle on a leaf."

Laurie arrived and hailed them on his way to dress. At the sight of him Laura remembered the accident again. She wanted to tell him. If Laurie agreed with the others, then it was bound to be all right. And she followed him into the hall.

"Laurie!"

"Hallo!" He was half-way upstairs, but when he turned round and saw Laura he suddenly puffed out his cheeks and goggled his eyes at her. "My word, Laura! You do look stunning," said Laurie. "What an absolutely topping hat!"

Laura said faintly "Is it?" and smiled up at Laurie and didn't tell him after all.

Soon after that people began coming in streams. The band struck up; the hired waiters ran from the house to the marquee. Wherever you looked there were couples strolling, bending to the flowers, greeting, moving on over the lawn. They were like bright birds that had alighted in the Sheridans' garden for this one afternoon, on their way to—where? Ah, what happiness it is to be with people who all are happy, to press hands, press cheeks, smile into eyes.

"Darling Laura, how well you look!"

"What a becoming hat, child!"

"Laura, you look quite Spanish. I've never seen you look so striking."

And Laura, glowing, answered softly, "Have you had tea? Won't you have an ice? The passion-fruit ices really are rather special." She ran to her father and begged him: "Daddy darling, can't the band have something to drink?"

And the perfect afternoon slowly ripened, slowly faded, slowly its petals closed.

"Never a more delightful garden-party . . ." "The greatest success . . ." "Quite the most . . ."

Laura helped her mother with the good-byes. They stood side by side in the porch till it was all over.

"All over, all over, thank heaven," said Mrs. Sheridan. "Round up the others, Laura. Let's go and have some fresh coffee. I'm exhausted. Yes, it's been very successful. But oh, these parties, these parties! Why will you children insist on giving parties!" And they all of them sat down in the deserted marquee.

"Have a sandwich, daddy dear. I wrote the flag."

"Thanks." Mr. Sheridan took a bite and the sandwich was gone. He took another. "I suppose you didn't hear of a beastly accident that happened to-day?" he said.

"My dear," said Mrs. Sheridan, holding up her hand, "we did. It nearly ruined the party. Laura insisted we should put it off."

"Oh, mother!" Laura didn't want to be teased about it.

"It was a horrible affair all the same," said Mr. Sheridan. "The chap was married too. Lived just below in the lane, and leaves a wife and half a dozen kiddies, so they say."

An awkward little silence fell. Mrs. Sheridan fidgeted with her cup. Really, it was very tactless of father . . .

Suddenly she looked up. There on the table were all those sandwiches, cakes, puffs, all uneaten, all going to be wasted. She had one of her brilliant ideas.

"I know," she said. "Let's make up a basket. Let's send that poor creature some of this perfectly good food. At any rate, it will be the greatest treat for the children. Don't you agree? And she's sure to have

27

neighbours calling in and so on. What a point to have it all ready prepared. Laura!" She jumped up. "Get me the big basket out of the stairs cupboard."

"But, mother, do you really think it's a good idea?" said Laura.

Again, how curious, she seemed to be different from them all. To take scraps from their party. Would the poor woman really like that?

"Of course! What's the matter with you to-day? An hour or two ago you were insisting on us being sympathetic."

Oh well! Laura ran for the basket. It was filled, it was now heaped by her mother.

"Take it yourself, darling," said she. "Run down just as you are. No, wait, take the arum lilies too. People of that class are so impressed by arum lilies."

"The stems will ruin her lace frock," said practical Jose.

So they would. Just in time. "Only the basket, then. And, Laura!"—her mother followed her out of the marquee—"don't on any account—"

"What, mother?"

No, better not put such ideas into the child's head! "Nothing! Run along."

It was just growing dusky as Laura shut their garden gates. A big dog ran by like a shadow. The road gleamed white, and down below in the hollow the little cottages were in deep shade. How quiet it seemed after the afternoon. Here she was going down the hill to somewhere where a man lay dead, and she couldn't realise it. Why couldn't she? She stopped a minute. And it seemed to her that kisses, voices, tinkling spoons, laughter, the smell of crushed grass were somehow inside her. She had no room for anything else. How strange! She looked up at the pale sky, and all she thought was, "Yes, it was the most successful party."

Now the broad road was crossed. The lane began, smoky and dark. Women in shawls and men's tweed caps hurried by. Men hung over the palings; the children played in the doorways. A low hum came from the mean little cottages. In some of them there was a flicker of light, and a shadow, crab-like, moved across the window. Laura bent her head and hurried on. She wished now she had put on a coat. How her frock shone! And the big hat with the velvet streamer—if only it was another hat! Were the people looking at her? They must be. It was a mistake to have come; she knew all along it was a mistake. Should she go back even now?

No, too late. This was the house. It must be. A dark knot of people stood outside. Beside the gate an old, old woman with a crutch sat in a chair, watching. She had her feet on a newspaper. The voices stopped as Laura drew near. The group parted. It was as though she was expected, as though they had known she was coming here.

Laura was terribly nervous. Tossing the velvet ribbon over her shoulder, she said to a woman standing by, "Is this Mrs. Scott's house?" and the woman, smiling queerly, said, "It is, my lass."

Oh, to be away from this! She actually said, "Help me, God," as she walked up the tiny path and knocked. To be away from those staring eyes, or to be covered up in anything, one of those women's shawls even. I'll just leave the basket and go, she decided. I shan't even wait for it to be emptied.

Then the door opened. A little woman in black showed in the gloom.

Laura said, "Are you Mrs. Scott?" But to her horror

the woman answered, "Walk in, please, miss," and she was shut in the passage.

"No," said Laura, "I don't want to come in. I only want to leave, this basket. Mother sent—"

The little woman in the gloomy passage seemed not to have heard her. "Step this way, please, miss," she said in an oily voice, and Laura followed her.

She found herself in a wretched little low kitchen, lighted by a smoky lamp. There was a woman sitting before the fire.

"Em," said the little creature who had let her in. "Em! It's a young lady." She turned to Laura. She said meaningly, "I'm 'er sister, miss. You'll excuse 'er, won't you?"

"Oh, but of course!" said Laura. "Please, please don't disturb her. I—I only want to leave—"

But at that moment the woman at the fire turned round. Her face, puffed up, red, with swollen eyes and swollen lips, looked terrible. She seemed as though she couldn't understand why Laura was there. What did it mean? Why was this stranger standing in the kitchen with a basket? What was it all about? And the poor face puckered up again.

"All right, my dear," said the other. "I'll thenk the young lady."

And again she began, "You'll excuse her, miss, I'm sure," and her face, swollen too, tried an oily smile.

Laura only wanted to get out, to get away. She was back in the passage. The door opened. She walked straight through into the bedroom, where the dead man was lying.

"You'd like a look at 'im, wouldn't you?" said Em's sister, and she brushed past Laura over to the bed. "Don't be afraid, my lass"—and now her voice sounded fond and sly, and fondly she drew down the sheet—" 'e looks a picture. There's nothing to show. Come along, my dear."

Laura came.

There lay a young man, fast asleep—sleeping so soundly, so deeply, that he was far, far away from them both. Oh, so remote, so peaceful. He was dreaming. Never wake him up again. His head was sunk in the pillow, his eyes were closed; they were blind under the closed eyelids. He was given up to his dream. What did garden-parties and baskets and lace frocks matter to him? He was far from all those things. He was wonderful, beautiful. While they were laughing and while the band was playing, this marvel had come to the lane. Happy . . . happy . . . All is well, said that sleeping face. This is just as it should be. I am content.

But all the same you had to cry, and she couldn't go out of the room without saying something to him. Laura gave a loud childish sob.

"Forgive my hat," she said.

And this time she didn't wait for Em's sister. She found her way out of the door, down the path past all those dark people. At the corner of the lane she met Laurie.

He stepped out of the shadow. "Is that you, Laura?"

"Yes."

"Mother was getting anxious. Was it all right?"

"Yes, quite. Oh, Laurie!" She took his arm, she pressed up against him.

"I say, you're not crying, are you?" asked her brother.

Laura shook her head. She was.

Laurie put his arm round her shoulder. "Don't cry," he said in his warm, loving voice. "Was it awful?"

"No," sobbed Laura. "It was simply marvellous. But, Laurie—" She stopped, she looked at her brother. "Isn't life," she stammered, "isn't life—" But what life was she couldn't explain. No matter. He quite understood.

"*Isn't* it, darling?" said Laurie.

AT LEHMANN'S

Certainly Sabina did not find life slow. She was on the trot from early morning until late at night. At five o'clock she tumbled out of bed, buttoned on her clothes, wearing a long-sleeved alpaca pinafore over her black frock, and groped her way downstairs into the kitchen.

Anna, the cook, had grown so fat during the summer that she adored her bed because she did not have to wear her corsets there, but could spread as much as she liked, roll about on the great mattress, calling upon Jesus and Holy Mary and Blessed Anthony himself that her life was not fit for a pig in a cellar.

Sabina was new to her work. Pink colour still flew in her cheeks; there was a little dimple on the left side of her mouth that even when she was most serious, most absorbed, popped out and gave her away. And Anna blessed that dimple. It meant an extra half-hour in bed for her; it made Sabina light the fire, turn out the kitchen and wash endless cups and saucers that had been left over from the evening before. Hans, the scullery boy, did not come until seven. He was the son of the butcher—a mean, undersized child very much like one of his father's sausages, Sabina thought. His red face was covered with pimples, and his nails indescribably filthy. When Herr Lehmann himself told Hans to get a hairpin and clean them he said they were stained from birth because his mother had always got so inky doing the accounts—and Sabina believed him and pitied him.

Winter had come very early to Mindelbau. By the end of October the streets were banked waist-high with snow, and the greater number of the "Cure Guests," sick unto death of cold water and herbs, had departed in nothing approaching peace. So the large salon was shut at Lehmann's and the breakfast-room was all the accommodation the café afforded. Here the floor had to be washed over, the tables rubbed, coffee-cups set out each with its little china platter of sugar, and newspapers and magazines hung on their hooks along the walls before Herr Lehmann appeared at seven-thirty and opened business.

As a rule his wife served in the shop leading into the café, but she had chosen the quiet season to have a baby, and, a big woman at the best of times, she had grown so enormous in the process that her husband told her she looked unappetising, and had better remain upstairs and sew.

Sabina took on the extra work without any thought of extra pay. She loved to stand behind the counter, cutting up slices of Anna's marvellous chocolate-spotted confections, or doing up packets of sugar almonds in pink and blue striped bags.

"You'll get varicose veins, like me," said Anna. "That's what the Frau's got too. No wonder the baby doesn't come! All her swelling's got into her legs." And Hans was immensely interested.

During the morning business was comparatively slack. Sabina answered the shop bell, attended to a few customers who drank a liqueur to warm their stomachs before the midday meal, and ran upstairs now and again to ask the Frau if she wanted anything. But in the afternoon six or seven choice spirits played cards, and everybody who was anybody drank tea or coffee.

"Sabina . . . Sabina . . ."

She flew from one table to the other, counting out handfuls of small change, giving orders to Anna through the "slide," helping the men with their heavy coats, always with that magical child air about her, that delightful sense of perpetually attending a party.

"How is the Frau Lehmann?" the women would whisper.

"She feels rather low, but as well as can be expected," Sabina would answer, nodding confidentially.

Frau Lehmann's bad time was approaching. Anna and her friends referred to it as her "journey to Rome," and Sabina longed to ask questions, yet, being ashamed of her ignorance, was silent, trying to puzzle it out for herself. She knew practically nothing except that the Frau had a baby inside her, which had to come out— very painful indeed. One could not have one without a husband—that she also realised. But what had the man got to do with it? So she wondered as she sat mending tea towels in the evening, head bent over her work, light shining on her brown curls. Birth—what was it? wondered Sabina. Death—such a simple thing. She had a little picture of her dead grandmother dressed in a black silk frock, tired hands clasping the crucifix that dragged between her flattened breasts, mouth curiously tight, yet almost secretly smiling. But the grandmother had been born once—that was the important fact.

As she sat there one evening, thinking, the Young Man entered the café, and called for a glass of port wine. Sabina rose slowly. The long day and the hot room made her feel a little languid, but as she poured out the wine she felt the Young Man's eyes fixed on her, looked down at him and dimpled.

"It's cold out," she said, corking the bottle.

The Young Man ran his hands through his snow-powdered hair and laughed.

"I wouldn't call it exactly tropical," he said. "But you're very snug in here—look as though you've been asleep."

Very languid felt Sabina in the hot room, and the Young Man's voice was strong and deep. She thought she had never seen anybody who looked so strong—as though he could take up the table in one hand—and his restless gaze wandering over her face and figure gave her a curious thrill deep in her body, half pleasure, half pain . . . She wanted to stand there, close beside him, while he drank his wine. A little silence followed. Then he took a book out of his pocket, and Sabina went back to her sewing. Sitting there in the corner, she listened to the sound of the leaves being turned and the loud ticking of the clock that hung over the gilt mirror. She wanted to look at him again—there was a something about him, in his deep voice, even in the way his clothes fitted. From the room above she heard the heavy drag-ging sound of Frau Lehmann's footsteps, and again the old thoughts worried Sabina. If she herself should one day look like that—feel like that! Yet it would be very sweet to have a little baby to dress and jump up and down.

"Fräulein—what's your name—what are you smiling at?" called the Young Man.

She blushed and looked up, hands quiet in her lap, looked across the empty tables and shook her head.

"Come here, and I'll show you a picture," he commanded.

She went and stood beside him. He opened the book, and Sabina saw a coloured sketch of a naked girl sitting on the edge of a great, crumpled bed, a man's opera hat on the back of her head.

He put his hand over the body, leaving only the face exposed, then scrutinised Sabina closely.

"Well?"

"What do you mean?" she asked, knowing perfectly well.

"Why, it might be your own photograph—the face, I mean—that's as far as I can judge."

"But the hair's done differently," said Sabina, laughing. She threw back her head, and the laughter bubbled in her round white throat.

"It's rather a nice picture, don't you think?" he asked. But she was looking at a curious ring he wore on the hand that covered the girl's body, and only nodded.

"Ever seen anything like it before?"

"Oh, there's plenty of those funny ones in the illustrated papers."

"How would you like to have your picture taken that way?"

"Me? I'd never let anybody see it. Besides, I haven't got a hat like that!"

"That's easily remedied."

Again a little silence, broken by Anna throwing up the slide.

Sabina ran into the kitchen.

"Here, take this milk and egg up to the Frau," said Anna. "Who've you got in there?"

"Got such a funny man! I think he's a little gone here," tapping her forehead.

Upstairs in the ugly room the Frau sat sewing, a black shawl round her shoulders, her feet encased in red woollen slippers. The girl put the milk on a table by her, then stood, polishing a spoon on her apron.

"Nothing else?"

"Na," said the Frau, heaving up in her chair. "Where's my man?"

"He's playing cards over at Snipold's. Do you want him?"

"Dear heaven, leave him alone. I'm nothing. I don't matter . . . And the whole day waiting here."

Her hand shook as she wiped the rim of the glass with her fat finger.

"Shall I help you to bed?"

"You go downstairs, leave me alone. Tell Anna not to let Hans grub the sugar—give him one on the ear."

"Ugly—ugly—ugly," muttered Sabina, returning to the café where the Young Man stood coat-buttoned, ready for departure.

"I'll come again to-morrow," said he. "Don't twist your hair back so tightly; it will lose all its curl."

"Well, you are a funny one," she said. "Good night."

By the time Sabina was ready for bed Anna was snoring. She brushed out her long hair and gathered it in her hands . . . Perhaps it would be a pity if it lost all its curl. Then she looked down at her straight chemise, and drawing it off, sat down on the side of the bed.

"I wish," she whispered, smiling sleepily, "there was a great big looking-glass in this room."

Lying down in the darkness, she hugged her little body.

"I wouldn't be the Frau for one hundred marks—not for a thousand marks. To look like that."

And half dreaming, she imagined herself heaving up in her chair with the port wine bottle in her hand as the Young Man entered the café.

Cold and dark the next morning. Sabina woke, tired, feeling as though something heavy had been pressing under her heart all night. There was a sound of footsteps shuffling along the passage. Herr Lehmann! She must have overslept herself. Yes, he was rattling the door-handle.

"One moment, one moment," she called, dragging on her stockings.

"Bina, tell Anna to go to the Frau—but quickly. I must ride for the nurse."

"Yes, yes!" she cried. "Has it come?"

But he had gone, and she ran over to Anna and shook her by the shoulder.

"The Frau—the baby—Herr Lehmann for the nurse," she stuttered.

"Name of God!" said Anna, flinging herself out of bed.

No complaints to-day. Importance—enthusiasm in Anna's whole bearing.

"You run downstairs and light the oven. Put on a pan of water"—speaking to an imaginary sufferer as she fastened her blouse—"Yes, yes, I know—we must be worse before we are better—I'm coming—patience."

It was dark all that day. Lights were turned on immediately the café opened, and business was very brisk. Anna, turned out of the Frau's room by the nurse, refused to work, and sat in a corner nursing herself, listening to sounds overhead. Hans was more sympathetic than Sabina. He also forsook work, and stood by the window, picking his nose.

"But why must I do everything?" said Sabina, washing glasses. "I can't help the Frau; she oughtn't to take such a time about it."

"Listen," said Anna, "they've moved her into the

back bedroom above here, so as not to disturb the people. That was a groan—that one!"

"Two small beers," shouted Herr Lehmann through the slide.

"One moment, one moment."

At eight o'clock the café was deserted. Sabina sat down in the corner without her sewing. Nothing seemed to have happened to the Frau. A doctor had come—that was all.

"Ach," said Sabina. "I think no more of it. I listen no more. Ach, I would like to go away—I hate this talk. I will not hear it. No, it is too much." She leaned both elbows on the table—cupped her face in her hands and pouted.

But the outer door suddenly opening, she sprang to her feet and laughed. It was the Young Man again. He ordered more port, and brought no book this time.

"Don't go and sit miles away," he grumbled. "I want to be amused. And here, take my coat. Can't you dry it somewhere?—snowing again."

"There's a warm place—the ladies' cloak-room," she said. "I'll take it in there—just by the kitchen."

She felt better, and quite happy again.

"I'll come with you," he said. "I'll see where you put it."

And that did not seem at all extraordinary. She laughed and beckoned to him.

"In here," she cried. "Feel how warm. I'll put more wood on that oven. It doesn't matter, they're all busy upstairs."

She knelt down on the floor, and thrust the wood into the oven, laughing at her own wicked extravagance.

The Frau was forgotten, the stupid day was forgotten. Here was someone beside her laughing, too. They were together in the little warm room stealing Herr Lehmann's wood. It seemed the most exciting adventure in the world. She wanted to go on laughing—or burst out crying—or—or—catch hold of the Young Man.

"What a fire," she shrieked, stretching out her hands.

"Here's a hand; pull up," said the Young Man. "There, now, you'll catch it to-morrow."

They stood opposite to each other, hands still clinging. And again that strange tremor thrilled Sabina.

"Look here," he said roughly, "are you a child, or are you playing at being one?"

"I—I—"

Laughter ceased. She looked up at him once, then down at the floor, and began breathing like a frightened little animal.

He pulled her closer still and kissed her mouth.

"Na, what are you doing?" she whispered.

He let go her hands, he placed his on her breasts, and the room seemed to swim round Sabina. Suddenly, from the room above, a frightful, tearing shriek.

She wrenched herself away, tightened herself, drew herself up.

"Who did that—who made that noise?"

In the silence the thin wailing of a baby.

"Achk!" shrieked Sabina, rushing from the room.

THE TIREDNESS OF ROSABEL

At the corner of Oxford Circus Rosabel bought a bunch
of violets, and that was practically the reason why she
had so little tea—for a scone and a boiled egg and a cup
of cocoa at Lyons are not ample sufficiency after a hard
day's work in a millinery establishment. As she swung
on to the step of the Atlas bus, grabbed her skirt with
one hand and clung to the railing with the other, Rosabel thought she would have sacrificed her soul for a
good dinner—roast duck and green peas, chestnut stuffing, pudding with brandy sauce—something hot and
strong and filling. She sat down next to a girl very much
her own age who was reading *Anna Lombard* in a cheap,
paper-covered edition, and the rain had tear-spattered
the pages. Rosabel looked out of the windows; the street
was blurred and misty, but light striking on the panes
turned their dullness to opal and silver, and the jewel-
lers' shops seen through this, were fairy palaces. Her feet
were horribly wet, and she knew the bottom of her skirt
and petticoat would be coated with black, greasy mud.
There was a sickening smell of warm humanity—it
seemed to be oozing out of everybody in the bus—and
everybody had the same expression, sitting so still, staring in front of them. How many times had she read
these advertisements—"Sapolio Saves Time, Saves
Labour"—"Heinz's Tomato Sauce"—and the inane,
annoying dialogue between doctor and judge concern-
ing the superlative merits of "Lamp-lough's Pyretic
Saline." She glanced at the book which the girl read so

earnestly, mouthing the words in a way that Rosabel detested, licking her first finger and thumb each time that she turned the page. She could not see very clearly; it was something about a hot, voluptuous night, a band playing, and a girl with lovely, white shoulders. Oh, heavens! Rosabel stirred suddenly and unfastened the two top buttons of her coat . . . she felt almost stifled. Through her half-closed eyes the whole row of people on the opposite seat seemed to resolve into one fatuous, staring face . . .

And this was her corner. She stumbled a little on her way out and lurched against the girl next her. "I beg your pardon," said Rosabel, but the girl did not even look up. Rosabel saw that she was smiling as she read.

Westbourne Grove looked as she had alway' imagined Venice to look at night, mysterious, dark, even the hansoms were like gondolas dodging up and down, and the lights trailing luridly—tongues of flame licking the wet street—magic fish swimming in the Grand Canal. She was more than glad to reach Richmond Road, but from the corner of the street until she came to No. 26 she thought of those four flights of stairs. Oh, why four flights! It was really criminal to expect people to live so high up. Every house ought to have a lift, something simple and inexpensive, or else an electric staircase like the one at Earl's Court—but four flights! When she stood in the hall and saw the first flight ahead of her and the stuffed albatross head on the landing, glimmering ghost-like in the light of the little gas jet, she almost cried. Well, they had to be faced; it was very like bicycling up a steep hill, but there was not the satisfaction of flying down the other side . . .

Her own room at last! She closed the door, lit the gas, took off her hat and coat, skirt, blouse, unhooked her old flannel dressing-gown from behind the door, pulled it on, then unlaced her boots—on consideration her stockings were not wet enough to change. She went over to the wash-stand. The jug had not been filled again to-day. There was just enough water to soak the sponge, and the enamel was coming off the basin—that was the second time she had scratched her chin.

It was just seven o'clock. If she pulled the blind up and put out the gas it was much more restful—Rosabel did not want to read. So she knelt down on the floor, pillowing her arms on the window-sill . . . just one little sheet of glass between her and the great wet world outside!

She began to think of all that had happened during the day. Would she ever forget that awful woman in the grey mackintosh who had wanted a trimmed motor-cap—"something purple with, something rosy each side"—or the girl who had tried on every hat in the shop and then said she would "call in tomorrow and decide definitely." Rosabel could not help smiling; the excuse was worn so thin . . .

But there had been one other—a girl with beautiful red hair and a white skin and eyes the colour of that green ribbon shot with gold they had got from Paris last week. Rosabel had seen her electric brougham at the door; a man had come in with her, quite a young man, and so well dressed.

"What is it exactly that I want, Harry?" she had said, as Rosabel took the pins out of her hat, untied her veil, and gave her a hand-mirror.

"You must have a black hat," he had answered, "a black hat with a feather that goes right round it and then round your neck and ties in a bow under your chin, and the ends tuck into your belt—a decent-sized feather."

The girl glanced at Rosabel laughingly. "Have you any hats like that?"

They had been very hard to please; Harry would demand the impossible, and Rosabel was almost in despair. Then she remembered the big, untouched box upstairs.

"Oh, one moment, Madam," she had said. "I think perhaps I can show you something that will please you better." She had run up, breathlessly, cut the cords, scattered the tissue paper, and yes, there was the very hat—rather large, soft, with a great, curled feather, and a black velvet rose, nothing else. They had been charmed. The girl had put it on and then handed it to Rosabel.

"Let me see how it looks on you," she said, frowning a little, very serious indeed.

Rosabel turned to the mirror and placed it on her brown hair, then faced them.

"Oh, Harry, isn't it adorable," the girl cried, "I must have that!" She smiled again at Rosabel. "It suits you beautifully."

A sudden, ridiculous feeling of anger had seized Rosabel. She longed to throw the lovely, perishable thing in the girl's face, and bent over the hat, flushing.

"It's exquisitely finished off inside, Madam," she said. The girl swept out to her brougham, and left Harry to pay and bring the box with him.

"I shall go straight home and put it on before I come out to lunch with you," Rosabel heard her say.

The man leant over her as she made out the bill, then, as he counted the money into her hand—"Ever been painted?" he said.

"No," said Rosabel shortly, realising the swift change in his voice, the slight tinge of insolence, of familiarity.

"Oh, well you ought to be," said Harry. "You've got such a damned pretty little figure."

Rosabel did not pay the slightest attention. How handsome he had been! She had thought of no one else all day; his face fascinated her; she could see clearly his fine, straight eyebrows, and his hair grew back from his forehead with just the slightest suspicion of crisp curl, his laughing, disdainful mouth. She saw again his slim hands counting the money into hers . . . Rosabel suddenly pushed the hair back from her face, her forehead was hot . . . if those slim hands could rest one moment . . . the luck of that girl!

Suppose they changed places. Rosabel would drive home with him, of course they were in love with each other, but not engaged, very nearly, and she would say—"I won't be one moment." He would wait in the brougham while her maid took the hat-box up the stairs, following Rosabel. Then the great, white and pink bedroom with roses everywhere in dull silver vases. She would sit down before the mirror and the little French maid would fasten her hat and find her a thin, fine veil and another pair of white suéde gloves—a button had come off the gloves she had worn that morning. She had scented her furs and gloves and handkerchief, taken a big muff and run downstairs. The butler opened the door, Harry was waiting, they drove away together . . . *That* was life, thought Rosabel! On the way to the Carlton they stopped at Gerard's, Harry bought her great sprays of Parma violets, filled her hands with them.

"Oh, they are sweet!" she said, holding them against her face.

47

"It is as you always should be," said Harry, "with your hands full of violets."

(Rosabel realised that her knees were getting stiff; she sat down on the floor and leant her head against the wall.) Oh, that lunch! The table covered with flowers, a band hidden behind a grove of palms playing music that fired her blood like wine—the soup, and oysters, and pigeons, and creamed potatoes, and champagne, of course, and afterwards coffee and cigarettes. She would lean over the table fingering her glass with one hand, talking with that charming gaiety which Harry so appreciated. Afterwards a matinée, something that gripped them both, and then tea at the "Cottage."

"Sugar? Milk? Cream?" The little homely questions seemed to suggest a joyous intimacy. And then home again in the dusk, and the scent of the Parma violets seemed to drench the air with their sweetness.

"I'll call for you at nine," he said as he left her.

The fire had been lighted in her boudoir, the curtains drawn, there were a great pile of letters waiting her—invitations for the Opera, dinners, balls, a week-end on the river, a motor tour—she glanced through them listlessly as she went upstairs to dress. A fire in her bedroom, too, and her beautiful, shining dress spread on the bed—white tulle over silver, silver shoes, silver scarf, a little silver fan. Rosabel knew that she was the most famous woman at the ball that night; men paid her homage, a foreign Prince desired to be presented to this English wonder. Yes, it was a voluptuous night, a band playing, and *her* lovely white shoulders . . .

But she became very tired. Harry took her home, and came in with her for just one moment. The fire was out in the drawing-room, but the sleepy maid waited for her in her boudoir. She took off her cloak, dismissed the servant, and went over to the fire-place, and stood peeling off her gloves; the firelight shone on her hair, Harry came across the room and caught her in his arms—"Rosabel, Rosabel, Rosabel . . ." Oh, the haven of those arms, and she was very tired.

(The real Rosabel, the girl crouched on the floor in the dark, laughed aloud, and put her hand up to her hot mouth.)

Of course they rode in the park next morning, the engagement had been announced in the *Court Circular*, all the world knew, all the world was shaking hands with her . . .

They were married shortly afterwards at St. George's, Hanover Square, and motored down to Harry's old ancestral home for the honeymoon; the peasants in the village curtseyed to them as they passed; under the folds of the rug he pressed her hands convulsively. And that night she wore again her white and silver frock. She was tired after the journey and went upstairs to bed . . . quite early . . .

The real Rosabel got up from the floor and undressed slowly, folding her clothes over the back of a chair. She slipped over her head her coarse, calico night-dress, and took the pins out of her hair—the soft, brown flood of it fell round her, warmly. Then she blew out the candle and groped her way into bed, pulling the blankets and grimy "honeycomb" quilt closely round her neck, cuddling down in the darkness . . .

So she slept and dreamed, and smiled in her sleep, and once threw out her arm to feel for something which was not there, dreaming still.

And the night passed. Presently the cold fingers of dawn closed over her uncovered hand; grey light flooded the dull room. Rosabel shivered, drew a little gasping breath, sat up. And because her heritage was that tragic optimism, which is all too often the only inheritance of youth, still half asleep, she smiled, with a little nervous tremor round her mouth.

THE DAUGHTERS OF THE
LATE COLONEL

I

The week after was one of the busiest weeks of their lives. Even when they went to bed it was only their bodies that lay down and rested; their minds went on, thinking things out, talking things over, wondering, deciding, trying to remember where . . .

Constantia lay like a statue, her hands by her sides, her feet just overlapping each other, the sheet up to her chin. She stared at the ceiling.

"Do you think father would mind if we gave his top-hat to the porter?"

"The porter?" snapped Josephine. "Why ever the porter? What a very extraordinary idea!"

"Because," said Constantia slowly, "he must often have to go to funerals. And I noticed at—at the cemetery that he only had a bowler." She paused. "I thought then how very much he'd appreciate a top-hat. We ought to give him a present, too. He was always very nice to father."

"But," cried Josephine, flouncing on her pillow and staring across the dark at Constantia, "father's head!" And suddenly, for one awful moment, she nearly giggled. Not, of course, that she felt in the least like giggling. It must have been habit. Years ago, when they had stayed awake at night talking, their beds had simply

51

heaved. And now the porter's head, disappearing, popped out, like a candle, under father's hat . . . The giggle mounted, mounted; she clenched her hands; she fought it down; she frowned fiercely at the dark and said "Remember" terribly sternly.

"We can decide to-morrow," she said.

Constantia had noticed nothing; she sighed.

"Do you think we ought to have our dressing-gowns dyed as well?"

"Black?" almost shrieked Josephine.

"Well, what else?" said Constantia. "I was thinking— it doesn't seem quite sincere, in a way, to wear black out of doors and when we're fully dressed, and then when we're at home—"

"But nobody sees us," said Josephine. She gave the bedclothes such a twitch that both her feet became uncovered and she had to creep up the pillows to get them well under again.

"Kate does," said Constantia. "And the postman very well might."

Josephine thought of her dark-red slippers, which matched her dressing-gown, and of Constantia's favourite indefinite green ones which went with hers. Black! Two black dressing-gowns and two pairs of black woolly slippers, creeping off to the bathroom like black cats.

"I don't think it's absolutely necessary," said she.

Silence. Then Constantia said, "We shall have to post the papers with the notice in them to-morrow to catch the Ceylon mail . . . How many letters have we had up till now?"

"Twenty-three."

Josephine had replied to them all, and twenty-three times when she came to "We miss our dear father so much" she had broken down and had to use her handkerchief, and on some of them even to soak up a very light-blue tear with an edge of blotting-paper. Strange! She couldn't have put it on—but twenty-three times. Even now, though, when she said over to herself sadly "We miss our dear father *so* much," she could have cried if she'd wanted to.

"Have you got enough stamps?" came from Constantia.

"Oh, how can I tell?" said Josephine crossly. "What's the good of asking me that now?"

"I was just wondering," said Constantia mildly.

Silence again. There came a little rustle, a scurry, a hop.

"A mouse," said Constantia.

"It can't be a mouse because there aren't any crumbs," said Josephine.

"But it doesn't know there aren't," said Constantia.

A spasm of pity squeezed her heart. Poor little thing! She wished she'd left a tiny piece of biscuit on the dressing-table. It was awful to think of it not finding anything. What would it do?

"I can't think how they manage to live at all," she said slowly.

"Who?" demanded Josephine.

And Constantia said more loudly than she meant to, "Mice."

Josephine was furious. "Oh, what nonsense, Con!" she said. "What have mice got to do with it? You're asleep."

"I don't think I am," said Constantia. She shut her eyes to make sure. She was.

Josephine arched her spine, pulled up her knees,

folded her arms so that her fists came under her ears, and pressed her cheek hard against the pillow.

II

Another thing which complicated matters was they had Nurse Andrews staying on with them that week. It was their own fault; they had asked her. It was Josephine's idea. On the morning—well, on the last morning, when the doctor had gone, Josephine had said to Constantia, "Don't you think it would be rather nice if we asked Nurse Andrews to stay on for a week as our guest?"

"Very nice," said Constantia.

"I thought," went on Josephine quickly, "I should just say this afternoon, after I've paid her, 'My sister and I would be very pleased, after all you've done for us, Nurse Andrews, if you would stay on for a week as our guest.' I'd have to put that in about being our guest in case—"

"Oh, but she could hardly expect to be paid!" cried Constantia.

"One never knows," said Josephine sagely.

Nurse Andrews had, of course, jumped at the idea. But it was a bother. It meant they had to have regular sit-down meals at the proper times, whereas if they'd been alone they could just have asked Kate if she wouldn't have minded bringing them a tray wherever they were. And meal-times now that the strain was over were rather a trial.

Nurse Andrews was simply fearful about butter. Really they couldn't help feeling that about butter, at least, she took advantage of their kindness. And she had that maddening habit of asking for just an inch more bread to finish what she had on her plate, and then, at the last mouthful, absent-mindedly—of course it wasn't absent-mindedly—taking another helping. Josephine got very red when this happened, and she fastened her small, bead-like eyes on the tablecloth as if she saw a minute strange insect creeping through the web of it. But Constantia's long, pale face lengthened and set, and she gazed away—away—far over the desert, to where that line of camels unwound like a thread of wool . . .

"When I was with Lady Tukes," said Nurse Andrews, "she had such a dainty little contrayvance for the buttah. It was a silvah Cupid balanced on the—on the bordah of a glass dish, holding a tayny fork. And when you wanted some buttah you simply pressed his foot and he bent down and speared you a piece. It was quite a gayme."

Josephine could hardly bear that. But "I think those things are very extravagant" was all she said.

"But whey?" asked Nurse Andrews, beaming through her eyeglasses. "No one, surely, would take more buttah than one wanted—would one?"

"Ring, Con," cried Josephine. She couldn't trust herself to reply.

And proud young Kate, the enchanted princess, came in to see what the old tabbies wanted now. She snatched away their plates of mock something or other and slapped down a white, terrified blancmange.

"Jam, please, Kate," said Josephine kindly.

Kate knelt and burst open the sideboard, lifted the lid of the jam-pot, saw it was empty, put it on the table, and stalked off.

"I'm afraid," said Nurse Andrews a moment later, "there isn't any."

"Oh, what a bother!" said Josephine. She bit her lip. "What had we better do?"

Constantia looked dubious. "We can't disturb Kate again," she said softly.

Nurse Andrews waited, smiling at them both. Her eyes wandered, spying at everything behind her eye-glasses. Constantia in despair went back to her camels. Josephine frowned heavily—concentrated. If it hadn't been for this idiotic woman she and Con would, of course, have eaten their blancmange without. Suddenly the idea came.

"I know," she said. "Marmalade. There's some marmalade in the sideboard. Get it, Con."

"I hope," laughed Nurse Andrews—and her laugh was like a spoon tinkling against a medicine-glass—"I hope it's not very bittah marmalayde."

III

But, after all, it was not long now, and then she'd be gone for good. And there was no getting over the fact that she had been very kind to father. She had nursed him day and night at the end. Indeed, both Constantia and Josephine felt privately she had rather overdone the not leaving him at the very last. For when they had gone in to say good-bye Nurse Andrews had sat beside his bed the whole time, holding his wrist and pretending to look at her watch. It couldn't have been necessary. It was so tactless, too. Supposing father had wanted to say something—something private to them. Not that he had. Oh, far from it! He lay there, purple, a dark, angry purple in the face, and never even looked at them when they came in. Then, as they were standing there, wondering what to do, he had suddenly opened one eye. Oh, what a difference it would have made, what a difference to their memory of him, how much easier to tell people about it, if he had only opened both! But no—one eye only. It glared at them a moment and then . . . went out.

IV

It had made it very awkward for them when Mr. Farolles, of St. John's, called the same afternoon.

"The end was quite peaceful, I trust?" were the first words he said as he glided towards them through the dark drawing-room.

"Quite," said Josephine faintly. They both hung their heads. Both of them felt certain that eye wasn't at all a peaceful eye.

"Won't you sit down?" said Josephine.

"Thank you, Miss Pinner," said Mr. Farolles gratefully. He folded his coat-tails and began to lower himself into father's arm-chair, but just as he touched it he almost sprang up and slid into the next chair instead.

He coughed. Josephine clasped her hands; Constantia looked vague.

"I want you to feel, Miss Pinner," said Mr. Farolles, "and you, Miss Constantia, that I'm trying to be helpful. I want to be helpful to you both, if you will let me. These are the times," said Mr. Farolles, very simply and earnestly, "when God means us to be helpful to one another."

"Thank you very much, Mr. Farolles," said Josephine and Constantia.

"Not at all," said Mr. Farolles gently. He drew his kid

gloves through his fingers and leaned forward. "And if either of you would like a little Communion, either or both of you, here *and* now, you have only to tell me. A little Communion is often very help—a great comfort," he added tenderly.

But the idea of a little Communion terrified them. What! In the drawing-room by themselves—with no—no altar or anything! The piano would be much too high, thought Constantia, and Mr. Farolles could not possibly lean over it with the chalice. And Kate would be sure to come bursting in and interrupt them, thought Josephine. And supposing the bell rang in the middle? It might be somebody important—about their mourning. Would they get up reverently and go out, or would they have to wait . . . in torture?

"Perhaps you will send round a note by your good Kate if you would care for it later," said Mr. Farolles.

"Oh yes, thank you very much!" they both said.

Mr. Farolles got up and took his black straw hat from the round table.

"And about the funeral," he said softly. "I may arrange that—as your dear father's old friend and yours, Miss Pinner—and Miss Constantia?"

Josephine and Constantia got up too.

"I should like it to be quite simple," said Josephine firmly, "and not too expensive. At the same time, I should like—"

"A good one that will last," thought dreamy Constantia, as if Josephine were buying a night-gown. But, of course, Josephine didn't say that. "One suitable to our father's position." She was very nervous.

"I'll run round to our good friend Mr. Knight," said Mr. Farolles soothingly. "I will ask him to come and see you. I am sure you will find him very helpful indeed."

V

Well, at any rate, all that part of it was over, though neither of them could possibly believe that father was never coming back. Josephine had had a moment of absolute terror at the cemetery, while the coffin was lowered, to think that she and Constantia had done this thing without asking his permission. What would father say when he found out? For he was bound to find out sooner or later. He always did. "Buried. You two girls had me *buried*!" She heard his stick thumping. Oh, what would they say? What possible excuse could they make? It sounded such an appallingly heartless thing to do. Such a wicked advantage to take of a person because he happened to be helpless at the moment. The other people seemed to treat it all as a matter of course. They were strangers; they couldn't be expected to understand that father was the very last person for such a thing to happen to. No, the entire blame for it all would fall on her and Constantia. And the expense, she thought, stepping into the tight-buttoned cab. When she had to show him the bills. What would he say then?

She heard him absolutely roaring. "And do you expect me to pay for this gimcrack excursion of yours?"

"Oh," groaned poor Josephine aloud, "we shouldn't have done it, Con!"

And Constantia, pale as a lemon in all that blackness, said in a frightened whisper, "Done what, Jug?"

"Let them bu-bury father like that," said Josephine, breaking down and crying into her new, queer-smelling mourning handkerchief.

"But what else could we have done?" asked Constantia wonderingly. "We couldn't have kept him, Jug—we couldn't have kept him unburied. At any rate, not in a flat that size."

Josephine blew her nose; the cab was dreadfully stuffy.

"I don't know," she said forlornly. "It is all so dreadful. I feel we ought to have tried to, just for a time at least. To make perfectly sure. One thing's certain"—and her tears sprang out again—"father will never forgive us for this—never!"

VI

Father would never forgive them. That was what they felt more than ever when, two mornings later, they went into his room to go through his things. They had discussed it quite calmly. It was even down on Josephine's list of things to be done. *Go through father's things and settle about them.* But that was a very different matter from saying after breakfast:

"Well, are you ready, Con?"

"Yes, Jug—when you are."

"Then I think we'd better get it over."

It was dark in the hall. It had been a rule for years never to disturb father in the morning, whatever happened. And now they were going to open the door without knocking even . . . Constantia's eyes were enormous at the idea; Josephine felt weak in the knees.

"You—you go first," she gasped, pushing Constantia.

But Constantia said, as she always had said on those occasions, "No, Jug, that's not fair. You're eldest."

Josephine was just going to say—what at other times she wouldn't have owned to for the world—what she kept for her very last weapon, "But you're tallest," when

60

they noticed that the kitchen door was open, and there stood Kate . . .

"Very stiff," said Josephine, grasping the door-handle and doing her best to turn it. As if anything ever deceived Kate!

It couldn't be helped. That girl was . . . Then the door was shut behind them, but—but they weren't in father's room at all. They might have suddenly walked through the wall by mistake into a different flat altogether. Was the door just behind them? They were too frightened to look. Josephine knew that if it was it was holding itself tight shut; Constantia felt that, like the doors in dreams, it hadn't any handle at all. It was the coldness which made it so awful. Or the whiteness—which? Everything was covered. The blinds were down, a cloth hung over the mirror, a sheet hid the bed; a huge fan of white paper filled the fire-place. Constantia timidly put out her hand; she almost expected a snowflake to fall. Josephine felt a queer tingling in her nose, as if her nose was freezing. Then a cab klop-klopped over the cobbles below, and the quiet seemed to shake into little pieces.

"I had better pull up a blind," said Josephine bravely.

"Yes, it might be a good idea," whispered Constantia.

They only gave the blind a touch, but it flew up and the cord flew after, rolling round the blind-stick, and the little tassel tapped as if trying to get fro. That was too much for Constantia.

"Don't you think—don't you think we might put it off for another day?" she whispered.

"Why?" snapped Josephine, feeling, as usual, much better now that she knew for certain that Constantia was terrified. "It's got to be done. But I do wish you wouldn't whisper, Con."

"I didn't know I was whispering," whispered Constantia.

"And why do you keep on staring at the bed?" said Josephine, raising her voice almost defiantly. "There's nothing *on* the bed."

"Oh, Jug, don't say so!" said poor Connie. "At any rate, not so loudly."

Josephine felt herself that she had gone too far. She took a wide swerve over to the chest of drawers, put out her hand, but quickly drew it back again.

"Connie!" she gasped, and she wheeled round and leaned with her back against the chest of drawers.

"Oh, Jug—what?"

Josephine could only glare. She had the most extraordinary feeling that she had just escaped something simply awful. But how could she explain to Constantia that father was in the chest of drawers? He was in the top drawer with his handkerchiefs and neckties, or in the next with his shirts and pyjamas, or in the lowest of all with his suits. He was watching there, hidden away— just behind the door-handle—ready to spring.

She pulled a funny old-fashioned face at Constantia, just as she used to in the old days when she was going to cry.

"I can't open," she nearly wailed.

"No, don't, Jug," whispered Constantia earnestly. "It's much better not to. Don't let's open anything. At any rate, not for a long time."

"But—but it seems so weak," said Josephine, breaking down.

"But why not be weak for once, Jug?" argued Constantia, whispering quite fiercely. "If it is weak." And her pale stare flew from the locked writing-table—so safe—to the huge glittering wardrobe, and she began to breathe in a queer, panting way. "Why shouldn't we be weak for once in our lives, Jug? It's quite excusable. Let's be weak—be weak, Jug. It's much nicer to be weak than to be strong."

And then she did one of those amazingly bold things that she'd done about twice before in their lives: she marched over to the wardrobe, turned the key, and took it out of the lock. Took it out of the lock and held it up to Josephine, showing Josephine by her extraordinary smile that she knew what she'd done—she'd risked deliberately father being in there among his overcoats.

If the huge wardrobe had lurched forward, had crashed down on Constantia, Josephine wouldn't have been surprised. On the contrary, she would have thought it the only suitable thing to happen. But nothing happened. Only the room seemed quieter than ever, and bigger flakes of cold air fell on Josephine's shoulders and knees. She began to shiver.

"Come, Jug," said Constantia, still with that awful callous smile; and Josephine followed just as she had that last time, when Constantia had pushed Benny into the round pond.

VII

But the strain told on them when they were back in the dining-room. They sat down, very shaky, and looked at each other.

"I don't feel I can settle to anything," said Josephine, "until I've had something. Do you think we could ask Kate for two cups of hot water?"

"I really don't see why we shouldn't," said Constantia carefully. She was quite normal again. "I won't ring. I'll go to the kitchen door and ask her."

"Yes, do," said Josephine, sinking down into a chair. "Tell her, just two cups, Con, nothing else—on a tray."

"She needn't even put the jug on, need she?" said Constantia, as though Kate might very well complain if the jug had been there.

"Oh no, certainly not! The jug's not at all necessary. She can pour it direct out of the kettle," cried Josephine, feeling that would be a labour-saving indeed.

Their cold lips quivered at the greenish brims. Josephine curved her small red hands round the cup; Constantia sat up and blew on the wavy steam, making it flutter from one side to the other.

"Speaking of Benny," said Josephine.

And though Benny hadn't been mentioned Constantia immediately looked as though he had.

"He'll expect us to send him something of father's, of course. But it's so difficult to know what to send to Ceylon."

"You mean things get unstuck so on the voyage," murmured Constantia.

"No, lost," said Josephine sharply. "You know there's no post. Only runners."

Both paused to watch a black man in white linen drawers running through the pale fields for dear life, with a large brown-paper parcel in his hands. Josephine's black man was tiny; he scurried along glistening like an ant. But there was something blind and tireless about Constantia's tall, thin fellow, which made him, she decided, a very unpleasant person indeed . . . On the veranda, dressed all in white and wearing a cork helmet, stood Benny. His right hand shook up and down, as father's did when he was impatient. And behind him, not in the least interested, sat Hilda, the unknown sister-in-law. She swung in a cane rocker and flicked over the leaves of the *Tatler*.

"I think his watch would be the most suitable present," said Josephine.

Constantia looked up; she seemed surprised.

"Oh, would you trust a gold watch to a native?"

"But, of course, I'd disguise it," said Josephine. "No one would know it was a watch." She liked the idea of having to make a parcel such a curious shape that no one could possibly guess what it was. She even thought for a moment of hiding the watch in a narrow cardboard corset-box that she'd kept by her for a long time, waiting for it to come in for something. It was such beautiful, firm cardboard. But, no, it wouldn't be appropriate for this occasion. It had lettering on it: *Medium Women's* 28. *Extra Firm Busks*. It would be almost too much of a surprise for Benny to open that and find father's watch inside.

"And, of course, it isn't as though it would be going—ticking, I mean," said Constantia, who was still thinking of the native love of jewellery. "At least," she added, "it would be very strange if after all that time it was."

VIII

Josephine made no reply. She had flown off on one of her tangents. She had suddenly thought of Cyril. Wasn't it more usual for the only grandson to have the watch? And then dear Cyril was so appreciative and a gold watch meant so much to a young man. Benny, in all probability, had quite got out of the habit of watches;

men so seldom wore waistcoats in those hot climates. Whereas Cyril in London wore them from year's end to year's end. And it would be so nice for her and Constantia, when he came to tea, to know it was there. "I see you've got on grandfather's watch, Cyril." It would be somehow so satisfactory.

Dear boy! What a blow his sweet, sympathetic little note had been! Of course they quite understood; but it was most unfortunate.

"It would have been such a point, having him," said Josephine.

"And he would have enjoyed it so," said Constantia, not thinking what she was saying.

However, as soon as he got back he was coming to tea with his aunties. Cyril to tea was one of their rare treats.

"Now, Cyril, you mustn't be frightened of our cakes. Your Auntie Con and I bought them at Buszard's this morning. We know what a man's appetite is. So don't be ashamed of making a good tea."

Josephine cut recklessly into the rich dark cake that stood for her winter gloves or the soling and heeling of Constantia's only respectable shoes. But Cyril was most unmanlike in appetite.

"I say, Aunt Josephine, I simply can't. I've only just had lunch, you know."

"Oh, Cyril, that can't be true! It's after four," cried Josephine. Constantia sat with her knife poised over the chocolate-roll.

"It is, all the same," said Cyril. "I had to meet a man at Victoria, and he kept me hanging about till . . . there was only time to get lunch and to come on here. And he gave me—phew"—Cyril put his hand to his forehead—"a terrific blowout," he said.

It was disappointing—to-day of all days. But still he couldn't be expected to know.

"But you'll have a meringue, won't you, Cyril?" said Aunt Josephine. "These meringues were bought specially for you. Your dear father was so fond of them. We were sure you are, too."

"I *am*, Aunt Josephine," cried Cyril ardently. "Do you mind if I take half to begin with?"

"Not at all, dear boy; but we mustn't let you off with that."

"Is your dear father still so fond of meringues?" asked Auntie Con gently. She winced faintly as she broke through the shell of hers.

"Well, I don't quite know, Auntie Con," said Cyril breezily.

At that they both looked up.

"Don't know?" almost snapped Josephine. "Don't know a thing like that about your own father, Cyril?"

"Surely," said Auntie Con softly.

Cyril tried to laugh it off. "Oh, well," he said, "it's such a long time since—" He faltered. He stopped. Their faces were too much for him.

"Even so," said Josephine.

And Auntie Con looked.

Cyril put down his teacup. "Wait a bit," he cried. "Wait a bit, Aunt Josephine. What am I thinking of?"

He looked up. They were beginning to brighten. Cyril slapped his knee.

"Of course," he said, "it was meringues. How could I have forgotten? Yes, Aunt Josephine, you're perfectly right. Father's most frightfully keen on meringues."

They didn't only beam. Aunt Josephine went scarlet with pleasure; Auntie Con gave a deep, deep sigh.

"And now, Cyril, you must come and see father," said Josephine. "He knows you were coming to-day."

"Right," said Cyril, very firmly and heartily. He got up from his chair; suddenly he glanced at the clock.

"I say, Auntie Con, isn't your clock a bit slow? I've got to meet a man at—at Paddington just after five. I'm afraid I shan't be able to stay very long with grandfather."

"Oh, he won't expect you to stay *very* long!" said Aunt Josephine.

Constantia was still gazing at the clock. She couldn't make up her mind if it was fast or slow. It was one or the other, she felt almost certain of that. At any rate, it had been.

Cyril still lingered. "Aren't you coming along, Auntie Con?"

"Of course," said Josephine, "we shall all go. Come on, Con."

IX

They knocked at the door, and Cyril followed his aunts into grandfather's hot, sweetish room.

"Come on," said Grandfather Pinner. "Don't hang about. What is it? What've you been up to?"

He was sitting in front of a roaring fire, clasping his stick. He had a thick rug over his knees. On his lap there lay a beautiful pale yellow silk handkerchief.

"It's Cyril, father," said Josephine shyly. And she took Cyril's hand and led him forward.

"Good afternoon, grandfather," said Cyril, trying to take his hand out of Aunt Josephine's. Grandfather Pinner shot his eyes at Cyril in the way he was famous for. Where was Auntie Con? She stood on the other side of Aunt Josephine; her long arms hung down in front of her; her hands were clasped. She never took her eyes off grandfather.

"Well," said Grandfather Pinner, beginning to thump, "what have you got to tell me?"

What had he, what had he got to tell him? Cyril felt himself smiling like a perfect imbecile. The room was stifling, too.

But Aunt Josephine came to his rescue. She cried brightly, "Cyril says his father is still very fond of meringues, father dear."

"Eh?" said Grandfather Pinner, curving his hand like a purple meringue-shell over one ear.

Josephine repeated, "Cyril says his father is still very fond of meringues."

"Can't hear," said old Colonel Pinner. And he waved Josephine away with his stick, then pointed with his stick to Cyril. "Tell me what she's trying to say," he said.

(My God!) "Must I?" said Cyril, blushing and staring at Aunt Josephine.

"Do, dear," she smiled. "It will please him so much."

"Come on, out with it!" cried Colonel Pinner testily, beginning to thump again.

And Cyril leaned forward and yelled, "Father's still very fond of meringues."

At that Grandfather Pinner jumped as though he had been shot.

"Don't shout!" he cried. "What's the matter with the boy? *Meringues!* What about 'em?"

"Oh, Aunt Josephine, must we go on?" groaned Cyril desperately.

"It's quite all right, dear boy," said Aunt Josephine, as though he and she were at the dentist's together. "He'll understand in a minute." And she whispered to Cyril, "He's getting a bit deaf, you know." Then she leaned forward and really bawled at Grandfather Pinner, "Cyril only wanted to tell you, father dear, that *his* father is still very fond of meringues."

Colonel Pinner heard that time, heard and brooded, looking Cyril up and down.

"What an esstrordinary thing!" said old Grandfather Pinner. "What an esstrordinary thing to come all this way here to tell me!"

And Cyril felt it *was*.

"Yes, I shall send Cyril the watch," said Josephine.

"That would be very nice," said Constantia. "I seem to remember last time he came there was some little trouble about the time."

X

They were interrupted by Kate bursting through the door in her usual fashion, as though she had discovered some secret panel in the wall.

"Fried or boiled?" asked the bold voice.

Fried or boiled? Josephine and Constantia were quite bewildered for the moment. They could hardly take it in.

"Fried or boiled what, Kate?" asked Josephine, trying to begin to concentrate.

Kate gave a loud sniff. "Fish."

"Well, why didn't you say so immediately?" Josephine reproached her gently. "How could you expect us to understand, Kate? There are a great many things in this world, you know, which are fried or boiled." And after such a display of courage she said quite brightly to Constantia, "Which do you prefer, Con?"

"I think it might be nice to have it fried," said Constantia. "On the other hand, of course, boiled fish is very nice. I think I prefer both equally well . . . Unless you . . . In that case—"

"I shall fry it," said Kate, and she bounced back, leaving their door open and slamming the door of her kitchen.

Josephine gazed at Constantia; she raised her pale eyebrows until they rippled away into her pale hair. She got up. She said in a very lofty, imposing way, "Do you mind following me into the drawing-room, Constantia? I've something of great importance to discuss with you."

For it was always to the drawing-room they retired when they wanted to talk over Kate.

Josephine closed the door meaningly. "Sit down, Constantia," she said, still very grand. She might have been receiving Constantia for the first time. And Con looked round vaguely for a chair, as though she felt indeed quite a stranger.

"Now the question is," said Josephine, bending forward, "whether we shall keep her or not."

"That is the question," agreed Constantia.

"And this time," said Josephine firmly, "we must come to a definite decision."

Constantia looked for a moment as though she might begin going over all the other times, but she pulled herself together and said, "Yes, Jug."

"You see, Con," explained Josephine, "everything is so changed now." Constantia looked up quickly. "I mean," went on Josephine, "we're not dependent on Kate as we were." And she blushed faintly. "There's not father to cook for."

That is perfectly true," agreed Constantia. "Father certainly doesn't want any cooking now whatever else—"

Josephine broke in sharply, "You're not sleepy, are you, Con?"

"Sleepy, Jug?" Constantia was wide-eyed.

"Well, concentrate more," said Josephine sharply, and she returned to the subject. "What it comes to is, if we did"—and this she barely breathed, glancing at the door—"give Kate notice"—she raised her voice again—"we could manage our own food."

"Why not?" cried Constantia. She couldn't help smiling. The idea was so exciting. She clasped her hands. "What should we live on, Jug?"

"Oh, eggs in various forms!" said Jug, lofty again. "And, besides, there are all the cooked foods."

"But I've always heard," said Constantia, "they are considered so very expensive."

"Not if one buys them in moderation," said Josephine. But she tore herself away from this fascinating bypath and dragged Constantia after her.

"What we've got to decide now, however, is whether we really do trust Kate or not."

Constantia leaned back. Her flat little laugh flew from her lips.

"Isn't it curious, Jug," said she, "that just on this one subject I've never been able to quite make up my mind?"

XI

She never had. The whole difficulty was to prove anything. How did one prove things, how could one? Suppose Kate had stood in front of her and deliberately made a face. Mightn't she very well have been in pain? Wasn't it impossible, at any rate, to ask Kate if she was making a face at her? If Kate answered "No"—and, of course, she would say "No"—what a position! How undignified! Then, again, Constantia suspected, she was almost certain that Kate went to her chest of drawers when she and Josephine were out, not to take things but to spy. Many times she had come back to find her amethyst cross in the most unlikely places, under her lace ties or on top of her evening Bertha. More than once she had laid a trap for Kate. She had arranged things in a special order and then called Josephine to witness.

"You see, Jug?"

"Quite, Con."

"Now we shall be able to tell."

But, oh dear, when she did go to look, she was as far off from a proof as ever! If anything was displaced, it might so very well have happened as she closed the drawer; a jolt might have done it so easily.

"You come, Jug, and decide. I really can't. It's too difficult."

But after a pause and a long glare Josephine would sigh, "Now you've put the doubt into my mind, Con, I'm sure I can't tell myself."

"Well, we can't postpone it again," said Josephine. "If we postpone it this time—"

XII

But at that moment in the street below a barrel-organ struck up. Josephine and Constantia sprang to their feet together.

"Run, Con," said Josephine. "Run quickly. There's sixpence on the—"

Then they remembered. It didn't matter. They would never have to stop the organ-grinder again. Never again would she and Constantia be told to make that monkey take his noise somewhere else. Never would sound that loud, strange bellow when father thought they were not hurrying enough. The organ-grinder might play there all day and the stick would not thump.

> It never will thump again,
> It never will thump again,

played the barrel-organ.

What was Constantia thinking? She had such a strange smile; she looked different. She couldn't be going to cry.

"Jug, Jug," said Constantia softly, pressing her hands together. "Do you know what day it is? It's Saturday. It's a week to-day, a whole week."

> A week since father died,
> A week since father died,

cried the barrel-organ. And Josephine, too, forgot to be practical and sensible; she smiled faintly, strangely. On the Indian carpet there fell a square of sunlight, pale red; it came and went and came—and stayed, deepened—until it shone almost golden.

"The sun's out," said Josephine, as though it really mattered.

A perfect fountain of bubbling notes shook from the barrel-organ, round, bright notes, carelessly scattered.

Constantia lifted her big, cold hands as if to catch them, and then her hands fell again. She walked over to the mantelpiece to her favourite Buddha. And the stone and gilt image, whose smile always gave her such a queer feeling, almost a pain and yet a pleasant pain, seemed to-day to be more than smiling. He knew something; he had a secret. "I know something that you don't know," said her Buddha. Oh, what was it, what could it be? And yet she had always felt there was . . . something.

The sunlight pressed through the windows, thieved its way in, flashed its light over the furniture and the photographs. Josephine watched it. When it came to mother's photograph, the enlargement over the piano, it lingered as though puzzled to find so little remained of mother, except the ear-rings shaped like tiny pagodas and a black feather boa. Why did the photographs of dead people always fade so? wondered Josephine. As soon as a person was dead their photograph died too. But, of course, this one of mother was very old. It was thirty-five years old. Josephine remembered standing on a chair and pointing out that feather boa to Constantia and telling her that it was a snake that had killed their mother in Ceylon . . . Would everything have been different if mother hadn't died? She didn't see why. Aunt Florence had lived with them until they had left school, and they had moved three times and had their yearly holiday and . . . and there'd been changes of servants, of course.

Some little sparrows, young sparrows they sounded, chirped on the window-ledge. *Yeep—eyeep—yeep.* But Josephine felt they were not sparrows, not on the window-ledge. It was inside her, that queer little crying noise. *Yeep—eyeep—yeep.* Ah, what was it crying, so weak and forlorn?

If mother had lived, might they have married? But there had been nobody for them to marry. There had been father's Anglo-Indian friends before he quarrelled with them. But after that she and Constantia never met a single man except clergymen. How did one meet men? Or even if they'd met them, how could they have got to know men well enough to be more than strangers? One read of people having adventures, being followed, and so on. But nobody had ever followed Constantia and her. Oh yes, there had been one year at Eastbourne a mysterious man at their boarding-house who had put a note on the jug of hot water outside their bedroom door! But by the time Connie had found it the steam had made the writing too faint to read; they couldn't even make out to which of them it was addressed. And he had left next day. And that was all. The rest had been looking after father and at the same time keeping out of father's way. But now? But now? The thieving sun touched Josephine gently. She lifted her face. She was drawn over to the window by gentle beams . . .

Until the barrel-organ stopped playing Constantia stayed before the Buddha, wondering, but not as usual, not vaguely. This time her wonder was like longing. She remembered the times she had come in here, crept out of bed in her night-gown when the moon was full, and lain on the floor with her arms outstretched, as though she was crucified. Why? The big, pale moon had made her do it. The horrible dancing figures on the carved screen had leered at her and she hadn't minded. She remembered too how, whenever they were at the seaside, she had gone off by herself and got as close to the sea as she could, and sung something, something she had made up, while she gazed all over that restless water. There had been this other life, running out, bringing things home in bags, getting things on approval, discussing them with Jug, and taking them back to get more things on approval, and arranging father's trays and trying not to annoy father. But it all seemed to have happened in a kind of tunnel. It wasn't real. It was only when she came out of the tunnel into the moonlight or by the sea or into a thunderstorm that she really felt herself. What did it mean? What was it she was always wanting? What did it all lead to? Now? Now?

She turned away from the Buddha with one of her vague gestures. She went over to where Josephine was standing. She wanted to say something to Josephine, something frightfully important, about—about the future and what . . .

"Don't you think perhaps—" she began.

But Josephine interrupted her. "I was wondering if now—" she murmured. They stopped; they waited for each other.

"Go on, Con," said Josephine.

"No, no, Jug; after you," said Constantia.

"No, say what you were going to say. You began," said Josephine.

"I . . . I'd rather hear what you were going to say first," said Constantia.

"Don't be absurd, Con."

"Really, Jug."

"Connie!"

"Oh, *Jug*!"

A pause. Then Constantia said faintly, "I can't say what I was going to say, Jug, because I've forgotten what it was . . . that I was going to say."

Josephine was silent for a moment. She stared at a big cloud where the sun had been. Then she replied shortly, "I've forgotten too."

LOVE À LA MODE

MR. AND MRS. WILLIAMS

I

That winter Mr. and Mrs. Williams of The Rowans, Wickenham, Surrey, astonished their friends by announcing that they were going for a three weeks' holiday to Switzerland. Switzerland! How very enterprising and exciting! There was quite a flutter in Wickenham households at the news. Husbands coming home from the city in the evening were greeted immediately with:

"My dear, have you heard the news about the Williams?"

"No! What's up now?"

"They're off to Switzerland."

"Switzerland! What the dickens are they going there for?"

That, of course, was only the extravagance of the moment. One knew perfectly well why people went. But nobody in Wickenham ever plunged so far away from home at that time of year. It was not considered "necessary"—as golf, bridge, a summer holiday at the sea, an account at Harrods' and a small car as soon as one could afford it, were considered necessary . . .

"Won't you find the initial expenditure very heavy?" asked stout old Mrs. Prean, meeting Mrs. Williams quite by chance at their nice obliging grocer's. And she brushed the crumbs of a sample cheese biscuit off her broad bosom.

"Oh, we shall get our kit over there," said Mrs. Williams.

"Kit" was a word in high favour among the Wickenham ladies. It was left over from the war, of course, with "cheery," "wash-out," "Hun," "Boche," and "Bolshy." As a matter of fact, Bolshy was post-war. But it belonged to the same mood. ("My dear, my housemaid is an absolute little Hun, and I'm afraid the cook is turning Bolshy . . .") There was a fascination in those words. To use them was like opening one's Red Cross cupboard again and gazing at the remains of the bandages, body-belts, tins of anti-insecticide and so on. One was stirred, one got a far-away thrill, like the thrill of hearing a distant band. It reminded you of those exciting, busy, of course anxious, but tremendous days when the whole of Wickenham was one united family. And, although one's husband was away, one had for a substitute three large photographs of him in uniform. One in a silver frame on the table by the bed, one in the regimental colours on the piano, and one in leather to match the dining-room chairs.

"Cook strongly advised us to buy nothing here," went on Mrs. Williams.

"*Cook!*" cried Mrs. Prean, greatly astounded. "What can—"

"Oh—*Thomas* Cook, of course, I mean," said Mrs. Williams, smiling brightly. Mrs. Prean subsided.

"But you will surely not depend upon the resources of a little Swiss village for clothes?" she persisted, deeply interested, as usual, in other people's affairs.

"Oh no, certainly not." Mrs. Williams was quite shocked. "We shall get all we need in the way of clothes from Harrods'."

That was what Mrs. Prean had wished to hear. That was as it should be.

"The great secret, my dear" (she always knew the great secret), "the great secret"—and she put her hand on Mrs. Williams' arm and spoke very distinctly—"is plenty of long-sleeved woven combies!"

"Thank you, m'm."

Both ladies started. There at their side was Mr. Wick, the nice grocer, holding Mrs. Prean's parcel by a loop of pink string. Dear me—how very awkward! He must have . . . he couldn't possibly not have . . . In the emotion of the moment Mrs. Prean, thinking to gloss it over tactfully, nodded significantly at Mrs. Williams and said, accepting the parcel, "And that is what I always tell my dear son!" But this was too swift for Mrs. Williams to follow.

Her embarrassment continued and, ordering the sardines, she just stopped herself from saying "Three large pairs, Mr. Wick, please," instead of "Three large tins."

II

As a matter of fact it was Mrs. Williams' Aunt Aggie's happy release which had made their scheme possible. Happy release it was! After fifteen years in a wheel-chair passing in and out of the little house at Ealing she had, to use the nurse's expression, "just glided away at the last." Glided away . . . it sounded as though Aunt Aggie had taken the wheel-chair with her. One saw her, in her absurd purple velvet, steering carefully among the stars and whimpering faintly, as was her terrestrial wont, when the wheel jolted over a particularly large one.

Aunt Aggie had left her dear niece Gwendolen two

hundred and fifty pounds. Not a vast sum by any means but quite a nice little windfall. Gwendolen, in that dashing mood that only women know, decided immediately to spend it—part of it on the house and the rest on a treat for Gerald. And the lawyer's letter happening to come at tea-time together with a copy of the *Sphere* full of the most fascinating, thrilling photographs of holiday-makers at Mürren and St. Moritz and Montana, the question of the treat was settled.

"You would like to go to Switzerland, wouldn't you, Gerald?"

"Very much."

"You're—awfully good at skating and all that kind of thing—aren't you?"

"Fairly."

"You do feel it's a thing to be done—don't you?"

"How do you mean?"

But Gwendolen only laughed. That was so like Gerald. She knew, in his heart of hearts, he was every bit as keen as she was. But he had this horror of showing his feelings—like all men. Gwendolen understood it perfectly and wouldn't have had him different for the world . . .

"I'll write to Cook's at once and tell them we don't want to go to a very fashionable place and we don't want one of those big jazzy hotels! I'd much prefer a really small out-of-the-way place where we could really go in for the sports seriously." This was quite untrue, but, like so many of Gwendolen's statements, it was made to please Gerald. "Don't you agree?"

Gerald lit his pipe for reply.

As you have gathered, the Christian names of Mr. and Mrs. Williams were Gwendolen and Gerald. How well they went together! They sounded married.

Gwendolen-Gerald. Gwendolen wrote them, bracketed, on bits of blotting-paper, on the backs of old envelopes, on the Stores' catalogue. They looked married. Gerald, when they were on their honeymoon, had made an awfully good joke about them. He had said one morning, "I say, has it ever struck you that both our names begin with *G*? Gwendolen-Gerald. You're a *G*," and he had pointed his razor at her—he was shaving—"and I'm a *G*. Two *G*s. Gee-Gee. See?"

Oh, Gwendolen saw immediately. It was really most witty. Quite brilliant! And so—sweet and unexpected of him to have thought of it. Gee-Gee. Oh, *very* good! She wished she could have told it to people. She had an idea that some people thought Gerald had not a very strong sense of humour. But it was a little too intimate. All the more precious for that reason, however.

"My dear, did you think of it at this moment? I mean—did you just make it up on the spot?"

Gerald, rubbing the lather with a finger, nodded. "Flashed into my mind while I was soaping my face," said he seriously. "It's a queer thing"—and he dipped the razor into the pot of hot water—"I've noticed it before. Shaving gives me ideas." It did, indeed, thought Gwendolen . . .

MARRIAGE À LA MODE

On his way to the station William remembered with a fresh pang of disappointment that he was taking nothing down to the kiddies. Poor little chaps! It was hard lines on them. Their first words always were as they ran to greet him, "What have you got for me, daddy?" and he had nothing. He would have to buy them some sweets at the station. But that was what he had done for the past four Saturdays; their faces had fallen last time when they saw the same old boxes produced again.

And Paddy had said, "I had red ribbing on mine *bee*-fore!"

And Johnny had said, "It's always pink on mine. I hate pink."

But what was William to do? The affair wasn't so easily settled. In the old days, of course, he would have taken a taxi off to a decent toyshop and chosen them something in five minutes. But nowadays they had Russian toys, French toys, Serbian toys—toys from God knows where. It was over a year since Isabel had scrapped the old donkeys and engines and so on because they were so "dreadfully sentimental" and "so appallingly bad for the babies' sense of form."

"It's so important," the new Isabel had explained, "that they should like the right things from the very beginning. It saves so much time later on. Really, if the poor pets have to spend their infant years staring at these horrors, one can imagine them growing up and asking to be taken to the Royal Academy."

And she spoke as though a visit to the Royal Academy was certain immediate death to anyone . . .

"Well, I don't know," said William slowly. "When I was their age I used to go to bed hugging an old towel with a knot in it."

The new Isabel looked at him, her eyes narrowed, her lips apart.

"*Dear* William! I'm sure you did!" She laughed in the new way.

Sweets it would have to be, however, thought William gloomily, fishing in his pocket for change for the taxi-man. And he saw the kiddies handing the boxes round—they were awfully generous little chaps—while Isabel's precious friends didn't hesitate to help themselves

What about fruit? William hovered before a stall just inside the station. What about a melon each? Would they have to share that, too? Or a pine-apple for Pad, and a melon for Johnny? Isabel's friends could hardly go sneaking up to the nursery at the children's meal-times. All the same, as he bought the melon William had a horrible vision of one of Isabel's young poets lapping up a slice, for some reason, behind the nursery door.

With his two very awkward parcels he strode off to his train. The platform was crowded, the train was in. Doors banged open and shut. There came such a loud hissing from the engine that people looked dazed as they scurried to and fro. William made straight for a first-class smoker, stowed away his suit-case and parcels, and taking a huge wad of papers out of his inner pocket, he flung down in the corner and began to read.

"Our client moreover is positive . . . We are inclined to reconsider . . . in the event of—" Ah, that was better. William pressed back his flattened hair and stretched his legs across the carriage floor. The familiar dull gnawing in his breast quietened down. "With regard to our decision—" He took out a blue pencil and scored a paragraph slowly.

Two men came in, stepped across him, and made for the farther corner. A young fellow swung his golf clubs into the rack and sat down opposite. The train gave a gentle lurch, they were off. William glanced up and saw the hot, bright station slipping away. A red-faced girl raced along by the carriages, there was something strained and almost desperate in the way she waved and called. "Hysterical!" thought William dully. Then a greasy, black-faced workman at the end of the platform grinned at the passing train. And William thought, "A filthy life!" and went back to his papers.

When he looked up again there were fields, and beasts standing for shelter under the dark trees. A wide river, with naked children splashing in the shallows, glided into sight and was gone again. The sky shone pale, and one bird drifted high like a dark fleck in a jewel.

"We have examined our client's correspondence files . . ." The last sentence he had read echoed in his mind. "We have examined . . ." William hung on to that sentence, but it was no good; it snapped in the middle, and the fields, the sky, the sailing bird, the water, all said, "Isabel." The same thing happened every Saturday afternoon. When he was on his way to meet Isabel there began those countless imaginary meetings. She was at the station, standing just a little apart from everybody else; she was sitting in the open taxi outside; she was at the garden gate; walking across the parched grass; at the door, or just inside the hall.

And her clear, light voice said, "It's William," or

"Hillo, William!" or "So William has come!" He touched her cool hand, her cool cheek.

The exquisite freshness of Isabel! When he had been a little boy, it was his delight to run into the garden after a shower of rain and shake the rose-bush over him. Isabel was that rosebush, petal-soft, sparkling and cool. And he was still that little boy. But there was no running into the garden now, no laughing and shaking. The dull, persistent gnawing in his breast started again. He drew up his legs, tossed the papers aside, and shut his eyes.

"What is it, Isabel? What is it?" he said tenderly. They were in their bedroom in the new house. Isabel sat on a painted stool before the dressing-table that was strewn with little black and green boxes.

"What is what, William?" And she bent forward, and her fine light hair fell over her cheek.

"Ah, you know!" He stood in the middle of the strange room and he felt a stranger. At that Isabel wheeled round quickly and faced him.

"Oh, William!" she cried imploringly, and she held up the hair-brush. "Please! Please don't be so dreadfully stuffy and—tragic. You're always saying or looking, or hinting that I've changed. Just because I've got to know really congenial people, and go about more, and am frightfully keen on—on everything, you behave as though I'd"—Isabel tossed back her hair and laughed—"killed our love or something. It's so awfully absurd"—she bit her lip—"and it's so maddening, William. Even this new house and the servants you grudge me."

"Isabel!"

"Yes, yes, it's true in a way," said Isabel quickly. "You think they are another bad sign. Oh, I know you do. I feel it," she said softly, "every time you come up the stairs. But we couldn't have gone on living in that other poky little hole, William. Be practical, at least! Why, there wasn't enough room for the babies even."

No, it was true. Every morning when he came back from chambers it was to find the babies with Isabel in the back drawing-room. They were having rides on the leopard skin thrown over the sofa back, or they were playing shops with Isabel's desk for a counter, or Pad was sitting on the hearthrug rowing away for dear life with a little brass fire-shovel, while Johnny shot at pirates with the tongs. Every evening they each had a pick-a-back up the narrow stairs to their fat old Nanny.

Yes, he supposed it was a poky little house. A little white house with blue curtains and a window-box of petunias. William met their friends at the door with "Seen our petunias? Pretty terrific for London, don't you think?"

But the imbecile thing, the absolutely extraordinary thing was that he hadn't the slightest idea that Isabel wasn't as happy as he. God, what blindness! He hadn't the remotest notion in those days that she really hated that inconvenient little house, that she thought the fat Nanny was ruining the babies, that she was desperately lonely, pining for new people and new music and pictures and so on. If they hadn't gone to that studio party at Moira Morrison's—if Moira Morrison hadn't said as they were leaving, "I'm going to rescue your wife, selfish man. She's like an exquisite little Titania"—if Isabel hadn't gone with Moira to Paris—if—if . . .

The train stopped at another station. Bettingford. Good heavens! They'd be there in ten minutes. William stuffed the papers back into his pockets; the young man opposite had long since disappeared. Now the other two got out. The late afternoon sun shone on women in cotton frocks and little sunburnt, barefoot children. It blazed on a silky yellow flower with coarse leaves which sprawled over a bank of rock. The air ruffling through the window smelled of the sea. Had Isabel the same crowd with her this week-end, wondered William?

And he remembered the holidays they used to have, the four of them, with a little farm girl, Rose, to look after the babies. Isabel wore a jersey and her hair in a plait; she looked about fourteen. Lord! how his nose used to peel! And the amount they ate, and the amount they slept in that immense feather bed with their feet locked together . . . William couldn't help a grim smile as he thought of Isabel's horror if she knew the full extent of his sentimentality.

"Hillo, William!" She was at the station after all, standing just as he had imagined, apart from the others, and—William's heart leapt—she was alone.

"Hallo, Isabel!" William stared. He thought she looked so beautiful that he had to say something, "You look very cool."

"Do I?" said Isabel. "I don't feel very cool. Come along, your horrid old train is late. The taxi's outside." She put her hand lightly on his arm as they passed the ticket collector. "We've all come to meet you," she said. "But we've left Bobby Kane at the sweet shop, to be called for."

"Oh!" said William. It was all he could say for the moment.

There in the glare waited the taxi, with Bill Hunt and Dennis Green sprawling on one side, their hats tilted over their faces, while on the other, Moira Morrison, in a bonnet like a huge strawberry, jumped up and down.

"No ice! No ice! No ice!" she shouted gaily.

And Dennis chimed in from under his hat. "*Only* to be had from the fishmonger's."

And Bill Hunt, emerging, added, "With *whole* fish in it."

"Oh, what a bore!" wailed Isabel. And she explained to William how they had been chasing round the town for ice while she waited for him. "Simply everything is running down the steep cliffs into the sea, beginning with the butter."

"We shall have to anoint ourselves with the butter," said Dennis. "May thy head, William, lack not ointment."

"Look here," said William, "how are we going to sit? I'd better get up by the driver."

"No, Bobby Kane's by the driver," said Isabel. "You're to sit between Moira and me." The taxi started. "What have you got in those mysterious parcels?"

"De-cap-it-ated heads!" said Bill Hunt, shuddering beneath his hat.

"Oh, fruit!" Isabel sounded very pleased. "Wise William! A melon and a pine-apple. How too nice!"

"No, wait a bit," said William, smiling. But he really was anxious. "I brought them down for the kiddies."

"Oh, my dear!" Isabel laughed, and slipped her hand through his arm. "They'd be rolling in agonies if they were to eat them. No"—she patted his hand—"you must bring them something next time. I refuse to part with my pineapple."

"Cruel Isabel! Do let me smell it!" said Moira. She flung her arms across William appealingly. "Oh!" The strawberry bonnet fell forward: she sounded quite faint.

"A Lady in Love with a Pine-apple," said Dennis, as the taxi drew up before a little shop with a striped blind. Out came Bobby Kane, his arms full of little packets.

"I do hope they'll be good. I've chosen them because of the colours. There are some round things which really look too divine. And just look at this nougat," he cried ecstatically, "just look at it! It's a perfect little ballet!"

But at that moment the shopman appeared. "Oh, I forgot. They're none of them paid for," said Bobby, looking frightened. Isabel gave the shopman a note, and Bobby was radiant again. "Hallo, William! I'm sitting by the driver." And bareheaded, all in white, with his sleeves rolled up to the shoulders, he leapt into his place. "Avanti!" he cried . . .

After tea the others went off to bathe, while William stayed and made his peace with the kiddies. But Johnny and Paddy were asleep, the rose-red glow had paled, bats were flying, and still the bathers had not returned. As William wandered downstairs, the maid crossed the hall carrying a lamp. He followed her into the sitting-room. It was a long room, coloured yellow. On the wall opposite William someone had painted a young man, over life-size, with very wobbly legs, offering a wide-eyed daisy to a young woman who had one very short arm and one very long, thin one. Over the chairs and sofa there hung strips of black material, covered with big splashes like broken eggs, and everywhere one looked there seemed to be an ash-tray full of cigarette ends. William sat down in one of the arm-chairs. Now-adays, when one felt with one hand down the sides, it wasn't to come upon a sheep with three legs or a cow that had lost one horn, or a very fat dove out of the Noah's Ark. One fished up yet another little paper-covered book of smudged-looking poems . . . He thought of the wad of papers in his pocket, but he was too hungry and tired to read. The door was open;

sounds came from the kitchen. The servants were talking as if they were alone in the house. Suddenly there came a loud screech of laughter and an equally loud "Sh!" They had remembered him. William got up and went through the french windows into the garden, and as he stood there in the shadow he heard the bathers coming up the sandy road; their voices rang through the quiet.

"I think it's up to Moira to use her little arts and wiles."

A tragic moan from Moira.

"We ought to have a gramophone for the week-ends that played 'The Maid of the Mountains.'"

"Oh no! Oh no!" cried Isabel's voice. "That's not fair to William. Be nice to him, my children! He's only staying until to-morrow evening."

"Leave him to me," cried Bobby Kane. "I'm awfully good at looking after people."

The gate swung open and shut. William moved on the terrace; they had seen him. "Hallo, William!" And Bobby Kane, flapping his towel, began to leap and pirouette on the parched lawn. "Pity you didn't come, William. The water was divine. And we all went to a little pub afterwards and had sloe gin."

The others had reached the house. "I say, Isabel," called Bobby, "would you like me to wear my Nijinsky dress to-night?"

"No," said Isabel, "nobody's going to dress. We're all starving. William's starving, too. Come along, *mes amis*, let's begin with sardines."

"I've found the sardines," said Moira, and she ran into the hall, holding a box high in the air.

"A Lady with a Box of Sardines," said Dennis gravely.

"Well, William, and how's London?" asked Bill Hunt, drawing the cork out of a bottle of whisky.

"Oh, London's not much changed," answered William.

"Good old London," said Bobby, very hearty, spearing a sardine.

But a moment later William was forgotten. Moira Morrison began wondering what colour one's legs really were under water.

"Mine are the palest, palest mushroom colour."

Bill and Dennis ate enormously. And Isabel filled glasses, and changed plates, and found matches, smiling blissfully. At one moment she said, "I do wish, Bill, you'd paint it."

"Paint what?" said Bill loudly, stuffing his mouth with bread.

"Us," said Isabel, "round the table. It would be so fascinating in twenty years' time."

Bill screwed up his eyes and chewed. "Light's wrong," he said rudely, "far too much yellow"; and went on eating. And that seemed to charm Isabel, too.

But after supper they were all so tired they could do nothing but yawn until it was late enough to go to bed . . .

It was not until William was waiting for his taxi the next afternoon that he found himself alone with Isabel. When he brought his suit-case down into the hall, Isabel left the others and went over to him. She stooped down and picked up the suitcase. "What a weight!" she said, and she gave a little awkward laugh. "Let me carry it! To the gate."

"No, why should you?" said William. "Of course not. Give it to me."

"Oh, please do let me," said Isabel. "I want to,

really." They walked together silently. William felt there was nothing to say now.

"There," said Isabel triumphantly, setting the suit-case down, and she looked anxiously along the sandy road. "I hardly seem to have seen you this time," she said breathlessly. "It's so short, isn't it? I feel you've only just come. Next time—" The taxi came into sight. "I hope they look after you properly in London. I'm so sorry the babies have been out all day, but Miss Neil had arranged it. They'll hate missing you. Poor William, going back to London." The taxi turned. "Goodbye!" She gave him a little hurried kiss; she was gone.

Fields, trees, hedges streamed by. They shook through the empty, blind-looking little town, ground up the steep pull to the station. The train was in. William made straight for a first-class smoker, flung back into the corner, but this time he let the papers alone. He folded his arms against the dull, persistent gnawing, and began in his mind to write a letter to Isabel.

The post was late as usual. They sat outside the house in long chairs under coloured parasols. Only Bobby Kane lay on the turf at Isabel's feet. It was dull, stifling; the day drooped like a flag.

"Do you think there will be Mondays in heaven?" asked Bobby childishly.

And Dennis murmured, "Heaven will be one long Monday."

But Isabel couldn't help wondering what had hap-pened to the salmon they had for supper last night. She had meant to have fish mayonnaise for lunch, and now . . .

Moira was asleep. Sleeping was her latest discovery.

"It's *so* wonderful. One simply shuts one's eyes, that's all. It's *so* delicious."

When the old ruddy postman came beating along the sandy road on his tricycle one felt the handle-bars ought to have been oars.

Bill Hunt put down his book. "Letters," he said complacently, and they all waited. But, heartless postman—O malignant world! There was only one, a fat one for Isabel. Not even a paper.

"And mine's only from William," said Isabel mournfully.

"From William—already?"

"He's sending you back your marriage lines as a gentle reminder."

"Does everybody have marriage lines? I thought they were only for servants."

"Pages and pages! Look at her! A Lady reading a Letter," said Dennis.

My darling, precious Isabel. Pages and pages there were. As Isabel read on her feeling of astonishment changed to a stifled feeling. What on earth had induced William . . . ? How extraordinary it was . . . What could have made him . . . ? She felt confused, more and more excited, even frightened. It was just like William. Was it? It was absurd, of course, it must be absurd, ridiculous. "Ha, ha, ha! Oh dear!" What was she to do? Isabel flung back in her chair and laughed till she couldn't stop laughing.

"Do, do tell us," said the others. "You must tell us."

"I'm longing to," gurgled Isabel. She sat up, gathered the letter, and waved it at them. "Gather round," she said. 'Listen, it's too marvellous. A love-letter!"

"A love-letter! But how divine!" *Darling, precious*

Isabel. But she had hardly begun before their laughter interrupted her.

"Go on, Isabel, it's perfect."

"It's the most marvellous find."

"Oh, do go on, Isabel!"

God forbid, my darling, that I should be a drag on your happiness.

"Oh! oh! oh!"

"Sh! sh! sh!"

And Isabel went on. When she reached the end they were hysterical: Bobby rolled on the turf and almost sobbed.

"You must let me have it just as it is, entire, for my new book," said Dennis firmly. "I shall give it a whole chapter."

"Oh, Isabel," moaned Moira, "that wonderful bit about holding you in his arms!"

"I always thought those letters in divorce cases were made up. But they pale before this."

"Let me hold it. Let me read it, mine own self," said Bobby Kane.

But, to their surprise, Isabel crushed the letter in her hand. She was laughing no longer. She glanced quickly at them all; she looked exhausted. "No, not just now. Not just now," she stammered.

And before they could recover she had run into the house, through the hall, up the stairs into her bedroom. Down she sat on the side of the bed. "How vile, odious, abominable, vulgar," muttered Isabel. She pressed her eyes with her knuckles and rocked to and fro. And again she saw them, but not four, more like forty, laughing, sneering, jeering, stretching out their hands while she read them William's letter. Oh, what a loathsome thing to have done. How could she have done it! *God forbid, my darling, that I should be a drag on your happiness.* William! Isabel pressed her face into the pillow. But she felt that even the grave bedroom knew her for what she was, shallow, tinkling, vain . . .

Presently from the garden below there came voices.

"Isabel, we're all going for a bathe. Do come!"

"Come, thou wife of William!"

"Call her once before you go, call once yet!"

Isabel sat up. Now was the moment, now she must decide. Would she go with them, or stay here and write to William. Which, which should it be? "I must make up my mind." Oh, but how could there be any question? Of course she would stay here and write.

"Titania!" piped Moira.

"Isa-bel?"

No, it was too difficult. "I'll—I'll go with them, and write to William later. Some other time. Later. Not now. But I shall *certainly* write," thought Isabel hurriedly.

And, laughing in the new way, she ran down the stairs.

BLISS

Although Bertha Young was thirty she still had moments like this when she wanted to run instead of walk, to take dancing steps on and off the pavement, to bowl a hoop, to throw something up in the air and catch it again, or to stand still and laugh at—nothing—at nothing, simply.

What can you do if you are thirty and, turning the corner of your own street, you are overcome, suddenly, by a feeling of bliss—absolute bliss!—as though you'd suddenly swallowed a bright piece of that late afternoon sun and it burned in your bosom, sending out a little shower of sparks into every particle, into every finger and toe? . . .

Oh, is there no way you can express it without being "drunk and disorderly"? How idiotic civilisation is! Why be given a body if you have to keep it shut up in a case like a rare, rare fiddle?

"No, that about the fiddle is not quite what I mean," she thought, running up the steps and feeling in her bag for the key—she'd forgotten it, as usual—and rattling the letter-box. "It's not what I mean, because—Thank you, Mary"—she went into the hall. "Is nurse back?"

"Yes, M'm."

"And has the fruit come?"

"Yes, M'm. Everything's come."

"Bring the fruit up to the dining-room, will you? I'll arrange it before I go upstairs."

It was dusky in the dining-room and quite chilly. But

all the same Bertha threw off her coat; she could not bear the tight clasp of it another moment, and the cold air fell on her arms.

But in her bosom there was still that bright glowing place—that shower of little sparks coming from it. It was almost unbearable. She hardly dared to breathe for fear of fanning it higher, and yet she breathed deeply, deeply. She hardly dared to look into the cold mirror—but she did look, and it gave her back a woman, radiant, with smiling, trembling lips, with big, dark eyes and an air of listening, waiting for something . . . divine to happen . . . that she knew must happen . . . infallibly.

Mary brought in the fruit on a tray and with it a glass bowl, and a blue dish, very lovely, with a strange sheen on it as though it had been dipped in milk.

"Shall I turn on the light, M'm?"

"No, thank you. I can see quite well."

There were tangerines and apples stained with strawberry pink. Some yellow pears, smooth as silk, some white grapes covered with a silver bloom and a big cluster of purple ones. These last she had bought to tone in with the new dining-room carpet. Yes, that did sound rather far-fetched and absurd, but it was really why she had bought them. She had thought in the shop: "I must have some purple ones to bring the carpet up to the table." And it had seemed quite sense at the time.

When she had finished with them and had made two pyramids of these bright round shapes, she stood away from the table to get the effect—and it really was most curious. For the dark table seemed to melt into the dusky light and the glass dish and the blue bowl to float in the air. This, of course, in her present mood, was so incredibly beautiful . . . She began to laugh.

"No, no. I'm getting hysterical." And she seized her bag and coat and ran upstairs to the nursery.

Nurse sat at a low table giving Little B her supper after her bath. The baby had on a white flannel gown and a blue woollen jacket, and her dark, fine hair was brushed up into a funny little peak. She looked up when she saw her mother and began to jump.

"Now, my lovey, eat it up like a good girl," said nurse, setting her lips in a way that Bertha knew, and that meant she had come into the nursery at another wrong moment.

"Has she been good, Nanny?"

"She's been a little sweet all the afternoon," whispered Nanny "We went to the park and I sat down on a chair and took her out of the pram and a big dog came along and put its head on my knee and she clutched its ear, tugged it. Oh, you should have seen her."

Bertha wanted to ask if it wasn't rather dangerous to let her clutch at a strange dog's ear. But she did not dare to. She stood watching them, her hands by her side, like the poor little girl in front of the rich little girl with the doll.

The baby looked up at her again, stared, and then smiled so charmingly that Bertha couldn't help crying:

"Oh, Nanny, do let me finish giving her her supper while you put the bath things away."

"Well, M'm, she oughtn't to be changed hands while she's eating," said Nanny, still whispering. "It unsettles her; it's very likely to upset her."

How absurd it was. Why have a baby if it has to be kept—not in a case like a rare, rare fiddle—but in another woman's arms?

"Oh, I must!" said she.

Very offended, Nanny handed her over.

"Now, don't excite her after her supper. You know you do, M'm. And I have such a time with her after!"

Thank heaven! Nanny went out of the room with the bath towels.

"Now I've got you to myself, my little precious," said Bertha, as the baby leaned against her.

She ate delightfully, holding up her lips for the spoon and then waving her hands. Sometimes she wouldn't let the spoon go; and sometimes, just as Bertha had filled it, she waved it away to the four winds.

When the soup was finished Bertha turned round to the fire.

"You're nice—you're very nice!" said she, kissing her warm baby. "I'm fond of you. I like you."

And, indeed, she loved Little B so much—her neck as she bent forward, her exquisite toes as they shone transparent in the firelight—that all her feeling of bliss came back again, and again she didn't know how to express it—what to do with it.

"You're wanted on the telephone," said Nanny, coming back in triumph and seizing *her* Little B.

Down she flew. It was Harry.

"Oh, is that you, Ber? Look here. I'll be late. I'll take a taxi and come along as quickly as I can, but get dinner put back ten minutes—will you? All right?"

"Yes, perfectly. Oh, Harry!"

"Yes?"

What had she to say? She'd nothing to say. She only wanted to get in touch with him for a moment. She couldn't absurdly cry: "Hasn't it been a divine day!"

"What is it?" rapped out the little voice.

"Nothing. *Entendu*," said Bertha, and hung up the

receiver, thinking how much more than idiotic civilisation was.

They had people coming to dinner. The Norman Knights—a very sound couple—he was about to start a theatre, and she was awfully keen on interior decoration, a young man, Eddie 'Warren, who had just published a little book of poems and whom everybody was asking to dine, and a "find" of Bertha's called Pearl Fulton. What Miss Fulton did, Bertha didn't know. They had met at the club and Bertha had fallen in love with her, as she always did fall in love with beautiful women who had something strange about them.

The provoking thing was that, though they had been about together and met a number of times and really talked, Bertha couldn't make her out. Up to a certain point Miss Fulton was rarely, wonderfully frank, but the certain point was there, and beyond that she would not go.

Was there anything beyond it? Harry said "No." Voted her dullish, and "cold like all blonde women, with a touch, perhaps, of anæmia of the brain." But Bertha wouldn't agree with him; not yet, at any rate.

"No, the way she has of sitting with her head a little on one side, and smiling, has something behind it, Harry, and I must find out what that something is."

"Most likely it's a good stomach," answered Harry.

He made a point of catching Bertha's heels with replies of that kind . . ."liver frozen, my dear girl," or "pure flatulence," or "kidney disease," . . . and so on. For some strange reason Bertha liked this, and almost admired it in him very much.

She went into the drawing-room and lighted the fire; then, picking up the cushions, one by one, that Mary had disposed so carefully, she threw them back on to the chairs and the couches. That made all the difference; the room came alive at once. As she was about to throw the last one she surprised herself by suddenly hugging it to her, passionately, passionately. But it did not put out the fire in her bosom. Oh, on the contrary!

The windows of the drawing-room opened on to a balcony overlooking the garden. At the far end, against the wall, there was a tall, slender pear tree in fullest, richest bloom; it stood perfect, as though becalmed against the jade-green sky. Bertha couldn't help feeling, even from this distance, that it had not a single bud or a faded petal. Down below, in the garden beds, the red and yellow tulips, heavy with flowers, seemed to lean upon the dusk. A grey cat, dragging its belly, crept across the lawn, and a black one, its shadow, trailed after. The sight of them, so intent and so quick, gave Bertha a curious shiver.

"What creepy things cats are!" she stammered, and she turned away from the window and began walking up and down . . .

How strong the jonquils smelled in the warm room. Too strong? Oh, no. And yet, as though overcome, she flung down on a couch and pressed her hands to her eyes.

"I'm too happy—too happy!" she murmured.

And she seemed to see on her eyelids the lovely pear tree with its wide open blossoms as a symbol of her own life.

Really—really—she had everything. She was young. Harry and she were as much in love as ever, and they got on together splendidly and were really good pals. She had an adorable baby. They didn't have to worry about money. They had this absolutely satisfactory house and garden. And friends—modern, thrilling friends, writers and painters and poets or people keen on social questions—just the kind of friends they wanted. And then there were books, and there was music, and she had found a wonderful little dressmaker, and they were going abroad in the summer, and their new cook made the most superb omelettes . . .

"I'm absurd. Absurd!" She sat up; but she felt quite dizzy, quite drunk. It must have been the spring.

Yes, it was the spring. Now she was so tired she could not drag herself upstairs to dress.

A white dress, a string of jade beads, green shoes and stockings. It wasn't intentional. She had thought of this scheme hours before she stood at the drawing-room window.

Her petals rustled softly into the hall, and she kissed Mrs. Norman Knight, who was taking off the most amusing orange coat with a procession of black monkeys round the hem and up the fronts.

". . . Why! Why! Why is the middle-class so stodgy—so utterly without a sense of humour! My dear, it's only by a fluke that I am here at all—Norman being the protective fluke. For my darling monkeys so upset the train that it rose to a man and simply ate me with its eyes. Didn't laugh—wasn't amused—that I should have loved. No, just stared—and bored me through and through."

"But the cream of it was," said Norman, pressing a large tortoiseshell-rimmed monocle into his eye, "you don't mind me telling this, Face, do you?" (In their home and among their friends they called each other Face and Mug.) "The cream of it was when she, being full fed, turned to the woman beside her and said: 'Haven't you ever seen a monkey before?'"

"Oh yes!" Mrs. Norman Knight joined in the laughter. "Wasn't that too absolutely creamy?"

And a funnier thing still was that now her coat was off she did look like a very intelligent monkey—who had even made that yellow silk dress out of scraped banana skins. And her amber ear-rings: they were like little dangling nuts.

"This is a sad, sad fall!" said Mug, pausing in front of Little B's perambulator. "When the perambulator comes into the hall—" and he waved the rest of the quotation away.

The bell rang. It was lean, pale Eddie Warren (as usual) in a state of acute distress.

"It *is* the right house, *isn't* it?" he pleaded.

"Oh, I think so—I hope so," said Bertha brightly.

"I have had such a *dreadful* experience with a taxi-man; he was *most* sinister. I couldn't get him to *stop*. The *more* I knocked and called the *faster* he went. And *in* the moonlight this *bizarre* figure with the *flattened* head *crouching* over the *lit-tle* wheel . . ."

He shuddered, taking off an immense white silk scarf. Bertha noticed that his socks were white, too—most charming.

"But how dreadful!" she cried.

"Yes, it really was," said Eddie, following her into the drawing-room. "I saw myself *driving* through Eternity in a *timeless* taxi."

He knew the Norman Knights. In fact, he was going to write a play for N. K. when the theatre scheme came off.

"Well, Warren, how's the play?" said Norman Knight, dropping his monocle and giving his eye a moment in which to rise to the surface before it was screwed down again.

And Mrs. Norman Knight: "Oh, Mr. Warren, what happy socks?"

"I *am* so glad you like them," said he, staring at his feet. "They seem to have got so *much* whiter since the moon rose." And he turned his lean sorrowful young face to Bertha. "There *is* a moon, you know."

She wanted to cry: "I am sure there is—often—often!"

He really was a most attractive person. But so was Face, crouched before the fire in her banana skins, and so was Mug, smoking a cigarette and saying as he flicked the ash: "Why doth the bridegroom tarry?"

"There he is, now."

Bang went the front door open and shut. Harry shouted: "Hullo, you people. Down in five minutes." And they heard him swarm up the stairs. Bertha couldn't help smiling; she knew how he loved doing things at high pressure. What, after all, did an extra five minutes matter? But he would pretend to himself that they mattered beyond measure. And then he would make a great point of coming into the drawing-room, extravagantly cool and collected.

Harry had such a zest for life. Oh, how she appreciated it in him. And his passion for fighting—for seeking in everything that came up against him another test of his power and of his courage—that, too, she understood. Even when it made him just occasionally, to other people, who didn't know him well, a little ridiculous perhaps . . . For there were moments when he rushed into battle where no battle was . . . She talked and laughed and positively forgot until he had come in (just as she had imagined) that Pearl Fulton had not turned up.

"I wonder if Miss Fulton has forgotten?"

"I expect so," said Harry. "Is she on the 'phone?"

"Ah! There's a taxi now." And Bertha smiled with that little air of proprietorship that she always assumed while her women finds were new and mysterious. "She lives in taxis." "She'll run to fat if she does," said Harry coolly, ringing the bell for dinner. "Frightful danger for blonde women."

"Harry—don't," warned Bertha, laughing up at him.

Came another tiny moment, while they waited, laughing and talking, just a trifle too much at their ease, a trifle too unaware. And then Miss Fulton, all in silver, with a silver fillet binding her pale blonde hair, came in smiling, her head a little on one side.

"Am I late?"

"No, not at all," said Bertha. "Come along." And she took her arm and they moved into the dining-room.

What was there in the touch of that cool arm that could fan—fan—start blazing—blazing—the fire of bliss that Bertha did not know what to do with?

Miss Fulton did not look at her; but then she seldom did look at people directly. Her heavy eyelids lay upon her eyes and the strange half-smile came and went upon her lips as though she lived by listening rather than seeing. But Bertha knew, suddenly, as if the longest, most intimate look had passed between them—as if they had said to each other: "You, too?"—that Pearl Fulton, stirring the beautiful red soup in the grey plate, was feeling just what she was feeling.

And the others? Face and Mug, Eddie and Harry, their spoons rising and falling—dabbing their lips with their napkins, crumbling bread, fiddling with the forks and glasses and talking.

"I met her at the Alpha show—the weirdest little person. She'd not only cut off her hair, but she seemed to have taken a dreadfully good snip off her legs and arms and her neck and her poor little nose as well."

"Isn't she very *liée* with Michael Oat?"

"The man who wrote *Love in False Teeth*?"

"He wants to write a play for me. One act. One man. Decides to commit suicide. Gives all the reasons why he should and why he shouldn't. And just as he has made up his mind either to do it or not to do it— curtain. Not half a bad idea."

"What's he going to call it—'Stomach Trouble'?"

"I *think* I've come across the *same* idea in a lit-tle French review, *quite* unknown in England."

No, they didn't share it. They were dears—dears— and she loved having them there, at her table, and giving them delicious food and wine. In fact, she longed to tell them how delightful they were, and what a dec- orative group they made, how they seemed to set one another off and how they reminded her of a play by Tchekof!

Harry was enjoying his dinner. It was part of his— well, not his nature, exactly, and certainly not his pose—his—something or other—to talk about food and to glory in his "shameless passion for the white flesh of the lobster" and "the green of pistachio ices—green and cold like the eyelids of Egyptian dancers."

When he looked up at her and said: "Bertha, this is a very admirable *soufflé*!" she almost could have wept with child-like pleasure.

Oh, why did she feel so tender towards the whole world to-night? Everything was good—was right. All that happened seemed to fill again her brimming cup of bliss.

And still, in the back of her mind, there was the pear tree. It would be silver now, in the light of poor dear

Eddie's moon, silver as Miss Fulton, who sat there turning a tangerine in her slender fingers that were so pale a light seemed to come from them.

What she simply couldn't make out—what was miraculous—was how she should have guessed Miss Fulton's mood so exactly and so instantly. For she never doubted for a moment that she was right, and yet what had she to go on? Less than nothing.

"I believe this does happen very, very rarely between women. Never between men," thought Bertha. "But while I am making the coffee in the drawing-room perhaps she will 'give a sign.'"

What she meant by that she did not know, and what would happen after that she could not imagine.

While she thought like this she saw herself talking and laughing. She had to talk because of her desire to laugh.

"I must laugh or die."

But when she noticed Face's funny little habit of tucking something down the front of her Lodice—as if she kept a tiny, secret hoard of nuts there, too—Bertha had to dig her nails into her hands—so as not to laugh too much.

It was over at last. And: "Come and see my new coffee machine," said Bertha.

"We only have a new coffee machine once a fort-night," said Harry. Face took her arm this time; Miss Fulton bent her head and followed after.

The fire had died down in the drawing-room to a red, flickering "nest of baby phœnixes," said Face.

"Don't turn up the light for a moment. It is so lovely." And down she crouched by the fire again. She was always cold. . ."without her little red flannel jacket, of course," thought Bertha.

At that moment Miss Fulton "gave the sign."

"Have you a garden?" said the cool, sleepy voice.

This was so exquisite on her part that all Bertha could do was to obey. She crossed the room, pulled the curtains apart, and opened those long windows.

"There!" she breathed.

And the two women stood side by side looking at the slender, flowering tree. Although it was so still it seemed, like the flame of a candle, to stretch up, to point, to quiver in the bright air, to grow taller and taller as they gazed—almost to touch the rim of the round, silver moon.

How long did they stand there? Both, as it were, caught in that circle of unearthly light, understanding each other perfectly, creatures of another world, and wondering what they were to do in this one with all this blissful treasure that burned in their bosoms and dropped, in silver flowers, from their hair and hands?

For ever—for a moment? And did Miss Fulton murmur: "Yes. Just *that*." Or did Bertha dream it?

Then the light was snapped on and Face made the coffee and Harry said: "My dear Mrs. Knight, don't ask me about my baby. I never see her. I shan't feel the slightest interest in her until she has a lover," and Mug took his eye out of the conservatory for a moment and then put it under glass again and Eddie Warren drank his coffee and set down the cup with a face of anguish as though he had drunk and seen the spider.

"What I want to do is to give the young men a show. I believe London is simply teeming with first-chop, unwritten plays. What I want to say to 'em is: 'Here's the theatre. Fire ahead.'"

"You know, my dear, I am going to decorate a room for the Jacob Nathans. Oh, I am so tempted to do a fried-fish scheme, with the backs of the chairs shaped like frying-pans and lovely chip potatoes embroidered all over the curtains."

"The trouble with our young writing men is that they are still too romantic. You can't put out to sea without being seasick and wanting a basin. Well, why won't they have the courage of those basins?"

"A *dreadful* poem about a *girl* who was *violated* by a beggar *without* a nose in a little wood . . ."

Miss Fulton sank into the lowest, deepest chair and Harry handed round the cigarettes.

From the way he stood in front of her shaking the silver box and saying abruptly: "Egyptian? Turkish? Virginian? They're all mixed up," Bertha realised that she not only bored him; he really disliked her. And she decided from the way Miss Fulton said: "No, thank you, I won't smoke," that she felt it, too, and was hurt.

"Oh, Harry, don't dislike her. You are quite wrong about her. She's wonderful, wonderful. And, besides, how can you feel so differently about someone who means so much to me. I shall try to tell you when we are in bed to-night what has been happening. What she and I have shared."

At those last words something strange and almost terrifying darted into Bertha's mind. And this something blind and smiling whispered to her: "Soon these people will go. The house will be quiet—quiet. The lights will be out. And you and he will be alone together in the dark room—the warm bed . . ."

She jumped up from her chair and ran over to the piano.

114

"What a pity someone does not play!" she cried. "What a pity somebody does not play."

For the first time in her life Bertha Young desired her husband.

Oh, she'd loved him—she'd been in love with him, of course, in every other way, but just not in that way. And equally, of course, she'd understood that he was different. They'd discussed it so often. It had worried her dreadfully at first to find that she was so cold, but after a time it had not seemed to matter. They were so frank with each other—such good pals. That was the best of being modern.

But now—ardently! ardently! The word ached in her ardent body! Was this what that feeling of bliss had been leading up to? But then, then—

"My dear," said Mrs. Norman Knight, "you know our shame. We are the victims of time and train. We live in Hampstead. It's been so nice."

"I'll come with you into the hall," said Bertha. "I loved having you. But you must not miss the last train. That's so awful, isn't it?"

"Have a whisky, Knight, before you go?" called Harry.

"No, thanks, old chap."

Bertha squeezed his hand for that as she shook it.

"Good night, good-bye," she cried from the top step, feeling that this self of hers was taking leave of them for ever.

When she got back into the drawing-room the others were on the move.

". . . Then you can come part of the way in my taxi."

"I shall be *so* thankful *not* to have to face *another* drive *alone* after my *dreadful* experience."

"You can get a taxi at the rank just at the end of the street. You won't have to walk more than a few yards."

"That's a comfort. I'll go and put on my coat."

Miss Fulton moved towards the hall and Bertha was following when Harry almost pushed past.

"Let me help you."

Bertha knew that he was repenting his rudeness—she let him go. What a boy he was in some ways—so impulsive—so—simple.

And Eddie and she were left by the fire.

"I *wonder* if you have seen Bilks' *new* poem called *Table d'Hôte*," said Eddie softly. "It's *so* wonderful. In the last Anthology. Have you got a copy? I'd *so* like to *show* it to you. It begins with an *incredibly* beautiful line: 'Why Must it Always be Tomato Soup?'"

"Yes," said Bertha. And she moved noiselessly to a table opposite the drawing-room door and Eddie glided noiselessly after her. She picked up the little book and gave it to him; they had not made a sound.

While he looked it up she turned her head towards the hall. And she saw . . . Harry with Miss Fulton's coat in his arms and Miss Fulton with her back turned to him and her head bent. He tossed the coat away, put his hands on her shoulders and turned her violently to him. His lips said: "I adore you," and Miss Fulton laid her moonbeam fingers on his cheeks and smiled her sleepy smile. Harry's nostrils quivered; his lips curled back in a hideous grin while he whispered: "To-morrow," and with her eyelids Miss Fulton said: "Yes."

"Here it is," said Eddie. "'Why Must it Always be Tomato Soup?' It's so *deeply* true, don't you feel? Tomato soup is so *dreadfully* eternal."

"If you prefer," said Harry's voice, very loud, from the hall, "I can 'phone you a cab to come to the door."

"Oh, no. It's not necessary," said Miss Fulton, and she came up to Bertha and gave her the slender fingers to hold.

"Good-bye. Thank you so much."

"Good-bye," said Bertha.

Miss Fulton held her hand a moment longer.

"Your lovely pear tree!" she murmured.

And then she was gone, with Eddie following, like the black cat following the grey cat.

"I'll shut up shop," said Harry, extravagantly cool and collected.

"Your lovely pear tree—pear tree—pear tree!"

Bertha simply ran over to the long windows.

"Oh, what is going to happen now?" she cried.

But the pear tree was as lovely as ever and as full of flower and as still.

This Flower

"But I tell you, my lord fool, out of this nettle, danger, we pluck this flower, safety."

As she lay there, looking up at the ceiling, she had her moment—yes, she had her moment! And it was not connected with anything she had thought or felt before, not even with those words the doctor had scarcely ceased speaking. It was single, glowing, perfect; it was like—a pearl, too flawless to match with another . . . Could she describe what happened? Impossible. It was as though, even if she had not been conscious (and she certainly had not been conscious all the time) that she was fighting against the stream of life—the stream of life indeed!—she had suddenly ceased to struggle. Oh, more than that! She had yielded, yielded absolutely, down to every minutest pulse and nerve, and she had fallen into the bright bosom of the stream and it had borne her . . . She was part of her room—part of the great bouquet of southern anemones, of the white net curtains that blew in stiff against the light breeze, of the mirrors, the white silky rugs; she was part of the high, shaking, quivering clamour, broken with little bells and crying voices that went streaming by outside—part of the leaves and the light.

Over. She sat up. The doctor had reappeared. This strange little figure with his stethoscope still strung round his neck—for she had asked him to examine her heart—squeezing and kneading his freshly washed hands, had told her . . .

It was the first time she had ever seen him. Roy, unable, of course, to miss the smallest dramatic opportunity, had obtained his rather shady Bloomsbury address from the man in whom he always confided everything, who, although he'd never met her, knew "all about them."

"My darling," Roy had said, "we'd better have an absolutely unknown man just in case it's—well, what we don't either of us want it to be. One can't be too careful in affairs of this sort. Doctors *do* talk. It's all damned rot to say they don't." Then, "Not that I care a straw who on earth knows. Not that I wouldn't—if you'd have me—blazon it on the skies, or take the front page of the *Daily Mirror* and have our two names on it, in a heart, you know—pierced by an arrow."

Nevertheless, of course, his love of mystery and intrigue, his passion for "keeping our secret beautifully" (his phrase!) had won the day, and off he'd gone in a taxi to fetch this rather sodden-looking little man.

She heard her untroubled voice saying, "Do you mind not mentioning anything of this to Mr. King? If you'd tell him that I'm a little run down and that my heart wants a rest. For I've been complaining about my heart."

Roy had been really *too* right about the kind of man the doctor was. He gave her a strange, quick, leering look, and taking off the stethoscope with shaking fingers he folded it into his bag that looked somehow like a broken old canvas shoe.

"Don't you worry, my dear," he said huskily. "I'll see you through."

Odious little toad to have asked a favour of! She sprang to her feet, and picking up her purple cloth jacket, went over to the mirror. There was a soft knock at the door, and Roy—he really did look pale, smiling his half-smile—came in and asked the doctor what he had to say.

"Well," said the doctor, taking up his hat, holding it against his chest and beating a tattoo on it, "all I've got to say is that Mrs.—h'm—Madam wants a bit of a rest. She's a bit run down. Her heart's a bit strained. Nothing else wrong."

In the street a barrel-organ struck up something gay, laughing, mocking, gushing, with little trills, shakes, jumbles of notes.

> That's *all* I got to say, to say,
> That's all I got to say,

it mocked. It sounded so near she wouldn't have been surprised if the doctor were turning the handle.

She saw Roy's smile deepen; his eyes took fire. He gave a little "Ah!" of relief and happiness. And just for one moment he allowed himself to gaze at her without caring a jot whether the doctor saw or not, drinking her up with that gaze she knew so well, as she stood tying the pale ribbons of her camisole and drawing on the little purple cloth jacket. He jerked back to the doctor, "She shall go away. She shall go away to the sea at once," said he, and then, terribly anxious, "What about her food?" At that, buttoning her jacket in the long mirror, she couldn't help laughing at him.

"That's all very well," he protested, laughing back delightfully at her and at the doctor. "But if I didn't manage her food, doctor, she'd never eat anything but caviare sandwiches and—and white grapes. About wine—oughtn't she to have wine?"

Wine would do her no harm.

"Champagne," pleaded Roy. How he was enjoying himself!

"Oh, as much champagne as she likes," said the doctor, "and a brandy and soda with her lunch if she fancies it."

Roy loved that; it tickled him immensely.

"Do you hear that?" he asked solemnly, blinking and sucking in his cheeks to keep from laughing. "Do you fancy a brandy and soda?"

And, in the distance, faint and exhausted, the barrel-organ:

> A brandy and so-da,
> A brandy and soda, please!
> A brandy and soda, please!

The doctor seemed to hear that, too. He shook hands with her, and Roy went with him into the passage to settle his fee.

She heard the front door close and then—rapid, rapid steps along the passage. This time he simply burst into her room, and she was in his arms, crushed up small while he kissed her with warm quick kisses, murmuring between them, "My darling, my beauty, my delight. You're mine, you're safe." And then three soft groans. "Oh! Oh! Oh! the relief!" Still keeping his arms round her he leant his head against her shoulder as though exhausted. "If you knew how frightened I've been," he murmured. "I thought we were in for it this time. I really did. And it would have been so—fatal—so fatal!"

JE NE PARLE PAS FRANÇAIS

I do not know why I have such a fancy for this little café. It's dirty and sad, sad. It's not as if it had anything to distinguish it from a hundred others—it hasn't; or as if the same strange types came here every day, whom one could watch from one's corner and recognise and more or less (with a strong accent on the less) get the hang of.

But pray don't imagine that those brackets are a confession of my humility before the mystery of the human soul. Not at all; I don't believe in the human soul. I never have. I believe that people are like portmanteaux—packed with certain things, started going, thrown about, tossed away, dumped down, lost and found, half emptied suddenly, or squeezed fatter than ever, until finally the Ultimate Porter swings them on to the Ultimate Train and away they rattle . . .

Not but what these portmanteaux can be very fascinating. Oh, but very! I see myself standing in front of them, don't you know, like a Customs official.

"Have you anything to declare? Any wines, spirits, cigars, perfumes, silks?"

And the moment of hesitation as to whether I am going to be fooled just before I chalk that squiggle, and then the other moment of hesitation just after, as to whether I have been, are perhaps the two most thrilling instants in life. Yes, they are, to me.

But before I started that long and rather far-fetched and not frightfully original digression, what I meant to say quite simply was that there are no portmanteaux to be examined here because the clientele of this café, ladies and gentlemen, does not sit down. No, it stands at the counter, and it consists of a handful of workmen who come up from the river, all powdered over with white flour, lime or something, and a few soldiers, bringing with them thin, dark girls with silver rings in their ears and market baskets on their arms.

Madame is thin and dark, too, with white cheeks and white hands. In certain lights she looks quite transparent, shining out of her black shawl with an extraordinary effect. When she is not serving she sits on a stool with her face turned, always, to the window. Her dark-ringed eyes search among and follow after the people passing, but not as if she was looking for somebody. Perhaps, fifteen years ago, she was; but now the pose has become a habit. You can tell from her air of fatigue and hopelessness that she must have given them up for the last ten years, at least . . .

And then there is the waiter. Not pathetic—decidedly not comic. Never making one of those perfectly insignificant remarks which amaze you so coming from a waiter (as though the poor wretch were a sort of cross between a coffee-pot and a wine bottle and not expected to hold so much as a drop of anything else). He is grey, flat-footed and withered, with long, brittle nails that set your nerves on edge while he scrapes up your two sous. When he is not smearing over the table or flicking at a dead fly or two, he stands with one hand on the back of a chair, in his far too long apron, and over his other arm the three-cornered dip of dirty napkin, waiting to be photographed in connection with some wretched murder. "Interior of Café where Body was Found." You've seen him hundreds of times.

Do you believe that every place has its hour of the

day when it really does come alive? That's not exactly what I mean. It's more like this. There does seem to be a moment when you realize that, quite by accident, you happen to have come on to the stage at exactly the moment you were expected. Everything is arranged for you—waiting for you. Ah, master of the situation! You fill with important breath. And at the same time you smile, secretly, slyly, because Life seems to be opposed to granting you these entrances, seems indeed to be engaged in snatching them from you and making them impossible, keeping you in the wings until it is too late, in fact . . . Just for once you've beaten the old hag.

I enjoyed one of these moments the first time I ever came in here. That's why I keep coming back, I suppose. Revisiting the scene of my triumph, or the scene of the crime where I had the old bitch by the throat for once and did what I pleased with her.

Query: Why am I so bitter against Life? And why do I see her as a rag-picker on the American cinema, shuffling along wrapped in a filthy shawl with her old claws crooked over a stick?

Answer: The direct result of the American cinema acting upon a weak mind.

Anyhow, the "short winter afternoon was drawing to a close", as they say, and I was drifting along, either going home or not going home, when I found myself in here, walking over to this seat in the corner.

I hung up my English overcoat and grey felt hat on that same peg behind me, and after I had allowed the waiter time for at least twenty photographers to snap their fill of him, I ordered a coffee.

He poured me out a glass of the familiar, purplish stuff with a green wandering light playing over it, and shuffled off, and I sat pressing my hands against the glass because it was bitterly cold outside.

Suddenly I realized that quite apart from myself, I was smiling. Slowly I raised my head and saw myself in the mirror opposite. Yes, there I sat, leaning on the table, smiling my deep, sly smile, the glass of coffee with its vague plume of steam before me and beside it the ring of white saucer with two pieces of sugar.

I opened my eyes very wide. There I had been for all eternity, as it were, and now at last I was coming to life . . .

It was very quiet in the café. Outside, one could just see through the dusk that it had begun to snow. One could just see the shapes of horses and carts and people, soft and white, moving through the feathery air. The waiter disappeared and reappeared with an armful of straw. He strewed it over the floor from the door to the counter and round about the stove with humble, almost adoring gestures. One would not have been surprised if the door had opened and the Virgin Mary had come in, riding upon an ass, her meek hands folded over her big belly . . .

That's rather nice, don't you think, that bit about the Virgin? It comes from the pen so gently; it has such a "dying fall". I thought so at the time and decided to make a note of it. One never knows when a little tag like that may come in useful to round off a paragraph. So, taking care to move as little as possible because the "spell" was still unbroken (you know that?), I reached over to the next table for a writing pad.

No paper or envelopes, of course. Only a morsel of pink blotting-paper, incredibly soft and limp and almost moist, like the tongue of a little dead kitten, which I've never felt.

I sat—but always underneath, in this state of expectation, rolling the little dead kitten's tongue round my finger and rolling the soft phrase round my mind while my eyes took in the girls' names and dirty jokes and drawings of bottles and cups that would not sit in the saucers, scattered over the writing pad.

They are always the same, you know. The girls always have the same names, the cups never sit in the saucers; all the hearts are stuck and tied up with ribbons.

But then, quite suddenly, at the bottom of the page, written in green ink, I fell on to that stupid, stale little phrase: *Je ne parle pas français.*

There! it had come—the moment—the *geste*! And although I was so ready, it caught me, it tumbled me over; I was simply overwhelmed. And the physical feeling was so curious, so particular. It was as if all of me, except my head and arms, all of me that was under the table, had simply dissolved, melted, turned into water. Just my head remained and two sticks of arms pressing on to the table. But, ah! the agony of that moment! How can I describe it? I didn't think of anything. I didn't even cry out to myself. Just for one moment I was not. I was Agony, Agony, Agony.

Then it passed, and the very second after I was thinking: "Good God! Am I capable of feeling as strongly as that? But I was absolutely unconscious! I hadn't a phrase to meet it with! I was overcome! I was swept off my feet! I didn't even try, in the dimmest way, to put it down!"

And up I puffed and puffed, blowing off finally with: "After all I must be first-rate. No second-rate mind could have experienced such an intensity of feeling so . . . purely."

★

The waiter has touched a spill at the red stove and lighted a bubble of gas under a spreading shade. It is no use looking out of the window, Madame; it is quite dark now. Your white hands hover over your dark shawl. They are like two birds that have come home to roost. They are restless, restless . . . You tuck them, finally, under your warm little armpits.

Now the waiter has taken a long pole and clashed the curtains together. "All gone", as children say.

And besides, I've no patience with people who can't let go of things, who will follow after and cry out. When a thing's gone, it's gone. It's over and done with. Let it go then! Ignore it, and comfort yourself, if you do want comforting, with the thought that you never do recover the same thing that you lose. It's always a new thing. The moment it leaves you it's changed. Why, that's even true of a hat you chase after; and I don't mean superficially—I mean profoundly speaking . . . I have made it a rule of my life never to regret and never to look back. Regret is an appalling waste of energy, and no one who intends to be a writer can afford to indulge in it. You can't get it into shape; you can't build on it; it's only good for wallowing in. Looking back, of course, is equally fatal to Art. It's keeping yourself poor. Art can't and won't stand poverty.

Je ne parle pas français. Je ne parle pas français. All the while I wrote that last page my other self has been chasing up and down out in the dark there. It left me just when I began to analyse my grand moment, dashed off distracted, like a lost dog who thinks at last, at last, he hears the familiar step again.

"Mouse! Mouse! Where are you? Are you near? Is that you leaning from the high window and stretching out your arms for the wings of the shutters? Are you this soft bundle moving towards me through the feathery snow? Are you this little girl pressing through the swing-doors of the restaurant? Is that your dark shadow bending forward in the cab? Where are you? Where are you? Which way must I turn? Which way shall I run? And every moment I stand here hesitating you are farther away again. Mouse! Mouse!"

Now the poor dog has come back into the café, his tail between his legs, quite exhausted.

"It was a . . . false . . . alarm. She's nowhere . . . to . . . be seen."

"Lie down then! Lie down! Lie down!"

My name is Raoul Duquette. I am twenty-six years old and a Parisian, a true Parisian. About my family—it really doesn't matter. I have no family; I don't want any. I never think about my childhood. I've forgotten it.

In fact, there's only one memory that stands out at all. That is rather interesting because it seems to me now so very significant as regards myself from the literary point of view. It is this.

When I was about ten our laundress was an African woman, very big, very dark, with a check handkerchief over her frizzy hair. When she came to our house she always took particular notice of me, and after the clothes had been taken out of the basket she would lift me up into it and give me a rock while I held tight to the handles and screamed for joy and fright. I was tiny for my age, and pale, with a lovely little half-open mouth—I feel sure of that.

One day when I was standing at the door, watching her go, she turned round and beckoned to me, nodding and smiling in a strange secret way. I never thought of not following. She took me into a little outhouse at the end of the passage, caught me up in her arms and began kissing me. Ah, those kisses! Especially those kisses inside my ears that nearly deafened me.

And then with a soft growl she tore open her bodice and put me to her. When she set me down she took from her pocket a little round fried cake covered with sugar and I reeled along the passage back to our door.

As this performance was repeated once a week it is no wonder that I remember it so vividly. Besides, from that very first afternoon, my childhood was, to put it prettily, "kissed away". I became very languid, very caressing, and greedy beyond measure. And so quickened, so sharpened, I seemed to understand everybody and be able to do what I liked with everybody.

I suppose I was in a state of more or less physical excitement, and that was what appealed to them. For all Parisians are more than half—oh, well, enough of that. And enough of my childhood, too. Bury it under a laundry basket instead of a shower of roses and *passons outre*.

I date myself from the moment that I became the tenant of a small bachelor flat on the fifth floor of a tall, not too shabby house, in a street that might or might not be discreet. Very useful, that . . . There I emerged, came out into the light and put out my two horns with a study and a bedroom and a kitchen on my back. And real furniture planted in the rooms. In the bedroom a wardrobe with a long glass, a big bed covered with a yellow puffed-up quilt, a bed table with a marbled top and a toilet set sprinkled with tiny apples. In my study—English writing table with drawers, writing chair with leather cushions, books, arm-chair, side table with paper-knife and lamp on it and some nude studies on the walls. I didn't use the kitchen except to throw old papers into.

Ah, I can see myself that first evening, after the furniture men had gone and I'd managed to get rid of my atrocious old concierge—walking about on tip-toe, arranging and standing in front of the glass with my hands in my pockets and saying to that radiant vision: "I am a young man who has his own flat. I write for two newspapers. I am going in for serious literature. I am starting a career. The book that I shall bring out will simply stagger the critics. I am going to write about things that have never been touched before. I am going to make a name for myself as a writer about the submerged world. But not as others have done before me. Oh, no! Very naively, with a sort of tender humour and from the inside, as though it were all quite simple, quite natural. I see my way quite perfectly. Nobody has ever done it as I shall do it because none of the others have lived my experiences. I'm rich—I'm rich."

All the same I had no more money than I have now. It's extraordinary how one can live without money . . . I have quantities of good clothes, silk underwear, two evening suits, four pairs of patent leather boots with light uppers, all sorts of little things, like gloves and powder boxes and a manicure set, perfumes, very good soap, and nothing is paid for. If I find myself in need of right-down cash—well, there's always an African laundress and an outhouse, and I am very frank and *bon enfant* about plenty of sugar on the little fried cake afterwards . . .

And here I should like to put something on record. Not from any strutting conceit, but rather with a mild sense of wonder. I've never yet made the first advances to any woman. It isn't as though I've known only one class of woman—not by any means. But from little prostitutes and kept women and elderly widows and shop girls and wives of respectable men, and even advanced modern literary ladies at the most select dinners and soirées (I've been there), I've met invariably with not only the same readiness, but with the same positive invitation. It surprised me at first. I used to look across the table and think "Is that very distinguished young lady, discussing *le Kipling* with the gentleman with the brown beard, really pressing my foot?" And I was never really certain until I had pressed hers.

Curious, isn't it? Why should I be able to have any woman I want? I don't look at all like a maiden's dream . . .

I am little and light with an olive skin, black eyes with long lashes, black silky hair cut short, tiny square teeth that show when I smile. My hands are supple and small. A woman in a bread shop once said to me: "You have the hands for making fine little pastries." I confess, without my clothes I am rather charming. Plump, almost like a girl, with smooth shoulders, and I wear a thin gold bracelet above my left elbow.

But, wait! Isn't it strange I should have written all that about my body and so on? It's the result of my bad life, my submerged life. I am like a little woman in a café who has to introduce herself with a handful of photographs. "Me in my chemise, coming out of an eggshell . . . Me upside down in a swing, with a frilly behind like a cauliflower . . ." You know the things.

If you think what I've written is merely superficial and impudent and cheap you're wrong. I'll admit it does sound so, but then it is not all. If it were, how could I have experienced what I did when I read that stale little phrase written in green ink, in the writing-pad? That proves there's more in me and that I really am important, doesn't it? Anything a fraction less than that moment of anguish I might have put on. But no! That was real.

"Waiter, a whisky."

I hate whisky. Every time I take it into my mouth my stomach rises against it, and the stuff they keep here is sure to be particularly vile. I only ordered it because I am going to write about an Englishman. We French are incredibly old-fashioned and out of date still in some ways. I wonder I didn't ask him at the same time for a pair of tweed knickerbockers, a pipe, some long teeth and a set of ginger whiskers.

"Thanks, *mon vieux*. You haven't got perhaps a set of ginger whiskers?"

"No, monsieur," he answers sadly. "We don't sell American drinks."

And having smeared a corner of the table he goes back to have another couple of dozen taken by artificial light.

Ugh! The smell of it! And the sickly sensation when one's throat contracts.

"It's bad stuff to get drunk on," says Dick Harmon, turning his little glass in his fingers and smiling his slow, dreaming smile. So he gets drunk on it slowly and dreamily and at a certain moment begins to sing very low, very low, about a man who walks up and down trying to find a place where he can get some dinner.

Ah! how I loved that song, and how I loved the way he sang it, slowly, slowly, in a dark, soft voice

> There was a man
> Walked up and down
> To get a dinner in the town . . .

It seemed to hold, in its gravity and muffled measure, all those tall grey buildings, those fogs, those endless streets, those sharp shadows of policemen that mean England.

And then—the subject! The lean, starved creature walking up and down with every house barred against him because he had no "home". How extraordinarily English that is ... I remember that it ended where he did at last "find a place" and ordered a little cake of fish, but when he asked for bread the waiter cried contemptuously, in a loud voice: "We don't serve bread with one fish ball."

What more do you want? How profound those songs are! There is the whole psychology of a people; and how un-French—how un-French!

"Once more, Deeck, once more!" I would plead, clasping my hands and making a pretty mouth at him. He was perfectly content to sing it for ever.

There again. Even with Dick. It was he who made the first advances.

I met him at an evening party given by the editor of a new review. It was a very select, very fashionable affair. One or two of the older men were there and the ladies were extremely *comme il faut*. They sat on cubist sofas in full evening dress and allowed us to hand them thimbles of cherry brandy and to talk to them about their poetry. For, as far as I can remember, they were all poetesses.

It was impossible not to notice Dick. He was the only Englishman present, and instead of circulating gracefully round the room as we all did, he stayed in one place leaning against the wall, his hands in his pockets, that dreamy half smile on his lips, and replying in excellent French in his low, soft voice to anybody who spoke to him.

"Who is he?"

"An Englishman. From London. A writer. And he is making a special study of modern French literature."

That was enough for me. My little book, *False Coins*, had just been published. I was a young, serious writer who was making a special study of modern English literature.

But I really had not time to fling my line before he said, giving himself a soft shake, coming right out of the water after the bait, as it were: "Won't you come and see me at my hotel? Come about five o'clock and we can have a talk before going out to dinner."

"Enchanted!"

I was so deeply, deeply flattered that I had to leave him then and there to preen and preen myself before the cubist sofas. What a catch! An Englishman, reserved, serious, making a special study of French literature . . .

That same night a copy of *False Coins* with a carefully cordial inscription was posted off, and a day or two later we did dine together and spent the evening talking.

Talking—but not only of literature. I discovered to my relief that it wasn't necessary to keep to the tendency of the modern novel, the need of a new form, or the reason why our young men appeared to be just missing it. Now and again, as if by accident, I threw in a card that seemed to have nothing to do with the game, just to see how he'd take it. But each time he gathered it into his hands with his dreamy look and smile unchanged. Perhaps he murmured: "That's very curious." But not as if it were curious at all.

That calm acceptance went to my head at last. It fascinated me. It led me on and on till I threw every card that I possessed at him and sat back and watched him arrange them in his hand.

"Very curious and interesting . . ."

By that time we were both fairly drunk, and he began to sing his song very soft, very low, about the man who walked up and down seeking his dinner.

But I was quite breathless at the thought of what I had done. I had shown somebody both sides of my life. Told him everything as sincerely and truthfully as I could. Taken immense pains to explain things about my submerged life that really were disgusting and never could possibly see the light of literary day. On the whole I had made myself out far worse than I was—more boastful, more cynical, more calculating.

And there sat the man I had confided in, singing to himself and smiling . . . It moved me so that real tears came into my eyes. I saw them glittering on my long silky lashes—so charming.

After that I took Dick about with me everywhere, and he came to my flat, and sat in the arm-chair, very indolent, playing with the paper-knife. I cannot think why his indolence and dreaminess always gave me the impression he had been to sea. And all his leisurely slow ways seemed to be allowing for the movement of the ship. This impression was so strong that often when we were together and he got up and left a little woman just when she did not expect him to get up and leave her, but quite the contrary, I would explain: "He can't help it, Baby. He has to go back to his ship." And I believed it far more than she did.

All the while we were together Dick never went with a woman. I sometimes wondered whether he wasn't completely innocent. Why didn't I ask him? Because I never did ask him anything about himself. But late one night he took out his pocket-book and a photograph dropped out of it. I picked it up and glanced at it before I gave it to him. It was of a woman. Not quite young. Dark, handsome, wild-looking, but so full in every line of a kind of haggard pride that even if Dick had not stretched out so quickly I wouldn't have looked longer.

"Out of my sight, you little perfumed fox-terrier of a Frenchman," said she. (In my very worst moments my nose reminds me of a fox-terrier's.)

"That is my Mother," said Dick, putting up the pocket-book.

But if he had not been Dick I should have been tempted to cross myself, just for fun.

This is how we parted. As we stood outside his hotel one night waiting for the concierge to release the catch of the outer door, he said, looking up at the sky: "I hope it will be fine to-morrow. I am leaving for England in the morning."

"You're not serious."

"Perfectly. I have to get back. I've some work to do that I can't manage here."

"But—but have you made all your preparations?"

"Preparations?" He almost grinned. "I've none to make."

"But—*enfin*, Dick, England is not the other side of the boulevard."

"It isn't much farther off," said he. "Only a few hours, you know." The door cracked open.

"Ah, I wish I'd known at the beginning of the evening!"

I felt hurt. I felt as a woman must feel when a man takes out his watch and remembers an appointment

137

that cannot possibly concern her, except that its claim is the stronger. "Why didn't you tell me?"

He put out his hand and stood, lightly swaying upon the step as though the whole hotel were his ship, and the anchor weighed.

"I forgot. Truly I did. But you'll write, won't you? Good night, old chap. I'll be over again one of these days."

And then I stood on the shore alone, more like a little fox-terrier than ever . . .

"But after all it was you who whistled to me, you who asked me to come! What a spectacle I've cut wagging my tail and leaping round you, only to be left like this while the boat sails off in its slow, dreamy way . . . Curse these English! No, this is too insolent altogether. Who do you imagine I am? A little paid guide to the night pleasures of Paris? . . . No, monsieur. I am a young writer, very serious, and extremely interested in modern English literature. And I have been insulted—insulted."

Two days after came a long, charming letter from him, written in French that was a shade too French, but saying how he missed me and counted on our friendship, on keeping in touch.

I read it standing in front of the (unpaid for) wardrobe mirror. It was early morning. I wore a blue kimono embroidered with white birds and my hair was still wet; it lay on my forehead, wet and gleaming.

"Portrait of Madame Butterfly," said I, "on hearing of the arrival of *ce cher Pinkerton*."

According to the books I should have felt immensely relieved and delighted. ". . . Going over to the window he drew apart the curtains and looked out at the Paris

trees, just breaking into buds and green . . . Dick! Dick!
My English friend!"

I didn't. I merely felt a little sick. Having been up for
my first ride in an aeroplane I didn't want to go up
again, just now.

That passed, and months after, in the winter, Dick
wrote that he was coming back to Paris to stay indef-
initely. Would I take rooms for him? He was bringing a
woman friend with him.

Of course I would. Away the little fox-terrier flew. It
happened most usefully, too; for I owed much money
at the hotel where I took my meals, and two English
people requiring rooms for an indefinite time was an
excellent sum on account.

Perhaps I did rather wonder, as I stood in the larger
of the two rooms with Madame, saying "Admirable,"
what the woman friend would be like, but only vaguely.
Either she would be very severe, flat back and front, or
she would be tall, fair, dressed in mignonette green,
name—Daisy, and smelling of rather sweetish lavender
water.

You see, by this time, according to my rule of not
looking back, I had almost forgotten Dick. I even got
the tune of his song about the unfortunate man a little
bit wrong when I tried to hum it . . .

I very nearly did not turn up at the station after all.
I had arranged to, and had, in fact, dressed with particular care for the occasion. For I intended to take a
new line with Dick this time. No more confidences and
tears on eyelashes. No, thank you!

"Since you left Paris," said I, knotting my black silver-
spotted tie in the (also unpaid for) mirror over the
mantelpiece, "I have been very successful, you know. I

have two more books in preparation, and then I have written a serial story, *Wrong Doors*, which is just on the point of publication and will bring me in a lot of money. And then my little book of poems," I cried, seizing the clothes-brush and brushing the velvet collar of my new indigo-blue overcoat, "my little book—*Left Umbrellas*—really did create," and I laughed and waved the brush, "an immense sensation!"

It was impossible not to believe this of the person who surveyed himself finally, from top to toe, drawing on his soft grey gloves. He was looking the part; he was the part.

That gave me an idea. I took out my notebook, and still in full view, jotted down a note or two . . . How can one look the part and not be the part? Or be the part and not look it? Isn't looking—being? Or being—looking? At any rate who is to say that it is not? . . .

This seemed to me extraordinarily profound at the time, and quite new. But I confess that something did whisper as, smiling, I put up the notebook: "You—literary? you look as though you've taken down a bet on a racecourse!" But I didn't listen. I went out, shutting the door of the flat with a soft, quick pull so as not to warn the concierge of my departure, and ran down the stairs quick as a rabbit for the same reason.

But ah! the old spider. She was too quick for me. She let me run down the last little ladder of the web and then she pounced. "One moment. One little moment, Monsieur," she whispered, odiously confidential. "Come in. Come in." And she beckoned with a dripping soup ladle. I went to the door, but that was not good enough. Right inside and the door shut before she would speak.

There are two ways of managing your concierge if you haven't any money. One is—to take the high hand, make her your enemy, bluster, refuse to discuss anything; the other is—to keep in with her, butter her up to the two knots of the black rag tying up her jaws, pretend to confide in her, and rely on her to arrange with the gas man and to put off the landlord.

I had tried the second. But both are equally detestable and unsuccessful. At any rate whichever you're trying is the worse, the impossible one.

It was the landlord this time . . . Imitation of the landlord by the concierge threatening to toss me out . . . Imitation of the concierge by the concierge taming the wild bull . . . Imitation of the landlord rampant again, breathing in the concierge's face. I was the concierge. No, it was too nauseous. And all the while the black pot on the gas ring bubbling away, stewing out the hearts and livers of every tenant in the place.

"Ah!" I cried, staring at the clock on the mantelpiece, and then, realizing that it didn't go, striking my forehead as though the idea had nothing to do with it. "Madame, I have a very important appointment with the director of my newspaper at nine-thirty. Perhaps to-morrow I shall be able to give you . . ."

Out, out. And down the métro and squeezed into a full carriage. The more the better. Everybody was one bolster the more between me and the concierge. I was radiant.

"Ah! pardon, Monsieur!" said the tall charming creature in black with a big full bosom and a great bunch of violets dropping from it. As the train swayed it thrust the bouquet right into my eyes. "Ah! pardon, Monsieur!"

But I looked up at her, smiling mischievously.

"There is nothing I love more, Madame, than flowers on a balcony."

At the very moment of speaking I caught sight of the huge man in a fur coat against whom my charmer was leaning. He poked his head over her shoulder and he went white to the nose; in fact his nose stood out a sort of cheese green.

"What was that you said to my wife?"

Gare Saint Lazare saved me. But you'll own that even as the author of *False Coins, Wrong Doors, Left Umbrellas,* and two in preparation, it was not too easy to go on my triumphant way.

At length, after countless trains had steamed into my mind, and countless Dick Harmons had come rolling towards me, the real train came. The little knot of us waiting at the barrier moved up close, craned forward, and broke into cries as though we were some kind of many-headed monster, and Paris behind us nothing but a great trap we had set to catch these sleepy innocents.

Into the trap they walked and were snatched and taken off to be devoured. Where was my prey?

"Good God!" My smile and my lifted hand fell together. For one terrible moment I thought this was the woman of the photograph, Dick's mother, walking towards me in Dick's coat and hat. In the effort—and you saw what an effort it was—to smile, his lips curled in just the same way and he made for me, haggard and wild and proud.

What had happened? What could have changed him like this? Should I mention it?

I waited for him and was even conscious of venturing a foxterrier wag or two to see if he could possibly respond, in the way I said: "Good evening, Dick! How are you, old chap? All right?"

"All right. All right." He almost gasped. "You've got the rooms?"

Twenty times, good God! I saw it all. Light broke on the dark waters and my sailor hadn't been drowned. I almost turned a somersault with amusement.

It was nervousness, of course. It was embarrassment. It was the famous English seriousness. What fun I was going to have! I could have hugged him.

"Yes, I've got the rooms," I nearly shouted. "But where is Madame?"

"She's been looking after the luggage," he panted. "Here she comes, now."

Not this baby walking beside the old porter as though he were her nurse and had just lifted her out of her ugly perambulator while he trundled the boxes on it.

"And she's not Madame," said Dick, drawling suddenly.

At that moment she caught sight of him and hailed him with her minute muff. She broke away from her nurse and ran up and said something, very quick, in English; but he replied in French: "Oh, very well. I'll manage."

But before he turned to the porter he indicated me with a vague wave and muttered something. We were introduced. She held out her hand in that strange boyish way Englishwomen do, and standing very straight in front of me with her chin raised and making—she too—the effort of her life to control her preposterous excitement, she said, wringing my hand (I'm sure she didn't know it was mine), *Je ne parle pas français.*

"But I'm sure you do," I answered, so tender, so

reassuring, I might have been a dentist about to draw her first little milk tooth.

"Of course she does." Dick swerved back to us. "Here, can't we get a cab or taxi or something? We don't want to stay in this cursed station all night. Do we?"

This was so rude that it took me a moment to recover; and he must have noticed, for he flung his arm round my shoulder in the old way, saying: "Ah, forgive me, old chap. But we've had such a loathsome, hideous journey. We've taken years to come. Haven't we?" To her. But she did not answer. She bent her head and began stroking her grey muff; she walked beside us stroking her grey muff all the way.

"Have I been wrong?" thought I. "Is this simply a case of frenzied impatience on their part? Are they merely 'in need of a bed', as we say? Have they been suffering agonies on the journey? Sitting, perhaps, very close and warm under the same travelling rug?" and so on and so on while the driver strapped on the boxes. That done—

"Look here, Dick. I go home by métro. Here is the address of your hotel. Everything is arranged. Come and see me as soon as you can."

Upon my life I thought he was going to faint. He went white to the lips.

"But you're coming back with us," he cried. "I thought it was all settled. Of course you're coming back. You're not going to leave us." No, I gave it up. It was too diffi- cult, too English for me.

"Certainly, certainly. Delighted. I only thought, perhaps . . ."

"You must come!" said Dick to the little fox-terrier. And again he made that big awkward turn towards her.

"Get in, Mouse."

And Mouse got in the black hole and sat stroking Mouse II and not saying a word.

Away we jolted and rattled like three little dice that life had decided to have a fling with.

I had insisted on taking the flap seat facing them because I would not have missed for anything those occasional flashing glimpses I had as we broke through the white circles of lamplight.

They revealed Dick, sitting far back in his corner, his coat collar turned up, his hands thrust in his pockets, and his broad dark hat shading him as if it were a part of him—a sort of wing he hid under. They showed her, sitting up very straight, her lovely little face more like a drawing than a real face—every line was so full of meaning and so sharp cut against the swimming dark.

For Mouse was beautiful. She was exquisite, but so fragile and fine that each time I looked at her it was as if for the first time. She came upon you with the same kind of shock that you feel when you have been drinking tea out of a thin innocent cup and suddenly, at the bottom, you see a tiny creature, half butterfly, half woman, bowing to you with her hands in her sleeves.

As far as I could make out she had dark hair and blue or black eyes. Her long lashes and the two little feathers traced above were most important.

She wore a long dark cloak such as one sees in old-fashioned pictures of Englishwomen abroad. Where her arms came out of it there was grey fur—fur round her neck, too, and her close-fitting cap was furry.

"Carrying out the mouse idea," I decided.

Ah, but how intriguing it was—how intriguing! Their excitement came nearer and nearer to me, while I ran out to meet it, bathed in it, flung myself far out of my depth, until at last I was as hard put to it to keep control as they.

But what I wanted to do was to behave in the most extraordinary fashion—like a clown. To start singing, with large extravagant gestures, to point out of the window and cry: "We are now passing, ladies and gentlemen, one of the sights for which *notre Paris* is justly famous"; to jump out of the taxi while it was going, climb over the roof and dive in by another door; to hang out of the window and look for the hotel through the wrong end of a broken telescope, which was also a peculiarly ear-splitting trumpet.

I watched myself do all this, you understand, and even managed to applaud in a private way by putting my gloved hands gently together, while I said to Mouse: "And is this your first visit to Paris?"

"Yes, I've not been here before."

"Ah, then you have a great deal to see."

And I was just going to touch lightly upon the objects of interest and the museums when we wrenched to a stop.

Do you know—it's very absurd—but as I pushed open the door for them and followed up the stairs to the bureau on the landing I felt somehow that this hotel was mine.

There was a vase of flowers on the window sill of the bureau and I even went so far as to re-arrange a bud or two and to stand off and note the effect while the manageress welcomed them. And when she turned to me and handed me the keys (the *garçon* was hauling up the boxes) and said: "Monsieur Duquette will show you your rooms"—I had a longing to tap Dick on the arm with a key and say, very confidentially: "Look here, old chap. As a friend of mine I'll be only too willing to make a slight reduction . . ."

Up and up we climbed. Round and round. Past an occasional pair of boots (why is it one never sees an attractive pair of boots outside a door?). Higher and higher.

"I'm afraid they're rather high up," I murmured idiotically. "But I chose them because . . ."

They so obviously did not care why I chose them that I went no further. They accepted everything. They did not expect anything to be different. This was just part of what they were going through—that was how I analysed it.

"Arrived at last." I ran from one side of the passage to the other, turning on the lights, explaining.

"This one I thought for you, Dick. The other is larger and it has a little dressing-room in the alcove."

My "proprietary" eye noted the clean towels and covers, and the bed linen embroidered in red cotton. I thought them rather charming rooms, sloping, full of angles, just the sort of rooms one would expect to find if one had not been to Paris before.

Dick dashed his hat down on the bed.

"Oughtn't I to help that chap with the boxes?" he asked—nobody.

"Yes, you ought," replied Mouse, "they're dreadfully heavy."

And she turned to me with the first glimmer of a smile: "Books, you know." Oh, he darted such a strange look at her before he rushed out. And he not only helped, he must have torn the box off the *garçon's* back, for he staggered back, carrying one, dumped it down and then fetched in the other.

"That's yours, Dick," said she.

"Well, you don't mind it standing here for the present, do you?" he asked, breathless, breathing hard (the box must have been tremendously heavy). He pulled out a handful of money. "I suppose I ought to pay this chap."

The *garçon*, standing by, seemed to think so too.

"And will you require anything further, Monsieur?"

"No! No!" said Dick impatiently.

But at that Mouse stepped forward. She said, too deliberately, not looking at Dick, with her quaint clipped English accent: "Yes, I'd like some tea. Tea for three."

And suddenly she raised her muff as though her hands were clasped inside it, and she was telling the pale, sweaty *garçon* by that action that she was at the end of her resources, that she cried out to him to save her with "Tea. Immediately!"

This seemed to me so amazingly in the picture, so exactly the gesture and cry that one would expect (though I couldn't have imagined it) to be wrung out of an Englishwoman faced with a great crisis, that I was almost tempted to hold up my hand and protest.

"No! No! Enough. Enough. Let us leave off there. At the word—tea. For really, really, you've filled your greediest subscriber so full that he will burst if he has to swallow another word."

It even pulled Dick up. Like someone who has been unconscious for a long long time he turned slowly to Mouse and slowly looked at her with his tired, haggard eyes, and murmured with the echo of his dreamy voice: "Yes. That's a good idea." And then: "You must be tired, Mouse. Sit down."

She sat down in a chair with lace tabs on the arms;

he leaned against the bed, and I established myself on a straight-backed chair, crossed my legs and brushed some imaginary dust off the knees of my trousers. (The Parisian at his ease.)

There came a tiny pause. Then he said: "Won't you take off your coat, Mouse?"

"No, thanks. Not just now."

Were they going to ask me? Or should I hold up my hand and call out in a baby voice: 'It's my turn to be asked.'

No, I shouldn't. They didn't ask me.

The pause became a silence. A real silence.

". . . Come, my Parisian fox-terrier! Amuse these sad English! It's no wonder they are such a nation for dogs."

But, after all—why should I? It was not my "job", as they would say. Nevertheless, I made a vivacious little bound at Mouse.

"What a pity it is that you did not arrive by daylight. There is such a charming view from these two windows. You know, the hotel is on a corner and each window looks down an immensely long, straight street."

"Yes," said she.

"Not that that sounds very charming," I laughed. "But there is so much animation—so many absurd little boys on bicycles and people hanging out of windows and—oh, well, you'll see for yourself in the morning . . . Very amusing. Very animated."

"Oh, yes," said she.

If the pale, sweaty *garçon* had not come in at that moment, carrying the tea-tray high on one hand as if the cups were cannonballs and he a heavy weight lifter on the cinema . . .

He managed to lower it on to a round table.

"Bring the table over here," said Mouse. The waiter seemed to be the only person she cared to speak to. She took her hands out of her muff, drew off her gloves and flung back the old-fashioned cape.

"Do you take milk and sugar?"

"No milk, thank you, and no sugar."

I went over for mine like a little gentleman. She poured out another cup.

"That's for Dick."

And the faithful fox-terrier carried it across to him and laid it at his feet, as it were.

"Oh, thanks," said Dick.

And then I went back to my chair and she sank back in hers.

But Dick was off again. He stared wildly at the cup of tea for a moment, glanced round him, put it down on the bed-table, caught up his hat and stammered at full gallop: "Oh, by the way, do you mind posting a letter for me? I want to get it off by to-night's post. I must. It's very urgent . . ." Feeling her eyes on him, he flung: "It's to my mother." To me: "I won't be long. I've got everything I want. But it must go off to-night. You don't mind? It . . . it won't take any time."

"Of course I'll post it. Delighted."

"Won't you drink your tea first?" suggested Mouse softly.

. . . Tea? Tea? Yes, of course. Tea . . . A cup of tea on the bed-table . . . In his racing dream he flashed the brightest, most charming smile at his little hostess.

"No, thanks. Not just now."

And still hoping it would not be any trouble to me he went out of the room and closed the door, and we heard him cross the passage.

I scalded myself with mine in my hurry to take the

cup back to the table and to say as I stood there: "You must forgive me if I am impertinent . . . if I am too frank. But Dick hasn't tried to disguise it—has he? There is something the matter. Can I help?"

(Soft music. Mouse gets up, walks the stage for a moment or so before she returns to her chair and pours him out, oh, such a brimming, such a burning cup that the tears come into the friend's eyes while he sips—while he drains it to the bitter dregs . . .)

I had time to do all this before she replied. First she looked in the teapot, filled it with hot water, and stirred it with a spoon.

"Yes, there is something the matter. No, I'm afraid you can't help, thank you." Again I got that glimmer of a smile. "I'm awfully sorry. I must be horrid for you."

Horrid, indeed! Ah, why couldn't I tell her that it was months and months since I had been so entertained?

"But you are suffering," I ventured softly, as though that was what I could not bear to see.

She didn't deny it. She nodded and bit her under-lip and I thought I saw her chin tremble.

"And there is really nothing I can do?" More softly still.

She shook her head, pushed back the table and jumped up.

"Oh, it will be all right soon," she breathed, walking over to the dressing-table and standing with her back towards me. "It will be all right. It can't go on like this."

"But of course it can't." I agreed, wondering whether it would look heartless if I lit a cigarette; I had a sudden longing to smoke.

In some way she saw my hand move to my breast pocket, half draw out my cigarette case and put it back again, for the next thing she said was: "Matches . . . in . . . candlestick. I noticed them."

And I heard from her voice that she was crying.

"Ah! thank you. Yes. Yes. I've found them." I lighted my cigarette and walked up and down, smoking.

It was so quiet it might have been two o'clock in the morning. It was so quiet you heard the boards creak and pop as one does in a house in the country. I smoked the whole cigarette and stabbed the end into my saucer before Mouse turned round and came back to the table.

"Isn't Dick being rather a long time?"

"You are very tired. I expect you want to go to bed," I said kindly. (And pray don't mind me if you do, said my mind.)

"But isn't he being a very long time?" she insisted.

I shrugged. "He is, rather."

Then I saw she looked at me strangely. She was listening.

"He's been gone ages," she said, and she went with little light steps to the door, opened it, and crossed the passage into his room.

I waited. I listened too, now. I couldn't have borne to miss a word. She had left the door open. I stole across the room and looked after her. Dick's door was open, too. But—there wasn't a word to miss.

You know I had the mad idea that they were kissing in that quiet room—a long comfortable kiss. One of those kisses that not only puts one's grief to bed, but nurses it and warms it and tucks it up and keeps it fast enfolded until it is sleeping sound. Ah! how good that is.

It was over at last. I heard some one move and tip-toed away.

It was Mouse. She came back. She felt her way into the room carrying the letter for me. But it wasn't in an envelope; it was just a sheet of paper and she held it by the corner as though it was still wet.

Her head was bent so low—so tucked in her furry collar that I hadn't a notion—until she let the paper fall and almost fell herself on to the floor by the side of the bed, leaned her cheek against it, flung out her hands as though the last of her poor little weapons was gone and now she let herself be carried away, washed out into the deep water.

Flash! went my mind. Dick has shot himself, and then a succession of flashes while I rushed in, saw the body, head unharmed, small blue hole over temple, roused hotel, arranged funeral, attended funeral, closed cab, new morning coat . . .

I stooped down and picked up the paper and would you believe it—so ingrained is my Parisian sense of *comme it faut*—I murmured "pardon" before I read it.

"Mouse, my little Mouse, It's not good. It's impossible. I can't see it through. Oh, I do love you. I do love you, Mouse, but I can't hurt her. People have been hurting her all her life. I simply dare not give her this final blow. You see, though she's stronger than both of us, she's so frail and proud. It would kill her—kill her, Mouse. And, oh God, I can't kill my mother! Not even for you. Not even for us. You do see that—don't you.

It all seemed so possible when we talked and planned, but the very moment the train started it was all over. I felt her drag me back to her—calling. I can hear her now as I write. And she's alone and she doesn't know. A man would have to be a devil to tell her and I'm not a devil, Mouse. She mustn't know. Oh, Mouse, some-where, somewhere in you don't you agree? It's all so unspeakably awful that I don't know if I want to go or not. Do I? Or is Mother just dragging me? I don't know. My head is too tired. Mouse, Mouse—what will you do? But I can't think of that, either. I dare not. I'd break down. And I must not break down. All I've got to do is—just to tell you this and go. I couldn't have gone off without telling you. You'd have been frightened. And you must not be frightened. You won't—will you? I can't bear—but no more of that. And don't write. I should not have the courage to answer your letters and the sight of your spidery handwriting—

Forgive me. Don't love me any more. Yes. Love me. Love me. Dick."

What do you think of that? Wasn't that a rare find? My relief at his not having shot himself was mixed with a wonderful sense of elation. I was even—more than even with my "that's very curious and interesting" Englishman . . .

She wept so strangely. With her eyes shut, with her face quite calm except for the quivering eyelids. The tears pearled down her cheeks and she let them fall.

But feeling my glance upon her she opened her eyes and saw me holding the letter.

"You've read it?"

Her voice was quite calm, but it was not her voice any more. It was like the voice you might imagine coming out of a tiny, cold seashell swept high and dry at last by the salt tide . . .

I nodded, quite overcome, you understand, and laid the letter down.

"It's incredible! incredible!" I whispered.

At that she got up from the floor, walked over to the wash-stand, dipped her handkerchief into the jug and sponged her eyes, saying: "Oh, no. It's not incredible at all." And still pressing the wet ball to her eyes she came back to me, to her chair with the lace tabs, and sank into it.

"I knew all along, of course," said the cold, salty little voice. "From the very moment that we started. I felt it all through me, but I still went on hoping—" and here she took the handkerchief down and gave me a final glimmer—"as one so stupidly does, you know."

"As one does."

Silence.

"But what will you do? You'll go back? You'll see him?"

That made her sit right up and stare across at me.

"What an extraordinary idea!" she said, more coldly than ever. "Of course I shall not dream of seeing him. As for going back—that is quite out of the question. I can't go back."

"But . . ."

"It's impossible. For one thing all my friends think I am married."

I put out my hand—"Ah, my poor little friend."

But she shrank away. (False move.)

Of course there was one question that had been at the back of my mind all this time. I hated it.

"Have you any money?"

"Yes, I have twenty pounds—here," and she put her hand on her breast. I bowed. It was a great deal more than I had expected.

"And what are your plans?"

Yes, I know. My question was the most clumsy, the most idiotic one I could have put. She had been so tame, so confiding, letting me, at any rate spiritually speaking, hold her tiny quivering body in one hand and

stroke her furry head—and now, I'd thrown her away.
Oh, I could have kicked myself.

She stood up. "I have no plans. But—it's very late.
You must go now, please."

How could I get her back? I wanted her back, I swear
I was not acting then.

"Do feel that I am your friend," I cried. "You will let
me come tomorrow, early? You will let me look after you
a little—take care of you a little? You'll use me just as
you think fit?"

I succeeded. She came out of her hole . . . timid . . .
but she came out.

"Yes, you're very kind. Yes. Do come to-morrow. I
shall be glad. It makes things rather difficult because—"
and again I clasped her boyish hand—"*je ne parle pas
français.*"

Not until I was half-way down the boulevard did it
come over me—the full force of it.

Why, they were suffering . . . those two . . . really
suffering. I have seen two people suffer as I don't suppose I ever shall again . . . And . . . "Good-night, my
little cat," said I, impudently, to the fattish old prosti-
tute picking her way home through the slush . . . I
didn't give her time to reply.

Of course you know what to expect. You anticipate,
fully, what I am going to write. It wouldn't be me,
otherwise.

I never went near the place again.

Yes, I still owe that considerable amount for lunches
and dinners, but that's beside the mark. It's vulgar to
mention it in the same breath with the fact that I never
saw Mouse again.

Naturally, I intended to. Started out—got to the

door—wrote and tore up letters—did all those things. But I simply could not make the final effort.

Even now I don't fully understand why. Of course I knew that I couldn't have kept it up. That had a great deal to do with it. But you would have thought, putting it at its lowest, curiosity couldn't have kept my fox-terrier nose away . . .

Je ne parle pas français. That was her swan song for me.

But how she makes me break my rule. Oh, you've seen for yourself, but I could give you countless examples.

. . . Evenings, when I sit in some gloomy café, and an automatic piano starts playing a "mouse" tune (there are dozens of tunes that evoke just her) I begin to dream things like . . .

A little house on the edge of the sea, somewhere far, far away. A girl outside in a frock rather like Red Indian women wear, hailing a light, bare-foot boy who runs up from the beach.

"What have you got?"

"A fish." I smile and give it to her.

. . . The same girl, the same boy, different costumes— sitting at an open window, eating fruit and leaning out and laughing.

"All the wild strawberries are for you, Mouse. I won't touch one."

. . . A wet night. They are going home together under an umbrella. They stop on the door to press their wet cheeks together.

And so on and so on until some dirty old gallant comes up to my table and sits opposite and begins to grimace and yap. Until I hear myself saying: "But I've got the little girl for you, *mon vieux*. So little . . . so tiny. And a virgin." I kiss the tips of my fingers—"A virgin"—and lay them upon my heart. "I give you my word of honour as a gentleman, a writer, serious, young, and extremely interested in modern English literature."

I must go. I must go. I reach down my coat and hat. Madame knows me. "You haven't dined yet?" she smiles.

"No, not yet, Madame."

I'd rather like to dine with her. Even to sleep with her afterwards. Would she be pale like that all over?

But no. She'd have large moles. They go with that kind of skin. And I can't bear them. They remind me somehow, disgustingly, of mushrooms.

THE LONELY VOICE

GERMANS AT MEAT

Bread soup was placed upon the table. "Ah," said the Herr Rat, leaning upon the table as he peered into the tureen, "that is what I need. My 'magen' has not been in order for several days. Bread soup, and just the right consistency. I am a good cook myself"—he turned to me.

"How interesting," I said, attempting to infuse just the right amount of enthusiasm into my voice.

"Oh yes—when one is not married it is necessary. As for me, I have had all I wanted from women without marriage." He tucked his napkin into his collar and blew upon his soup as he spoke. "Now at nine o'clock I make myself an English breakfast, but not much. Four slices of bread, two eggs, two slices of cold ham, one plate of soup, two cups of tea—that is nothing to you."

He asserted the fact so vehemently that I had not the courage to refute it.

All eyes were suddenly turned upon me. I felt I was bearing the burden of the nation's preposterous breakfast—I who drank a cup of coffee while buttoning my blouse in the morning.

"Nothing at all," cried Herr Hoffmann from Berlin. "Ach, when I was in England in the morning I used to eat."

He turned up his eyes and his moustache, wiping the soup drippings from his coat and waistcoat.

"Do they really eat so much?" asked Fräulein Stiege-lauer. "Soup and baker's bread and pig's flesh, and tea and coffee and stewed fruit, and honey and eggs, and cold fish and kidneys, and hot fish and liver? All the ladies eat too, especially the ladies?"

"Certainly. I myself have noticed it, when I was living in a hotel in Leicester Square," cried the Herr Rat. "It was a good hotel, but they could not make tea—now—"

"Ah, that's one thing I *can* do," said I, laughing brightly. "I can make very good tea. The great secret is to warm the teapot."

"Warm the teapot," interrupted the Herr Rat, pushing away his soup plate. "What do you warm the teapot for? Ha! ha! that's very good! One does not eat the teapot, I suppose?"

He fixed his cold blue eyes upon me with an expression which suggested a thousand premeditated invasions.

"So that is the great secret of your English tea? All you do is to warm the teapot."

I wanted to say that was only the preliminary canter, but could not translate it, and so was silent.

The servant brought in veal, with sauerkraut and potatoes.

"I eat sauerkraut with great pleasure," said the Traveller from North Germany, "but now I have eaten so much of it that I cannot retain it. I am immediately forced to—"

"A beautiful day," I cried, turning to Fräulein Stiegelauer. "Did you get up early?"

"At five o'clock I walked for ten minutes in the wet grass. Again in bed. At half-past five I fell asleep and woke at seven, when I made an 'overbody' washing! Again in bed. At eight o'clock I had a cold-water poultice, and at half-past eight I drank a cup of mint tea. At

nine I drank some malt coffee, and began my 'cure.'
Pass me the sauerkraut, please. You do not eat it?"

"No, thank you. I still find it a little strong."

"Is it true," asked the Widow, picking her teeth with
a hairpin as she spoke, "that you are a vegetarian?"

"Why, yes; I have not eaten meat for three years."

"Im-possible! Have you any family?"

"No."

"There now, you see, that's what you're coming to!
Who ever heard of having children upon vegetables? It
is not possible. But you never have large families in
England now; I suppose you are too busy with your
suffragetting. Now I have had nine children, and they
are all alive, thank God. Fine, healthy babies—though
after the first one was born I had to—"

"How *wonderful*!" I cried.

"Wonderful," said the Widow contemptuously,
replacing the hairpin in the knob which was balanced
on the top of her head. "Not at all! A friend of mine
had four at the same time. Her husband was so pleased
he gave a supper-party and had them placed on the
table. Of course she was very proud."

"Germany," boomed the Traveller, biting round a
potato which he had speared with his knife, "is the
home of the Family."

Followed an appreciative silence.

The dishes were changed for beef, red currants and
spinach. They wiped their forks upon black bread and
started again.

"How long are you remaining here?" asked the Herr
Rat.

"I do not know exactly. I must be back in London in
September."

"Of course you will visit München?"

"I am afraid I shall not have time. You see, it is important not to break into my 'cure.'"

"But you *must* go to München. You have not seen Germany if you have not been to München. All the Exhibitions, all the Art and Soul life of Germany are in München. There is the Wagner Festival in August, and Mozart and a Japanese collection of pictures—and there is the beer! You do not know what good beer is until you have been to München. Why, I see fine ladies every afternoon, but fine ladies, I tell you, drinking glasses so high." He measured a good wash-stand pitcher in height, and I smiled.

"If I drink a great deal of München beer I sweat so," said Herr Hoffmann. "When I am here, in the fields or before my baths, I sweat, but I enjoy it; but in the town it is not at all the same thing."

Prompted by the thought, he wiped his neck and face with his dinner napkin and carefully cleaned his ears.

A glass dish of stewed apricots was placed upon the table.

"Ah, fruit!" said Fräulein Stiegelauer, "that is so necessary to health. The doctor told me this morning that the more fruit I could eat the better."

She very obviously followed the advice.

Said the Traveller: "I suppose you are frightened of an invasion too, eh? Oh, that's good. I've been reading all about your English play in a newspaper. Did you see it?"

"Yes." I sat upright. "I assure you we are not afraid."

"Well, then, you ought to be," said the Herr Rat. "You have got no army at all—a few little boys with their veins full of nicotine poisoning."

"Don't be afraid," Herr Hoffmann said. "We don't want England. If we did we would have had her long ago. We really do not want you."

He waved his spoon airily, looking across at me as though I were a little child whom he would keep or dismiss as he pleased.

"We certainly do not want Germany," I said.

"This morning I took a half bath. Then this afternoon I must take a knee bath and an arm bath," volunteered the Herr Rat; "then I do my exercises for an hour, and my work is over. A glass of wine and a couple of rolls with some sardines—"

They were handed cherry cake with whipped cream.

"What is your husband's favourite meat?" asked the Widow.

"I really do not know," I answered.

"You really do not know? How long have you been married?"

"Three years."

"But you cannot be in earnest! You would not have kept house as his wife for a week without knowing that fact."

"I really never asked him; he is not at all particular about his food."

A pause. They all looked at me, shaking their heads, their mouths full of cherry stones.

"No wonder there is a repetition in England of that dreadful state of things in Paris," said the Widow, folding her dinner napkin. "How can a woman expect to keep her husband if she does not know his favourite food after three years?"

"*Mahlzeit!*"

"*Mahlzeit!*"

I closed the door after me.

THE BARON

"Who is he?" I said. "And why does he sit always alone, with his back to us, too?"

"Ah!" whispered the Frau Oberregierungsrat, "he is a *Baron*."

She looked at me very solemnly, and yet with the slightest possible contempt—a "fancy-not-recognising-that-at-the-first-glance" expression.

"But, poor soul, he cannot help it," I said. "Surely that unfortunate fact ought not to debar him from the pleasures of intellectual intercourse."

If it had not been for her fork I think she would have crossed herself.

"Surely you cannot understand. He is one of the First Barons."

More than a little unnerved, she turned and spoke to the Frau Doktor on her left.

"My omelette is empty—*empty*," she protested, "and this is the third I have tried!"

I looked at the First of the Barons. He was eating salad—taking a whole lettuce leaf on his fork and absorbing it slowly, rabbit-wise—a fascinating process to watch.

Small and slight, with scanty black hair and beard and yellow-toned complexion, he invariably wore black serge clothes, a rough linen shirt, black sandals, and the largest black-rimmed spectacles that I had ever seen.

The Herr Oberlehrer, who sat opposite me, smiled benignantly.

"It must be very interesting for you, gnädige Frau, to be able to watch . . . of course this is a *very fine house*. There was a lady from the Spanish Court here in the summer; she had a liver. We often spoke together."

I looked gratified and humble.

"Now, in England, in your 'boarding-'ouse,' one does not find the First Class, as in Germany."

"No, indeed," I replied, still hypnotised by the Baron, who looked like a little yellow silkworm.

"The Baron comes every year," went on the Herr Oberlehrer, "for his nerves. He has never spoken to any of the guests—*yet*." A smile crossed his face. I seemed to see his visions of some splendid upheaval of that silence—a dazzling exchange of courtesies in a dim future, a splendid sacrifice of a newspaper to this Exalted One, a "danke schön" to be handed down to future generations.

At that moment the postman, looking like a German army officer, came in with the mail. He threw my letters into my milk pudding, and then turned to a waitress and whispered. She retired hastily. The manager of the pension came in with a little tray. A picture postcard was deposited on it, and reverently bowing his head, the manager of the pension carried it to the Baron.

Myself, I felt disappointed that there was not a salute of twenty-five guns.

At the end of the meal we were served with coffee. I noticed the Baron took three lumps of sugar, putting two in his cup and wrapping up the third in a corner of his pocket-handkerchief. He was always the first to enter the dining-room and the last to leave; and in a vacant chair beside him he placed a little black leather bag.

In the afternoon, leaning from my window, I saw him

pass down the street, walking tremulously and carrying the bag. Each time he passed a lamp-post he shrank a little, as though expecting it to strike him, or maybe the sense of plebeian contamination . . .

I wondered where he was going, and why he carried the bag. Never had I seen him at the Casino or the Bath Establishment. He looked forlorn, his feet slipped in his sandals. I found myself pitying the Baron.

That evening a party of us were gathered in the salon discussing the day's "kur" with feverish animation. The Frau Oberregierungsrat sat by me knitting a shawl for her youngest of nine daughters, who was in that very interesting, frail condition . . ."But it is bound to be quite satisfactory," she said to me. "The dear married a banker—the desire of her life."

There must have been eight or ten of us gathered together, we who were married exchanging confidences as to the underclothing and peculiar characteristics of our husbands, the unmarried discussing the over-clothing and peculiar fascinations of Possible Ones.

"I knit them myself," I heard the Frau Lehrer cry, "of thick grey wool. He wears one a month, with two soft collars."

"And then," whispered Fräulein Lisa, "he said to me, 'Indeed you please me. I shall, perhaps, write to your mother.'"

Small wonder that we were a little violently excited, a little expostulatory.

Suddenly the door opened and admitted the Baron.

Followed a complete and deathlike silence.

He came in slowly, hesitated, took up a toothpick from a dish on the top of the piano, and went out again.

When the door was closed we raised a triumphant

cry! It was the first time he had ever been known to enter the salon. Who could tell what the Future held?

Days lengthened into weeks. Still we were together, and still the solitary little figure, head bowed as though under the weight of the spectacles, haunted me. He entered with the black bag, he retired with the black bag—and that was all.

At last the manager of the pension told us the Baron was leaving the next day.

"Oh," I thought, "surely he cannot drift into obscurity—be lost without one word! Surely he will honour the Frau Oberregierungsrat or the Frau Feldleutnantswitwe *once* before he goes."

In the evening of that day it rained heavily. I went to the post-office, and as I stood on the steps, umbrella-less, hesitating before plunging into the slushy road, a little, hesitating voice seemed to come from under my elbow.

I looked down. It was the First of the Barons with the black bag and an umbrella. Was I mad? Was I sane? He was asking me to share the latter. But I was exceedingly nice, a trifle diffident, appropriately reverential. Together we walked through the mud and slush.

Now, there is something peculiarly intimate in sharing an umbrella.

It is apt to put one on the same footing as brushing a man's coat for him—a little daring, naive.

I longed to know why he sat alone, why he carried the bag, what he did all day. But he himself volunteered some information.

"I fear," he said, "that my luggage will be damp. I invariably carry it with me in this bag—one requires so little—for servants are untrustworthy."

"A wise idea," I answered. And then: "Why have you denied us the pleasure—"

"I sit alone that I may eat more," said the Baron, peering into the dusk; "my stomach requires a great deal of food. I order double portions, and eat them in peace."

Which sounded finely Baronial.

"And what do you do all day?"

"I imbibe nourishment in my room," he replied, in a voice that closed the conversation and almost repented of the umbrella.

When we arrived at the pension there was very nearly an open riot.

I ran half-way up the stairs, and thanked the Baron audibly from the landing.

He distinctly replied: "Not at all!"

It was very friendly of the Herr Oberlehrer to have sent me a bouquet that evening, and the Frau Oberregierungsrat asked me for my pattern of a baby's bonnet!

Next day the Baron was gone.

Sic transit gloria German mundi.

A DILL PICKLE

And then, after six years, she saw him again. He was seated at one of those little bamboo tables decorated with a Japanese vase of paper daffodils. There was a tall plate of fruit in front of him, and very carefully, in a way she recognised immediately as his "special" way, he was peeling an orange.

He must have felt that shock of recognition in her, for he looked up and met her eyes. Incredible! He didn't know her! She smiled; he frowned. She came towards him. He closed his eyes an instant, but opening them his face lit up as though he had struck a match in a dark room. He laid down the orange and pushed back his chair, and she took her little warm hand out of her muff and gave it to him.

"Vera!" he exclaimed. "How strange. Really, for a moment I didn't know you. Won't you sit down? You've had lunch? Won't you have some coffee?"

She hesitated, but of course she meant to.

"Yes, I'd like some coffee." And she sat down opposite him.

"You've changed. You've changed very much," he said, staring at her with that eager, lighted look. "You look so well. I've never seen you look so well before."

"Really?" She raised her veil and unbuttoned her high fur collar. "I don't feel very well. I can't bear this weather, you know."

"Ah, no. You hate the cold . . ."

"Loathe it." She shuddered. "And the worst of it is that the older one grows . . ."

He interrupted her. "Excuse me," and tapped on the table for the waitress. "Please bring some coffee and cream." To her: "You are sure you won't eat anything? Some fruit, perhaps. The fruit here is very good."

"No, thanks. Nothing."

"Then that's settled." And smiling just a hint too broadly he took up the orange again. "You were saying—the older one grows—"

"The colder," she laughed. But she was thinking how well she remembered that trick of his—the trick of interrupting her—and how it used to exasperate her six years ago. She used to feel then as though he, quite suddenly, in the middle of what she was saying, put his hand over her lips, turned from her, attended to something different, and then took his hand away, and with just the same slightly too broad smile, gave her his attention again . . . Now we are ready. That is settled.

"The colder!" He echoed her words, laughing too. "Ah, ah. You still say the same things. And there is another thing about you that is not changed at all— your beautiful voice—your beautiful way of speaking." Now he was very grave; he leaned towards her, and she smelled the warm, stinging scent of the orange peel. "You have only to say one word and I would know your voice among all other voices. I don't know what it is— I've often wondered—that makes your voice such a—haunting memory . . . Do you remember that first afternoon we spent together at Kew Gardens? You were so surprised because I did not know the names of any flowers. I am still just as ignorant for all your telling me. But whenever it is very fine and warm, and I see some bright colours—it's awfully strange—I hear your voice saying: 'Geranium, marigold and verbena.' And I feel those three words are all I recall of some forgotten, heavenly language . . . You remember that afternoon?"

"Oh, yes, very well." She drew a long, soft breath, as though the paper daffodils between them were almost too sweet to bear. Yet, what had remained in her mind of that particular afternoon was an absurd scene over the tea-table. A great many people taking tea in a Chinese pagoda, and he behaving like a maniac about the wasps—waving them away, flapping at them with his straw hat, serious and infuriated out of all proportion to the occasion. How delighted the sniggering tea drinkers had been. And how she had suffered.

But now, as he spoke, that memory faded. His was the truer. Yes, it had been a wonderful afternoon, full of geranium and marigold and verbena, and—warm sunshine. Her thoughts lingered over the last two words as though she sang them.

In the warmth, as it were, another memory unfolded. She saw herself sitting on a lawn. He lay beside her, and suddenly, after a long silence, he rolled over and put his head in her lap.

"I wish," he said, in a low, troubled voice, "I wish that I had taken poison and were about to die—here now!"

At that moment a little girl in a white dress, holding a long, dripping white lily, dodged from behind a bush, stared at them, and dodged back again. But he did not see. She leaned over him.

"Ah, why do you say that? I could not say that."

But he gave a kind of soft moan, and taking her hand he held it to his cheek.

"Because I know I am going to love you too much— far too much. And I shall suffer so terribly, Vera, because you never, never will love me."

He was certainly far better looking now than he had been then. He had lost all that dreamy vagueness and indecision. Now he had the air of a man who has found his place in life, and fills it with a confidence and an assurance which was, to say the least, impressive. He must have made money, too. His clothes were admirable, and at that moment he pulled a Russian cigarette-case out of his pocket.

"Won't you smoke?"

"Yes, I will." She hovered over them. "They look very good."

"I think they are. I get them made for me by a little man in St. James's Street. I don't smoke very much. I'm not like you—but when I do, they must be delicious, very fresh cigarettes. Smoking isn't a habit with me; it's a luxury—like perfume. Are you still so fond of perfumes? Ah, when I was in Russia . . ."

She broke in: "You've really been to Russia?"

"Oh yes. I was there for over a year. Have you forgotten how we used to talk of going there?"

"No, I've not forgotten."

He gave a strange half-laugh and leaned back in his chair. "Isn't it curious. I have really carried out all those journeys that we planned. Yes, I have been to all those places that we talked of, and stayed in them long enough to—as you used to say—'air oneself' in them. In fact, I have spent the last three years of my life travelling all the time. Spain, Corsica, Siberia, Russia, Egypt. The only country left is China, and I mean to go there, too, when the war is over."

As he spoke, so lightly, tapping the end of his cigarette against the ash-tray, she felt the strange beast that had slumbered so long within her bosom stir, stretch itself, yawn, prick up its ears, and suddenly bound to its feet, and fix its longing, hungry stare upon those far-away places. But all she said was, smiling gently: "How I envy you."

He accepted that. "It has been," he said, "very wonderful—especially Russia. Russia was all that we had imagined, and far, far more. I even spent some days on a river boat on the Volga. Do you remember that boatman's song that you used to play?"

"Yes." It began to play in her mind as she spoke.

"Do you ever play it now?"

"No, I've no piano."

He was amazed at that. "But what has become of your beautiful piano?"

She made a little grimace. "Sold. Ages ago."

"But you were so fond of music," he wondered.

"I've no time for it now," said she.

He let it go at that. "That river life," he went on, "is something quite special. After a day or two you cannot realise that you have ever known another. And it is not necessary to know the language—the life of the boat creates a bond between you and the people that's more than sufficient. You eat with them, pass the day with them, and in the evening there is that endless singing."

She shivered, hearing the boatman's song break out again loud and tragic, and seeing the boat floating on the darkening river with melancholy trees on either side . . ." Yes, I should like that," said she, stroking her muff.

"You'd like almost everything about Russian life," he said warmly. "It's so informal, so impulsive, so free with-out question. And then the peasants are so splendid. They are such human beings—yes, that is it. Even the man who drives your carriage has—has some real part in what is happening. I remember the evening a party of us, two friends of mine and the wife of one of them, went for a picnic by the Black Sea. We took supper and champagne and ate and drank on the grass. And while we were eating the coachman came up. 'Have a dill pickle,' he said. He wanted to share with us. That seemed to me so right, so—you know what I mean?"

And she seemed at that moment to be sitting on the grass beside the mysteriously Black Sea, black as velvet, and rippling against the banks in silent, velvet waves. She saw the carriage drawn up to one side of the road, and the little group on the grass, their faces and hands white in the moonlight. She saw the pale dress of the woman outspread and her folded parasol, lying on the grass like a huge pearl crochet-hook. Apart from them, with his supper in a cloth on his knees, sat the coachman. "Have a dill pickle," said he, and although she was not certain what a dill pickle was, she saw the greenish glass jar with a red chilli like a parrot's beak glimmering through. She sucked in her cheeks; the dill pickle was terribly sour . . .

"Yes, I know perfectly what you mean," she said.

In the pause that followed they looked at each other. In the past when they had looked at each other like that they had felt such a boundless understanding between them that their souls had, as it were, put their arms round each other and dropped into the same sea, content to be drowned, like mournful lovers. But now, the surprising thing was that it was he who held back. He who said:

"What a marvellous listener you are. When you look at me with those wild eyes I feel that I could tell you things that I would never breathe to another human being."

Was there just a hint of mockery in his voice or was it her fancy? She could not be sure.

"Before I met you," he said, "I had never spoken of myself to anybody. How well I remember one night, the night that I brought you the little Christmas tree, telling you all about my childhood. And of how I was so miserable that I ran away and lived under a cart in our yard for two days without being discovered. And you listened, and your eyes shone, and I felt that you had even made the little Christmas tree listen too, as in a fairy story."

But of that evening she had remembered a little pot of caviare. It had cost seven and sixpence. He could not get over it. Think of it—a tiny jar like that costing seven and sixpence. While she ate it he watched her, delighted and shocked.

"No, really, that is eating money. You could not get seven shillings into a little pot that size. Only think of the profit they must make . . ." And he had begun some immensely complicated calculations . . . But now good-bye to the caviare. The Christmas tree was on the table, and the little boy lay under the cart with his head pillowed on the yard dog.

"The dog was called Bosun," she cried delightedly.

But he did not follow. "Which dog? Had you a dog? I don't remember a dog at all."

"No, no. I mean the yard dog when you were a little boy." He laughed and snapped the cigarette-case to.

"Was he? Do you know I had forgotten that. It seems such ages ago. I cannot believe that it is only six years. After I had recognised you to-day—I had to take such a leap—I had to take a leap over my whole life to get back to that time. I was such a kid then." He drummed on the table. "I've often thought how I must have bored you. And now I understand so perfectly why you wrote to me as you did—although at the time that letter nearly finished my life. I found it again the other day, and I couldn't help laughing as I read it. It was so clever— such a true picture of me." He glanced up. "You're not going?"

She had buttoned her collar again and drawn down her veil.

"Yes, I am afraid I must," she said, and managed a smile. Now she knew that he had been mocking.

"Ah no, please," he pleaded. "Don't go just for a moment," and he caught up one of her gloves from the table and clutched at it as if that would hold her. "I see so few people to talk to nowadays, that I have turned into a sort of barbarian," he said. "Have I said something to hurt you?"

"Not a bit," she lied. But as she watched him draw her glove through his fingers, gently, gently, her anger really did die down, and besides, at the moment he looked more like himself of six years ago . . .

"What I really wanted then," he said softly, "was to be a sort of carpet—to make myself into a sort of carpet for you to walk on so that you need not be hurt by the sharp stones and the mud that you hated so. It was nothing more positive than that—nothing more selfish. Only I did desire, eventually, to turn into a magic carpet and carry you away to all those lands you longed to see."

As he spoke she lifted her head as though she drank something; the strange beast in her bosom began to purr . . .

"I felt that you were more lonely than anybody else in the world," he went on, "and yet, perhaps, that you were the only person in the world who was really, truly alive. Born out of your time," he murmured, stroking the glove, "fated."

Ah, God! What had she done! How had she dared to

throw away her happiness like this. This was the only man who had ever understood her. Was it too late? Could it be too late? *She* was that glove that he held in his fingers . . .

"And then the fact that you had no friends and never had made friends with people. How I understood that, for neither had I. Is it just the same now?"

"Yes," she breathed. "Just the same. I am as alone as ever."

"So am I," he laughed gently, "just the same."

Suddenly with a quick gesture he handed her back the glove and scraped his chair on the floor. "But what seemed to me so mysterious then is perfectly plain to me now. And to you, too, of course . . . It simply was that we were such egoists, so self-engrossed, so wrapped up in ourselves that we hadn't a corner in our hearts for anybody else. Do you know," he cried, naive and hearty, and dreadfully like another side of that old self again, "I began studying a Mind System when I was in Russia, and I found that we were not peculiar at all. It's quite a well-known form of . . ."

She had gone. He sat there, thunder-struck, astounded beyond words . . . And then he asked the waitress for his bill.

"But the cream has not been touched," he said. "Please do not charge me for it."

Mr. Reginald Peacock's Day

If there was one thing that he hated more than another it was the way she had of waking him in the morning. She did it on purpose, of course. It was her way of establishing her grievance for the day, and he was not going to let her know how successful it was. But really, really, to wake a sensitive person like that was positively dangerous! It took him hours to get over it—simply hours. She came into the room buttoned up in an over-all, with a handkerchief over her head—thereby proving that she had been up herself and slaving since dawn—and called in a low, warning voice: "Reginald!"

"Eh! What! What's that? What's the matter?"

"It's time to get up; it's half-past eight." And out she went, shutting the door quietly after her, to gloat over her triumph, he supposed.

He rolled over in the big bed, his heart still beating in quick, dull throbs, and with every throb he felt his energy escaping him, his—his inspiration for the day stifling under those thudding blows. It seemed that she took a malicious delight in making life more difficult for him than—Heaven knows—it was, by denying him his rights as an artist, by trying to drag him down to her level. What was the matter with her? What the hell did she want? Hadn't he three times as many pupils now as when they were first married, earned three times as much, paid for every stick and stone that they possessed, and now had begun to shell out for Adrian's kindergarten? . . . And had he ever reproached her for not having a penny to her name? Never a word—never a sign! The truth was that once you married a woman she became insatiable, and the truth was that nothing was more fatal for an artist than marriage, at any rate until he was well over forty . . . Why had he married her? He asked himself this question on an average about three times a day, but he never could answer it satisfactorily. She had caught him at a weak moment, when the first plunge into reality had bewildered and overwhelmed him for a time. Looking back, he saw a pathetic, youthful creature, half child, half wild untamed bird, totally incompetent to cope with bills and creditors and all the sordid details of existence. Well—she had done her best to clip his wings, if that was any satisfaction for her, and she could congratulate herself on the success of this early morning trick. One ought to wake exquisitely, reluctantly, he thought, slipping down in the warm bed. He began to imagine a series of enchanting scenes which ended with his latest, most charming pupil putting her bare, scented arms round his neck and covering him with her long, perfumed hair. "Awake, my love!" . . .

As was his daily habit, while the bath water ran, Reginald Peacock tried his voice.

"When her mother tends her before
the laughing mirror,
Looping up her laces, tying up her hair,"

he sang, softly at first, listening to the quality, nursing his voice until he came to the third line:

"Often she thinks, were this wild thing wedded . . ."

and upon the word "wedded" he burst into such a shout of triumph that the tooth-glass on the bathroom shelf trembled and even the bath tap seemed to gush stormy applause . . .

Well, there was nothing wrong with his voice, he thought, leaping into the bath and soaping his soft, pink body all over with a loofah shaped like a fish. He could fill Covent Garden with it! "*Wedded*," he shouted again, seizing the towel with a magnificent operatic gesture, and went on singing while he rubbed as though he had been Lohengrin tipped out by an unwary Swan and drying himself in the greatest haste before that tiresome Elsa came along, along . . .

Back in his bedroom, he pulled the blind up with a jerk, and standing upon the pale square of sunlight that lay upon the carpet like a sheet of cream blotting-paper, he began to do his exercises—deep breathing, bending forward and back, squatting like a frog and shooting out his legs—for if there was one thing he had a horror of it was of getting fat, and men in his profession had a dreadful tendency that way. However, there was no sign of it at present. He was, he decided, just right, just in good proportion. In fact, he could not help a thrill of satisfaction when he saw himself in the glass, dressed in a morning coat, dark grey trousers, grey socks and a black tie with a silver thread in it. Not that he was vain— he couldn't stand vain men—no; the sight of himself gave him a thrill of purely artistic satisfaction. "*Voilà tout!*" said he, passing his hand over his sleek hair.

That little, easy French phrase blown so lightly from his lips, like a whiff of smoke, reminded him that some-one had asked him again, the evening before, if he was English. People seemed to find it impossible to believe that he hadn't some Southern blood. True, there was an emotional quality in his singing that had nothing of the

John Bull in it . . . The door-handle rattled and turned
round and round. Adrian's head popped through.

"Please, father, mother says breakfast is quite ready,
please."

"Very well," said Reginald. Then, just as Adrian disappeared: "Adrian!"

"Yes, father."

"You haven't said 'good morning.'"

A few months ago Reginald had spent a week-end in
a very aristocratic family, where the father received his
little sons in the morning and shook hands with them.
Reginald thought the practice charming, and introduced it immediately, but Adrian felt dreadfully silly at
having to shake hands with his own father every morning. And why did his father always sort of sing to him
instead of talk? . . .

In excellent temper, Reginald walked into the dining-
room and sat down before a pile of letters, a copy of
the *Times* and a little covered dish. He glanced at the
letters and then at his breakfast. There were two thin
slices of bacon and one egg.

"Don't you want any bacon?" he asked.

"No, I prefer a cold baked apple. I don't feel the need
of bacon every morning."

Now, did she mean that there was no need for him
to have bacon every morning, either, and that she
grudged having to cook it for him?

"If you don't want to cook the breakfast," said he,
"why don't you keep a servant? You know we can afford
one, and you know how I loathe to see my wife doing
the work. Simply because all the women we have had
in the past have been failures and utterly upset my
régime, and made it almost impossible for me to have
any pupils here, you've given up trying to find a decent

woman. It's not impossible to train a servant—is it? I mean, it doesn't require genius?"

"But I prefer to do the work myself; it makes life so much more peaceful . . . Run along, Adrian darling, and get ready for school."

"Oh no, that's not it!" Reginald pretended to smile. "You do the work yourself, because, for some extraordinary reason, you love to humiliate me. Objectively, you may not know that, but, subjectively, it's the case." This last remark so delighted him that he cut open an envelope as gracefully as if he had been on the stage . . .

"DEAR MR. PEACOCK,

I feel I cannot go to sleep until I have thanked you again for the wonderful joy your singing gave me this evening. Quite unforgettable. You make me wonder, as I have not wondered since I was a girl, if this is *all*. I mean, if this ordinary world is *all*. If there is not, perhaps, for those of us who understand, divine beauty and richness awaiting us if we only have the *courage* to see it. And to make it ours . . . The house is so quiet. I wish you were here now that I might thank you in person. You are doing a great thing. You are teaching the world to escape from life!

Yours, most sincerely,

ÆNONE FELL.

P.S.—I am in every afternoon this week . . .

The letter was scrawled in violet ink on thick, hand-made paper. Vanity, that bright bird, lifted its wings again, lifted them until he felt his breast would break.

"Oh well, don't let us quarrel," said he, and actually flung out a hand to his wife.

But she was not great enough to respond.

"I must hurry and take Adrian to school," said she. "Your room is quite ready for you."

Very well—very well—let there be open war between them! But he was hanged if he'd be the first to make it up again!

He walked up and down his room and was not calm again until he heard the outer door close upon Adrian and his wife. Of course, if this went on, he would have to make some other arrangement. That was obvious. Tied and bound like this, how could he help the world to escape from life? He opened the piano and looked up his pupils for the morning. Miss Betty Brittle, the Countess Wilkowska and Miss Marian Morrow. They were charming, all three.

Punctually at half-past ten the door-bell rang. He went to the door. Miss Betty Brittle was there, dressed in white, with her music in a blue silk case.

"I'm afraid I'm early," she said, blushing and shy, and she opened her big blue eyes very wide. "Am I?"

"Not at all, dear lady. I am only too charmed," said Reginald. "Won't you come in?"

"It's such a heavenly morning," said Miss Brittle. "I walked across the Park. The flowers were too marvellous."

"Well, think about them while you sing your exercises," said Reginald, sitting down at the piano. "It will give your voice colour and warmth."

Oh, what an enchanting idea! What a *genius* Mr. Peacock was. She parted her pretty lips and began to sing like a pansy.

"Very good, very good, indeed," said Reginald,

playing chords that would waft a hardened criminal to heaven. "Make the notes round. Don't be afraid. Linger over them, breathe them like a perfume."

How pretty she looked, standing there in her white frock, her little blonde head tilted, showing her milky throat.

"Do you ever practise before a glass?" asked Reginald. "You ought to, you know; it makes the lips more flexible. Come over here."

They went over to the mirror and stood side by side.

"Now sing—moo-e-koo-e-oo-e-a!"

But she broke down and blushed more brightly than ever.

"Oh," she cried, "I can't. It makes me feel so silly. It makes me want to laugh. I do look so absurd!"

"No, you don't. Don't be afraid," said Reginald, but laughed, too, very kindly. "Now, try again!"

The lesson simply flew and Betty Brittle quite got over her shyness.

"When can I come again?" she asked, tying the music up again in the blue silk case. "I want to take as many lessons as I can just now. Oh, Mr. Peacock, I *do* enjoy them so much. May I come the day after to-morrow?"

"Dear lady, I shall be only too charmed," said Reginald, bowing her out.

Glorious girl! And when they had stood in front of the mirror, her white sleeve had just touched his black one. He could feel—yes, he could actually feel a warm, glowing spot, and he stroked it. She loved her lessons. His wife came in.

"Reginald, can you let me have some money? I must pay the dairy. And will you be in for dinner to-night?"

"Yes, you know I'm singing at Lord Timbuck's at

half-past nine. Can you make me some clear soup with an egg in it?"

"Yes. And the money, Reginald. It's eight and six-pence."

"Surely that's very heavy—isn't it?"

"No, it's just what it ought to be. And Adrian must have milk."

There she was—off again. Now she was standing up for Adrian against him.

"I have not the slightest desire to deny my child a proper amount of milk," said he. "Here is ten shillings."

The door-bell rang. He went to the door.

"Oh," said the Countess Wilkowska, "the stairs. I have not a breath." And she put her hand over her heart as she followed him into the music-room. She was all in black, with a little black hat with a floating veil—violets in her bosom.

"Do not make me sing exercises to-day," she cried, throwing out her hands in her delightful foreign way. "No, to-day, I want only to sing songs . . . And may I take off my violets? They fade so soon."

"They fade so soon—they fade so soon," played Reginald on the piano.

"May I put them here?" asked the Countess, dropping them in a little vase that stood in front of one of Reginald's photographs.

"Dear lady, I should be only too charmed!"

She began to sing, and all was well until she came to the phrase: "You love me. Yes, I *know* you love me!" Down dropped his hands from the keyboard, he wheeled round, facing her.

"No, no; that's not good enough. You can do better than that," cried Reginald ardently. "You must sing as

if you were in love. Listen; let me try and show you."
And he sang.

"Oh yes, yes. I see what you mean," stammered the
little Countess. "May I try it again?"

"Certainly. Do not be afraid. Let yourself go. Confess yourself. Make proud surrender!" he called above
the music. And she sang.

"Yes; better that time. But I still feel you are capable
of more. Try it with me. There must be a kind of exult-
ant defiance as well—don't you feel?" And they sang
together. Ah! now she was sure she understood. "May
I try once again?"

"You love me. Yes, I *know* you love me."

The lesson was over before that phrase was quite
perfect. The little foreign hands trembled as they put
the music together.

"And you are forgetting your violets," said Reginald
softly.

"Yes, I think I will forget them," said the Countess,
biting her underlip. What fascinating ways these foreign
women have!

"And you will come to my house on Sunday and
make music?" she asked.

"Dear lady, I shall be only too charmed!" said
Reginald.

> "Weep ye no more, sad fountains,
>   Why need ye flow so fast?"

sang Miss Marion Morrow, but her eyes filled with
tears and her chin trembled.

"Don't sing just now," said Reginald. "Let me play it
for you." He played so softly.

"Is there anything the matter?" asked Reginald.
"You're not quite happy this morning."

No, she wasn't; she was awfully miserable.

"You don't care to tell me what it is?"

It really was nothing particular. She had those moods sometimes when life seemed almost unbearable.

"Ah, I know," he said; "if I could only help!"

"But you do; you do! Oh, if it were not for my lessons I don't feel I could go on."

"Sit down in the arm-chair and smell the violets and let me sing to you. It will do you just as much good as a lesson."

Why weren't all men like Mr. Peacock?

"I wrote a poem after the concert last night—just about what I felt. Of course, it wasn't *personal*. May I send it to you?"

"Dear lady, I should be only too charmed!"

By the end of the afternoon he was quite tired and lay down on a sofa to rest his voice before dressing. The door of his room was open. He could hear Adrian and his wife talking in the dining-room.

"Do you know what that teapot reminds me of, mummy? It reminds me of a little sitting-down kitten."

"Does it, Mr. Absurdity?"

Reginald dozed. The telephone bell woke him.

"Ænone Fell is speaking. Mr. Peacock, I have just heard that you are singing at Lord Timbuck's to-night. Will you dine with me, and we can go on together afterwards?" And the words of his reply dropped like flowers down the telephone.

"Dear lady, I should be only too charmed."

What a triumphant evening! The little dinner *tête-à-tête* with Ænone Fell, the drive to Lord Timbuck's in her white motor-car, when she thanked him again for the unforgettable joy. Triumph upon triumph! And Lord Timbuck's champagne simply flowed.

"Have some more champagne, Peacock," said Lord Timbuck. Peacock, you notice—not Mr. Peacock—but Peacock, as if he were one of them. And wasn't he? He was an artist. He could sway them all. And wasn't he teaching them all to escape from life? How he sang! And as he sang, as in a dream he saw their feathers and their flowers and their fans, offered to him, laid before him, like a huge bouquet.

"Have another glass of wine, Peacock."

"I could have any one I liked by lifting a finger," thought Peacock, positively staggering home.

But as he let himself into the dark flat his marvellous sense of elation began to ebb away. He turned up the light in the bedroom. His wife lay asleep, squeezed over to her side of the bed. He remembered suddenly how she had said when he had told her he was going out to dinner: "You might have let me know before!" And how he had answered: "Can't you possibly speak to me without offending against even good manners?" It was incredible, he thought, that she cared so little for him—incredible that she wasn't interested in the slightest in his triumphs and his artistic career. When so many women in her place would have given their eyes . . . Yes, he knew it . . . Why not acknowledge it? . . . And there she lay, an enemy, even in her sleep . . . Must it ever be thus? he thought, the champagne still working. Ah, if we only were friends, how much I could tell her now! About this evening; even about Timbuck's manner to me, and all that they said to me and so on and so on. If only I felt that she was here to come back to—that I could confide in her—and so on and so on.

In his emotion he pulled off his evening boot and simply hurled it in the corner. The noise woke his wife with a terrible start. She sat up, pushing back her hair.

And he suddenly decided to have one more try to treat her as a friend, to tell her everything, to win her. Down he sat on the side of the bed and seized one of her hands. But of all those splendid things he had to say, not one could he utter. For some fiendish reason, the only words he could get out were: "Dear lady, I should be so charmed—so charmed!"

MISS BRILL

Although it was so brilliantly fine—the blue sky powdered with gold and the great spots of light like white wine splashed over the Jardins Publiques—Miss Brill was glad that she had decided on her fur. The air was motionless, but when you opened your mouth there was just a faint chill, like a chill from a glass of iced water before you sip, and now and again a leaf came drifting—from nowhere, from the sky. Miss Brill put up her hand and touched her fur. Dear little thing! It was nice to feel it again. She had taken it out of its box that afternoon, shaken out the moth-powder, given it a good brush, and rubbed the life back into the dim little eyes. "What has been happening to me?" said the sad little eyes. Oh, how sweet it was to see them snap at her again from the red eiderdown! . . . But the nose, which was of some black composition, wasn't at all firm. It must have had a knock, somehow. Never mind—a little dab of black sealing-wax when the time came—when it was absolutely necessary . . . Little rogue! Yes, she really felt like that about it. Little rogue biting its tail just by her left ear. She could have taken it off and laid it on her lap and stroked it. She felt a tingling in her hands and arms, but that came from walking, she supposed. And when she breathed, something light and sad—no, not sad, exactly—something gentle seemed to move in her bosom.

There were a number of people out this afternoon, far more than last Sunday. And the band sounded louder and gayer. That was because the Season had begun. For although the band played all the year round on Sundays, out of season it was never the same. It was like someone playing with only the family to listen; it didn't care how it played if there weren't any strangers present. Wasn't the conductor wearing a new coat, too? She was sure it was new. He scraped with his foot and flapped his arms like a rooster about to crow, and the bandsmen sitting in the green rotunda blew out their cheeks and glared at the music. Now there came a little "flutey" bit—very pretty!—a little chain of bright drops. She was sure it would be repeated. It was; she lifted her head and smiled.

Only two people shared her "special" seat: a fine old man in a velvet coat, his hands clasped over a huge carved walking-stick, and a big old woman, sitting upright, with a roll of knitting on her embroidered apron. They did not speak. This was disappointing, for Miss Brill always looked forward to the conversation. She had become really quite expert, she thought, at listening as though she didn't listen, at sitting in other people's lives just for a minute while they talked round her.

She glanced, sideways, at the old couple. Perhaps they would go soon. Last Sunday, too, hadn't been as interesting as usual. An Englishman and his wife, he wearing a dreadful Panama hat and she button boots. And she'd gone on the whole time about how she ought to wear spectacles; she knew she needed them; but that it was no good getting any; they'd be sure to break and they'd never keep on. And he'd been so patient. He'd suggested everything—gold rims, the kind that curved round your ears, little pads inside the bridge. No, nothing would please her. "They'll always be sliding down my nose!" Miss Brill had wanted to shake her.

The old people sat on the bench, still as statues. Never mind, there was always the crowd to watch. To and fro, in front of the flower-beds and the band rotunda, the couples and groups paraded, stopped to talk, to greet, to buy a handful of flowers from the old beggar who had his tray fixed to the railings. Little children ran among them, swooping and laughing; little boys with big white silk bows under their chins; little girls, little French dolls, dressed up in velvet and lace. And sometimes a tiny staggerer came suddenly rocking into the open from under the trees, stopped, stared, as suddenly sat down "flop," until its small high-stepping mother, like a young hen, rushed scolding to its rescue. Other people sat on the benches and green chairs, but they were nearly always the same, Sunday after Sunday, and—Miss Brill had often noticed—there was something funny about nearly all of them. They were odd, silent, nearly all old, and from the way they stared they looked as though they'd just come from dark little rooms or even—even cupboards!

Behind the rotunda the slender trees with yellow leaves down drooping, and through them just a line of sea, and beyond the blue sky with gold-veined clouds.

Tum-tum-tum tiddle-um! tiddle-um! turn tiddley-um tum ta! blew the band.

Two young girls in red came by and two young soldiers in blue met them, and they laughed and paired and went off arm in arm. Two peasant women with funny straw hats passed, gravely, leading beautiful smoke-coloured donkeys. A cold, pale nun hurried by. A beautiful woman came along and dropped her bunch of violets, and a little boy ran after to hand them to her, and she took them and threw them away as if they'd been poisoned. Dear me! Miss Brill didn't know whether to admire that or not! And now an ermine toque and a gentleman in grey met just in front of her. He was tall, stiff, dignified, and she was wearing the ermine toque she'd bought when her hair was yellow. Now everything, her hair, her face, even her eyes, was the same colour as the shabby ermine, and her hand, in its cleaned glove, lifted to dab her lips, was a tiny yellowish paw. Oh, she was so pleased to see him— delighted! She rather thought they were going to meet that afternoon. She described where she'd been— everywhere, here, there, along by the sea. The day was so charming—didn't he agree? And wouldn't he, per- haps? . . . But he shook his head, lighted a cigarette, slowly breathed a great deep puff into her face and, even while she was still talking and laughing, flicked the match away and walked on. The ermine toque was alone; she smiled more brightly than ever. But even the band seemed to know what she was feeling and played more softly, played tenderly, and the drum beat "The Brute! The Brute!" over and over. What would she do? What was going to happen now? But as Miss Brill won- dered, the ermine toque turned, raised her hand as though she'd seen someone else, much nicer, just over there, and pattered away. And the band changed again and played more quickly, more gaily than ever, and the old couple on Miss Brill's seat got up and marched away, and such a funny old man with long whiskers hob- bled along in time to the music and was nearly knocked over by four girls walking abreast.

Oh, how fascinating it was! How she enjoyed it! How she loved sitting here, watching it all! It was like a play. It was exactly like a play. Who could believe the sky at the back wasn't painted? But it wasn't till a little brown dog trotted on solemnly and then slowly trotted off, like a little "theatre" dog, a little dog that had been drugged, that Miss Brill discovered what it was that made it so exciting. They were all on the stage. They weren't only the audience, not only looking on; they were acting. Even she had a part and came every Sunday. No doubt somebody would have noticed if she hadn't been there; she was part of the performance, after all. How strange she'd never thought of it like that before! And yet it explained why she made such a point of starting from home at just the same time each week—so as not to be late for the performance—and it also explained why she had quite a queer, shy feeling at telling her English pupils how she spent her Sunday afternoons. No wonder! Miss Brill nearly laughed out loud. She was on the stage. She thought of the old invalid gentleman to whom she read the newspaper four afternoons a week while he slept in the garden. She had got quite used to the frail head on the cotton pillow, the hollowed eyes, the open mouth and the high pinched nose. If he'd been dead she mightn't have noticed for weeks; she wouldn't have minded. But suddenly he knew he was having the paper read to him by an actress! "An actress!" The old head lifted; two points of light quivered in the old eyes. "An actress—are ye?" And Miss Brill smoothed the newspaper as though it were the manuscript of her part and said gently: "Yes, I have been an actress for a long time."

The band had been having a rest. Now they started again. And what they played was warm, sunny, yet there was just a faint chill—a something, what was it?—not sadness—no, not sadness—a something that made you want to sing. The tune lifted, lifted, the light shone; and it seemed to Miss Brill that in another moment all of them, all the whole company, would begin singing. The young ones, the laughing ones who were moving together, they would begin, and the men's voices, very resolute and brave, would join them. And then she too, she too, and the others on the benches—they would come in with a kind of accompaniment—something low, that scarcely rose or fell, something so beautiful—moving . . . And Miss Brill's eyes filled with tears and she looked smiling at all the other members of the company. Yes, we understand, we understand, she thought—though what they understood she didn't know.

Just at that moment a boy and a girl came and sat down where the old couple had been. They were beautifully dressed; they were in love. The hero and heroine, of course, just arrived from his father's yacht. And still soundlessly singing, still with that trembling smile, Miss Brill prepared to listen.

"No, not now," said the girl. "Not here, I can't."

"But why? Because of that stupid old thing at the end there?" asked the boy. "Why does she come here at all—who wants her? Why doesn't she keep her silly old mug at home?"

"It's her fu-fur which is so funny," giggled the girl. "It's exactly like a fried whiting."

"Ah, be off with you!" said the boy in an angry whisper. Then: "Tell me, ma petite chère—"

"No, not here," said the girl. "Not yet."

On her way home she usually bought a slice of honey-cake at the baker's. It was her Sunday treat. Sometimes there was an almond in her slice, sometimes not. It made a great difference. If there was an almond it was like carrying home a tiny present—a surprise—something that might very well not have been there. She hurried on the almond Sundays and struck the match for the kettle in quite a dashing way.

But to-day she passed the baker's by, climbed the stairs, went into the little dark room—her room like a cupboard—and sat down on the red eiderdown. She sat there for a long time. The box that the fur came out of was on the bed. She unclasped the necklet quickly; quickly, without looking, laid it inside. But when she put the lid on she thought she heard something crying.

THE FLY

"Y'are very snug in here," piped old Mr. Woodifield, and he peered out of the great, green-leather armchair by his friend the boss's desk as a baby peers out of its pram. His talk was over; it was time for him to be off. But he did not want to go. Since he had retired, since his . . . stroke, the wife and the girls kept him boxed up in the house every day of the week except Tuesday. On Tuesday he was dressed and brushed and allowed to cut back to the City for the day. Though what he did there the wife and girls couldn't imagine. Made a nuisance of himself to his friends, they supposed . . . Well, perhaps so. All the same, we cling to our last pleasures as the tree clings to its last leaves. So there sat old Woodifield, smoking a cigar and staring almost greedily at the boss, who rolled in his office chair, stout, rosy, five years older than he, and still going strong, still at the helm. It did one good to see him.

Wistfully, admiringly, the old voice added, "It's snug in here, upon my word!"

"Yes, it's comfortable enough," agreed the boss, and he flipped the *Financial Times* with a paper-knife. As a matter of fact he was proud of his room; he liked to have it admired, especially by old Woodifield. It gave him a feeling of deep, solid satisfaction to be planted there in the midst of it in full view of that frail old figure in the muffler.

"I've had it done up lately," he explained, as he had explained for the past—how many?—weeks. "New carpet," and he pointed to the bright red carpet with a pattern of large white rings. "New furniture," and he nodded towards the massive bookcase and the table with legs like twisted treacle. "Electric heating!" He waved almost exultantly towards the five transparent, pearly sausages glowing so softly in the tilted copper pan.

But he did not draw old Woodifield's attention to the photograph over the table of a grave-looking boy in uniform standing in one of those spectral photographers' parks with photographers' storm-clouds behind him. It was not new. It had been there for over six years.

"There was something I wanted to tell you," said old Woodifield, and his eyes grew dim remembering. "Now what was it? I had it in my mind when I started out this morning." His hands began to tremble, and patches of red showed above his beard.

Poor old chap, he's on his last pins, thought the boss. And, feeling kindly, he winked at the old man, and said jokingly, "I tell you what. I've got a little drop of something here that'll do you good before you go out into the cold again. It's beautiful stuff. It wouldn't hurt a child." He took a key off his watch-chain, unlocked a cupboard below his desk, and drew forth a dark, squat bottle. "That's the medicine," said he. "And the man from whom I got it told me on the strict Q.T. it came from the cellars at Windsor Castle."

Old Woodifield's mouth fell open at the sight. He couldn't have looked more surprised if the boss had produced a rabbit.

"It's whisky, ain't it?" he piped feebly.

The boss turned the bottle and lovingly showed him the label. Whisky it was.

"D'you know," said he, peering up at the boss wonderingly, "they won't let me touch it at home." And he looked as though he was going to cry.

"Ah, that's where we know a bit more than the ladies," cried the boss, swooping across for two tumblers that stood on the table with the water-bottle, and pouring a generous finger into each. "Drink it down. It'll do you good. And don't put any water with it. It's sacrilege to tamper with stuff like this. Ah!" He tossed off his, pulled out his handkerchief, hastily wiped his moustaches, and cocked an eye at old Woodifield, who was rolling his in his chaps.

The old man swallowed, was silent a moment, and then said faintly, "It's nutty!"

But it warmed him; it crept into his chill old brain— he remembered.

"That was it," he said, heaving himself out of his chair. "I thought you'd like to know. The girls were in Belgium last week having a look at poor Reggie's grave, and they happened to come across your boy's. They're quite near each other, it seems."

Old Woodifield paused, but the boss made no reply. Only a quiver in his eyelids showed that he heard.

"The girls were delighted with the way the place is kept," piped the old voice. "Beautifully looked after. Couldn't be better if they were at home. You've not been across, have yer?"

"No, no!" For various reasons the boss had not been across.

"There's miles of it," quavered old Woodifield, "and it's all as neat as a garden. Flowers growing on all the graves. Nice broad paths." It was plain from his voice how much he liked a nice broad path.

The pause came again. Then the old man brightened wonderfully.

"D'you know what the hotel made the girls pay for a pot of jam?" he piped. "Ten francs! Robbery, I call it. It was a little pot, so Gertrude says, no bigger than a half-crown. And she hadn't taken more than a spoonful when they charged her ten francs. Gertrude brought the pot away with her to teach 'em a lesson. Quite right, too; it's trading on our feelings. They think because we're over there having a look round we're ready to pay anything. That's what it is." And he turned towards the door.

"Quite right, quite right!" cried the boss, though what was quite right he hadn't the least idea. He came round by his desk, followed the shuffling footsteps to the door, and saw the old fellow out. Woodifield was gone.

For a long moment the boss stayed, staring at nothing, while the grey-haired office messenger, watching him, dodged in and out of his cubby-hole like a dog that expects to be taken for a run. Then: "I'll see nobody for half an hour, Macey," said the boss. "Understand? Nobody at all."

"Very good, sir."

The door shut, the firm heavy steps recrossed the bright carpet, the fat body plumped down in the spring chair, and leaning forward, the boss covered his face with his hands. He wanted, he intended, he had arranged to weep . . .

It had been a terrible shock to him when old Woodifield sprang that remark upon him about the boy's grave. It was exactly as though the earth had opened and he had seen the boy lying there with Woodifield's girls staring down at him. For it was strange. Although over six years had passed away, the boss never thought of the boy except as lying unchanged, unblemished in his uniform, asleep for ever. "My son!" groaned the boss. But no tears came yet. In the past, in the first months and even years after the boy's death, he had only to say those words to be overcome by such grief that nothing short of a violent fit of weeping could relieve him. Time, he had declared then, he had told everybody, could make no difference. Other men perhaps might recover, might live their loss down, but not he. How was it possible? His boy was an only son. Ever since his birth the boss had worked at building up this business for him; it had no other meaning if it was not for the boy. Life itself had come to have no other meaning. How on earth could he have slaved, denied himself, kept going all those years without the promise for ever before him of the boy's stepping into his shoes and carrying on where he left off?

And that promise had been so near being fulfilled. The boy had been in the office learning the ropes for a year before the war. Every morning they had started off together; they had come back by the same train. And what congratulations he had received as the boy's father! No wonder; he had taken to it marvellously. As to his popularity with the staff, every man jack of them down to old Macey couldn't make enough of the boy. And he wasn't in the least spoilt. No, he was just his bright natural self, with the right word for everybody, with that boyish look and his habit of saying, "Simply splendid!"

But all that was over and done with as though it never had been. The day had come when Macey had handed him the telegram that brought the whole place crashing about his head. "Deeply regret to inform you . . ." And he had left the office a broken man, with his life in ruins.

Six years ago, six years . . . How quickly time passed! It might have happened yesterday. The boss took his hands from his face; he was puzzled. Something seemed to be wrong with him. He wasn't feeling as he wanted to feel. He decided to get up and have a look at the boy's photograph. But it wasn't a favourite photograph of his; the expression was unnatural. It was cold, even stern-looking. The boy had never looked like that.

At that moment the boss noticed that a fly had fallen into his broad inkpot, and was trying feebly but desperately to clamber out again. Help! help! said those struggling legs. But the sides of the inkpot were wet and slippery; it fell back again and began to swim. The boss took up a pen, picked the fly out of the ink, and shook it on to a piece of blotting-paper. For a fraction of a second it lay still on the dark patch that oozed round it. Then the front legs waved, took hold, and, pulling its small, sodden body up, it began the immense task of cleaning the ink from its wings. Over and under, over and under, went a leg along a wing as the stone goes over and under the scythe. Then there was a pause, while the fly, seeming to stand on the tips of its toes, tried to expand first one wing and then the other. It succeeded at last, and, sitting down, it began, like a minute cat, to clean its face. Now one could imagine that the little front legs rubbed against each other lightly, joyfully. The horrible danger was over; it had escaped; it was ready for life again.

But just then the boss had an idea. He plunged his pen back into the ink, leaned his thick wrist on the blotting-paper, and as the fly tried its wings down came a great heavy blot. What would it make of that? What indeed! The little beggar seemed absolutely cowed, stunned, and afraid to move because of what would happen next. But then, as if painfully, it dragged itself forward. The front legs waved, caught hold, and, more slowly this time, the task began from the beginning.

He's a plucky little devil, thought the boss, and he felt a real admiration for the fly's courage. That was the way to tackle things; that was the right spirit. Never say die; it was only a question of . . . But the fly had again finished its laborious task, and the boss had just time to refill his pen, to shake fair and square on the new-cleaned body yet another dark drop. What about it this time? A painful moment of suspense followed. But behold, the front legs were again waving; the boss felt a rush of relief. He leaned over the fly and said to it tenderly, "You artful little b . . ." And he actually had the brilliant notion of breathing on it to help the drying process. All the same, there was something timid and weak about its efforts now, and the boss decided that this time should be the last, as he dipped the pen deep into the inkpot.

It was. The last blot fell on the soaked blotting-paper, and the draggled fly lay in it and did not stir. The back legs were stuck to the body; the front legs were not to be seen.

"Come on," said the boss. "Look sharp!" And he stirred it with his pen—in vain. Nothing happened or was likely to happen. The fly was dead.

The boss lifted the corpse on the end of the paper-knife and flung it into the waste-paper basket. But such a grinding feeling of wretchedness seized him that he felt positively frightened. He started forward and pressed the bell for Macey.

"Bring me some fresh blotting-paper," he said

sternly, "and look sharp about it." And while the old dog padded away he fell to wondering what it was he had been thinking about before. What was it? It was . . . He took out his handkerchief and passed it inside his collar. For the life of him he could not remember.

PRELUDE

I

There was not an inch of room for Lottie and Kezia in the buggy. When Pat swung them on top of the luggage they wobbled; the grandmother's lap was full and Linda Burnell could not possibly have held a lump of a child on hers for any distance. Isabel, very superior, was perched beside the new handy-man on the driver's seat. Holdalls, bags and boxes were piled upon the floor. "These are absolute necessities that I will not let out of my sight for one instant," said Linda Burnell, her voice trembling with fatigue and excitement.

Lottie and Kezia stood on the patch of lawn just inside the gate all ready for the fray in their coats with brass anchor buttons and little round caps with battleship ribbons. Hand in hand, they stared with round solemn eyes, first at the absolute necessities and then at their mother.

"We shall simply have to leave them. That is all. We shall simply have to cast them off," said Linda Burnell. A strange little laugh flew from her lips; she leaned back against the buttoned leather cushions and shut her eyes, her lips trembling with laughter. Happily at that moment Mrs. Samuel Josephs, who had been watching the scene from behind her drawingroom blind, waddled down the garden path.

"Why nod leave the chudren with be for the afterdoon, Brs. Burnell? They could go on the dray with the

211

storeban when he comes in the eveding. Those thigs on the path have to go, dod't they?"

"Yes, everything outside the house is supposed to go," said Linda Burnell, and she waved a white hand at the tables and chairs standing on their heads on the front lawn. How absurd they looked! Either they ought to be the other way up, or Lottie and Kezia ought to stand on their heads, too. And she longed to say: "Stand on your heads, children, and wait for the storeman." It seemed to her that would be so exquisitely funny that she could not attend to Mrs. Samuel Josephs.

The fat creaking body leaned across the gate, and the big jelly of a face smiled. "Dod't you worry, Brs. Burnell. Loddie and Kezia can have tea with by chudren in the dursery, and I'll see theb on the dray afterwards."

The grandmother considered. "Yes, it really is quite the best plan. We are very obliged to you, Mrs. Samuel Josephs. Children, say 'thank you' to Mrs. Samuel Josephs."

Two subdued chirrups: "Thank you, Mrs. Samuel Josephs."

"And be good little girls, and—come closer—" they advanced, "don't forget to tell Mrs. Samuel Josephs when you want to . . ."

"No, granma."

"Dod't worry, Brs. Burnell."

At the last moment Kezia let go Lottie's hand and darted towards the buggy.

"I want to kiss my granma good-bye again."

But she was too late. The buggy rolled off up the road, Isabel bursting with pride, her nose turned up at all the world, Linda Burnell prostrated, and the grandmother rummaging among the very curious oddments she had had put in her black silk reticule at the last moment, for something to give her daughter. The buggy twinkled away in the sunlight and fine golden dust up the hill and over. Kezia bit her lip, but Lottie, carefully finding her handkerchief first, set up a wail.

"Mother! Granma!"

Mrs. Samuel Josephs, like a huge warm black silk tea-cosy, enveloped her.

"It's all right, by dear. Be a brave child. You come and blay in the dursery!"

She put her arm round weeping Lottie and led her away. Kezia followed, making a face at Mrs. Samuel Josephs' placket, which was undone as usual, with two long pink corset laces hanging out of it . . .

Lottie's weeping died down as she mounted the stairs, but the sight of her at the nursery door with swollen eyes and a blob of a nose gave great satisfaction to the S. J. 's, who sat on two benches before a long table covered with American cloth and set out with immense plates of bread and dripping and two brown jugs that faintly steamed.

"Hullo! You've been crying!"

"Ooh! Your eyes have gone right in."

"Doesn't her nose look funny."

"You're all red-and-patchy."

Lottie was quite a success. She felt it and swelled, smiling timidly.

"Go and sid by Zaidee, ducky," said Mrs. Samuel Josephs, "and Kezia, you sid ad the end by Boses."

Moses grinned and gave her a nip as she sat down; but she pretended not to notice. She did hate boys.

"Which will you have?" asked Stanley, leaning across the table very politely, and smiling at her. "Which will

213

you have to begin with—strawberries and cream or bread and dripping?"

"Strawberries and cream, please," said she.

"Ah-h-h-h." How they all laughed and beat the table with their teaspoons. Wasn't that a take-in! Wasn't it now! Didn't he fox her! Good old Stan!

"Ma! She thought it was real."

Even Mrs. Samuel Josephs, pouring out the milk and water, could not help smiling. "You bustn't tease theb on their last day," she wheezed.

But Kezia bit a big piece out of her bread and dripping, and then stood the piece up on her plate. With the bite out it made a dear little sort of a gate. Pooh! She didn't care! A tear rolled down her cheek, but she wasn't crying. She couldn't have cried in front of those awful Samuel Josephs. She sat with her head bent, and as the tear dripped slowly down, she caught it with a neat little whisk of her tongue and ate it before any of them had seen.

II

After tea Kezia wandered back to their own house. Slowly she walked up the back steps, and through the scullery into the kitchen. Nothing was left in it but a lump of gritty yellow soap in one corner of the kitchen window-sill and a piece of flannel stained with a blue bag in another. The fire-place was choked up with rubbish. She poked among it but found nothing except a hair-tidy with a heart painted on it that had belonged to the servant girl. Even that she left lying, and she trailed through the narrow passage into the drawing-room. The Venetian blind was pulled down but not drawn close.

Long pencil rays of sunlight shone through and the wavy shadow of a bush outside danced on the gold lines. Now it was still, now it began to flutter again, and now it came almost as far as her feet. Zoom! Zoom! a blue-bottle knocked against the ceiling; the carpet-tacks had little bits of red fluff sticking to them.

The dining-room window had a square of coloured glass at each corner. One was blue and one was yellow. Kezia bent down to have one more look at a blue lawn with blue arum lilies growing at the gate, and then at a yellow lawn with yellow lilies and a yellow fence. As she looked a little Chinese Lottie came out on to the lawn and began to dust the tables and chairs with a corner of her pinafore. Was that really Lottie? Kezia was not quite sure until she had looked through the ordinary window.

Upstairs in her father's and mother's room she found a pill box black and shiny outside and red in, holding a blob of cotton wool.

"I could keep a bird's egg in that," she decided.

In the servant girl's room there was a stay-button stuck in a crack of the floor, and in another crack some beads and a long needle. She knew there was nothing in her grandmother's room; she had watched her pack. She went over to the window and leaned against it, pressing her hands against the pane.

Kezia liked to stand so before the window. She liked the feeling of the cold shining glass against her hot palms, and she liked to watch the funny white tops that came on her fingers when she pressed them hard against the pane. As she stood there, the day flickered out and dark came. With the dark crept the wind snuffling and howling. The windows of the empty house shook, a creaking came from the walls and floors, a piece of loose iron on the roof banged forlornly. Kezia was suddenly quite, quite still, with wide open eyes and knees pressed together. She was frightened. She wanted to call Lottie and to go on calling all the while she ran downstairs and out of the house. But IT was just behind her, waiting at the door, at the head of the stairs, at the bottom of the stairs, hiding in the passage, ready to dart out at the back door. But Lottie was at the back door, too.

"Kezia!" she called cheerfully. "The storeman's here. Everything is on the dray and three horses, Kezia. Mrs. Samuel Josephs has given us a big shawl to wear round us, and she says to button up your coat. She won't come out because of asthma."

Lottie was very important.

"Now then, you kids," called the storeman. He hooked his big thumbs under their arms and up they swung. Lottie arranged the shawl "most beautifully" and the store-man tucked up their feet in a piece of old blanket.

"Lift up. Easy does it."

They might have been a couple of young ponies. The storeman felt over the cords holding his load, unhooked the brake-chain from the wheel, and whistling, he swung up beside them.

"Keep close to me," said Lottie, "because otherwise you pull the shawl away from my side, Kezia."

But Kezia edged up to the storeman. He towered beside her big as a giant and he smelled of nuts and new wooden boxes.

III

It was the first time that Lottie and Kezia had ever been out so late. Everything looked different—the painted wooden houses far smaller than they did by day, the gardens far bigger and wilder. Bright stars speckled the sky and the moon hung over the harbour dabbling the waves with gold. They could see the lighthouse shining on Quarantine Island, and the green lights on the old coal hulks.

"There comes the Picton boat," said the storeman, pointing to a little steamer all hung with bright beads.

But when they reached the top of the hill and began to go down the other side the harbour disappeared, and although they were still in the town they were quite lost. Other carts rattled past. Everybody knew the storeman.

"Night, Fred."

"Night O," he shouted.

Kezia liked very much to hear him. Whenever a cart appeared in the distance she looked up and waited for his voice. He was an old friend; and she and her grandmother had often been to his place to buy grapes. The storeman lived alone in a cottage that had a glasshouse against one wall built by himself. All the glasshouse was spanned and arched over with one beautiful vine. He took her brown basket from her, lined it with three large leaves, and then he felt in his belt for a little horn knife, reached up and snapped off a big blue cluster and laid it on the leaves so tenderly that Kezia held her breath to watch. He was a very big man. He wore brown velvet trousers, and he had a long brown beard. But he never wore a collar, not even on Sunday. The back of his neck was burnt bright red.

"Where are we now?" Every few minutes one of the children asked him the question.

"Why, this is Hawk Street, or Charlotte Crescent."

"Of course it is," Lottie pricked up her ears at the last name; she always felt that Charlotte Crescent belonged specially to her. Very few people had streets with the same name as theirs.

"Look, Kezia, there is Charlotte Crescent. Doesn't it look different?" Now everything familiar was left behind. Now the big dray rattled into unknown country, along new roads with high clay banks on either side, up steep, steep hills, down into bushy valleys, through wide shallow rivers. Further and further. Lottie's head wagged; she drooped, she slipped half into Kezia's lap and lay there But Kezia could not open her eyes wide enough. The wind blew and she shivered; but her cheeks and ears burned.

"Do stars ever blow about?" she asked.

"Not to notice," said the storeman.

"We've got a nuncle and a naunt living near our new house," said Kezia. "They have got two children, Pip, the eldest is called, and the youngest's name is Rags. He's got a ram. He has to feed it with a nenamuel teapot and a glove top over the spout. He's going to show us. What is the difference between a ram and a sheep?"

"Well, a ram has horns and runs for you."

Kezia considered. "I don't want to see it frightfully," she said. "I hate rushing animals like dogs and parrots. I often dream that animals rush at me—even camels—and while they are rushing, their heads swell e-enormous."

The storeman said nothing. Kezia peered up at him, screwing up her eyes. Then she put her finger out and stroked his sleeve; it felt hairy. "Are we near?" she asked.

"Not far off, now," answered the storeman. "Getting tired?"

"Well, I'm not an atom bit sleepy," said Kezia. "But

my eyes keep curling up in such a funny sort of way."
She gave a long sigh, and to stop her eyes from curling
she shut them . . . When she opened them again they
were clanking through a drive that cut through the
garden like a whip-lash, looping suddenly an island of
green, and behind the island, but out of sight until you
came upon it, was the house. It was long and low built,
with a pillared veranda and balcony all the way round.
The soft white bulk of it lay stretched upon the green
garden like a sleeping beast. And now one and now
another of the windows leaped into light. Someone was
walking through the empty rooms carrying a lamp.
From the window downstairs the light of a fire flickered.
A strange beautiful excitement seemed to stream from
the house in quivering ripples.

"Where are we?" said Lottie, sitting up. Her reefer
cap was all on one side and on her cheek there was the
print of an anchor button she had pressed against while
sleeping. Tenderly the storeman lifted her, set her cap
straight, and pulled down her crumpled clothes. She
stood blinking on the lowest veranda step watching
Kezia, who seemed to come flying through the air to
her feet.

"Ooh!" cried Kezia, flinging up her arms. The
grandmother came out of the dark hall carrying a little
lamp. She was smiling.

"You found your way in the dark?" said she.

"Perfectly well."

But Lottie staggered on the lowest veranda step like
a bird fallen out of the nest. If she stood still for a
moment she fell asleep; if she leaned against anything
her eyes closed. She could not walk another step.

"Kezia," said the grandmother, "can I trust you to
carry the lamp?"

"Yes, my granma."

The old woman bent down and gave the bright breathing thing into her hands and then she caught up drunken Lottie. "This way."

Through a square hall filled with bales and hundreds of parrots (but the parrots were only on the wall-paper) down a narrow passage where the parrots persisted in flying past Kezia with her lamp.

"Be very quiet," warned the grandmother, putting down Lottie and opening the dining-room door. "Poor little mother has got such a headache."

Linda Burnell, in a long cane chair, with her feet on a hassock and a plaid over her knees, lay before a crackling fire. Burnell and Beryl sat at the table in the middle of the room eating a dish of fried chops and drinking tea out of a brown china teapot. Over the back of her mother's chair leaned Isabel. She had a comb in her fingers and in a gentle absorbed fashion she was combing the curls from her mother's forehead. Outside the pool of lamp and firelight the room stretched dark and bare to the hollow windows.

"Are those the children?" But Linda did not really care; she did not even open her eyes to see.

"Put down the lamp, Kezia," said Aunt Beryl, "or we shall have the house on fire before we are out of the packing cases. More tea, Stanley?"

"Well, you might just give me five-eighths of a cup," said Burnell, leaning across the table. "Have another chop, Beryl. Tip-top meat, isn't it? Not too lean and not too fat." He turned to his wife. "You're sure you won't change your mind, Linda darling?"

"The very thought of it is enough." She raised one eyebrow in the way she had. The grandmother brought the children bread and milk and they sat up to table, flushed and sleepy behind the wavy steam.

"I had meat for my supper," said Isabel, still combing gently.

"I had a whole chop for my supper, the bone and all and Worcester sauce. Didn't I, father?"

"Oh, don't boast, Isabel," said Aunt Beryl.

Isabel looked astounded. "I wasn't boasting, was I, Mummy? I never thought of boasting. I thought they would like to know. I only meant to tell them."

"Very well. That's enough," said Burnell. He pushed back his plate, took a tooth-pick out of his pocket and began picking his strong white teeth.

"You might see that Fred has a bite of something in the kitchen before he goes, will you, mother?"

"Yes, Stanley." The old woman turned to go.

"Oh, hold on half a jiffy. I suppose nobody knows where my slippers were put? I suppose I shall not be able to get at them for a month or two—what?"

"Yes," came from Linda. "In the top of the canvas holdall marked 'urgent necessities.'"

"Well, you might get them for me, will you, mother?"

"Yes, Stanley."

Burnell got up, stretched himself, and going over to the fire he turned his back to it and lifted up his coat tails.

"By Jove, this is a pretty pickle. Eh, Beryl?"

Beryl, sipping tea, her elbows on the table, smiled over the cup at him. She wore an unfamiliar pink pinafore; the sleeves of her blouse were rolled up to her shoulders showing her lovely freckled arms, and she had let her hair fall down her back in a long pigtail.

"How long do you think it will take to get straight—couple of weeks—eh?" he chaffed.

"Good heavens, no," said Beryl airily. "The worst is over already. The servant girl and I have simply slaved all day, and ever since mother came she has worked like a horse, too. We have never sat down for a moment. We have had a day."

Stanley scented a rebuke.

"Well, I suppose you did not expect me to rush away from the office and nail carpets—did you?"

"Certainly not," laughed Beryl. She put down her cup and ran out of the dining-room.

"What the hell does she expect us to do?" asked Stanley. "Sit down and fan herself with a palm-leaf fan while I have a gang of professionals to do the job? By Jove, if she can't do a hand's turn occasionally without shouting about it in return for . . ."

And he gloomed as the chops began to fight the tea in his sensitive stomach. But Linda put up a hand and dragged him down to the side of her long chair.

"This is a wretched time for you, old boy," she said. Her cheeks were very white, but she smiled and curled her fingers into the big red hand she held. Burnell became quiet. Suddenly he began to whistle "Pure as a lily, joyous and free"—a good sign.

"Think you're going to like it?" he asked.

"I don't want to tell you, but I think I ought to, mother," said Isabel. "Kezia is drinking tea out of Aunt Beryl's cup."

IV

They were taken off to bed by the grandmother. She went first with a candle; the stairs rang to their climbing feet. Isabel and Lottie lay in a room to themselves, Kezia curled in her grandmother's soft bed.

"Aren't there going to be any sheets, my granma?"

"No, not to-night."

"It's tickly," said Kezia, "but it's like Indians." She dragged her grandmother down to her and kissed her under the chin. "Come to bed soon and be my Indian brave."

"What a silly you are," said the old woman, tucking her in as she loved to be tucked.

"Aren't you going to leave me a candle?"

"No. Sh—h. Go to sleep."

"Well, can I have the door left open?"

She rolled herself up into a round but she did not go to sleep. From all over the house came the sound of steps. The house itself creaked and popped. Loud whispering voices came from downstairs. Once she heard Aunt Beryl's rush of high laughter, and once she heard a loud trumpeting from Burnell blowing his nose. Outside the window hundreds of black cats with yellow eyes sat in the sky watching her—but she was not frightened. Lottie was saying to Isabel:

"I'm going to say my prayers in bed to-night."

"No, you can't, Lottie." Isabel was very firm. "God only excuses you saying your prayers in bed if you've got a temperature." So Lottie yielded:

"Gentle Jesus meek anmile,
            Look pon a little chile.
            Pity me, simple Lizzie,
        Suffer me to come to thee."

And then they lay down back to back, their little behinds just touching, and fell asleep.

★

Standing in a pool of moonlight Beryl Fairfield undressed herself. She was tired, but she pretended to be more tired than she really was—letting her clothes fall, pushing back with a languid gesture her warm, heavy hair.

"Oh, how tired I am—very tired."

She shut her eyes a moment, but her lips smiled. Her breath rose and fell in her breast like two fanning wings. The window was wide open; it was warm, and somewhere out there in the garden a young man, dark and slender, with mocking eyes, tiptoed among the bushes, and gathered the flowers into a big bouquet, and slipped under her window and held it up to her. She saw herself bending forward. He thrust his head among the bright waxy flowers, sly and laughing. "No, no," said Beryl. She turned from the window and dropped her nightgown over her head.

"How frightfully unreasonable Stanley is sometimes," she thought, buttoning. And then, as she lay down, there came the old thought, the cruel thought—ah, if only she had money of her own.

A young man, immensely rich, has just arrived from England. He meets her quite by chance . . . The new governor is unmarried . . . There is a ball at Government house . . . Who is that exquisite creature in *eau-de-nil* satin? Beryl Fairfield . . .

"The thing that pleases me," said Stanley, leaning against the side of the bed and giving himself a good scratch on his shoulders and back before turning in, "is that I've got the place dirt cheap, Linda. I was talking about it to little Wally Bell to-day and he said he simply could not understand why they had accepted my figure. You see land about here is bound to become more and more valuable . . . in about ten years' time . . . of course we shall have to go very slow and cut down expenses as fine as possible. Not asleep—are you?"

"No, dear, I've heard every word," said Linda.

He sprang into bed, leaned over her and blew out the candle.

"Good night, Mr. Business Man," said she, and she took hold of his head by the ears and gave him a quick kiss. Her faint far-away voice seemed to come from a deep well.

"Good night, darling." He slipped his arm under her neck and drew her to him.

"Yes, clasp me," said the faint voice from the deep well.

Pat the handy-man sprawled in his little room behind the kitchen. His sponge-bag, coat and trousers hung from the door-peg like a hanged man. From the edge of the blanket his twisted toes protruded, and on the floor beside him there was an empty cane bird-cage. He looked like a comic picture.

"Honk, honk," came from the servant girl. She had adenoids.

Last to go to bed was the grandmother.

"What. Not asleep yet?"

"No, I'm waiting for you," said Kezia. The old woman sighed and lay down beside her. Kezia thrust her head under her grandmother's arm and gave a little squeak. But the old woman only pressed her faintly, and sighed again, took out her teeth, and put them in a glass of water beside her on the floor.

In the garden some tiny owls, perched on the branches of a lace-bark tree, called: "More pork; more pork." And far away in the bush there sounded a harsh rapid chatter: "Ha-ha-ha . . . Ha-ha-ha."

V

Dawn came sharp and chill with red clouds on a faint green sky and drops of water on every leaf and blade. A breeze blew over the garden, dropping dew and dropping petals, shivered over the drenched paddocks, and was lost in the sombre bush. In the sky some tiny stars floated for a moment and then they were gone—they were dissolved like bubbles. And plain to be heard in the early quiet was the sound of the creek in the paddock running over the brown stones, running in and out of the sandy hollows, hiding under clumps of dark berry bushes, spilling into a swamp of yellow water flowers and cresses.

And then at the first beam of sun the birds began. Big cheeky birds, starlings and mynahs, whistled on the lawns, the little birds, the goldfinches and linnets and fan-tails, flicked from bough to bough. A lovely kingfisher perched on the paddock fence preening his rich beauty, and a *tui* sang his three notes and laughed and sang them again.

"How loud the birds are," said Linda in her dream. She was walking with her father through a green paddock sprinkled with daisies. Suddenly he bent down and parted the grasses and showed her a tiny ball of fluff just at her feet. "Oh, papa, the darling." She made a cup of her hands and caught the tiny bird and stroked its head with her finger. It was quite tame. But a funny thing happened. As she stroked it began to swell, it ruffled and pouched, it grew bigger and bigger and its round eyes seemed to smile knowingly at her. Now her arms were hardly wide enough to hold it and she dropped it into her apron. It had become a baby with a big naked head and a gaping bird-mouth, opening and shutting. Her father broke into a loud clattering laugh and she woke to see Burnell standing by the windows rattling the Venetian blind up to the very top.

"Hullo," he said. "Didn't wake you, did I? Nothing much wrong with the weather this morning."

He was enormously pleased. Weather like this set a final seal on his bargain. He felt, somehow, that he had bought the lovely day, too—got it chucked in dirt cheap with the house and ground. He dashed off to his bath and Linda turned over and raised herself on one elbow to see the room by daylight. All the furniture had found a place—all the old paraphernalia, as she expressed it. Even the photographs were on the mantelpiece and the medicine bottles on the shelf above the washstand. Her clothes lay across a chair—her outdoor things, a purple cape and a round hat with a plume in it. Looking at them she wished that she was going away from this house, too. And she saw herself driving away from them all in a little buggy, driving away from everybody and not even waving.

Back came Stanley girt with a towel, glowing and slapping his thighs. He pitched the wet towel on top of her hat and cape, and standing firm in the exact centre of a square of sunlight he began to do his exercises. Deep breathing, bending and squatting like a frog and shooting out his legs. He was so delighted with his firm, obedient body that he hit himself on the chest and gave a loud "Ah." But this amazing vigour seemed to set him worlds away from Linda. She lay on the white tumbled bed and watched him as if from the clouds.

"Oh, damn! Oh, blast!" said Stanley, who had butted into a crisp white shirt only to find that some idiot had fastened the neck-band and he was caught. He stalked over to Linda waving his arms.

"You look like a big fat turkey," said she.

"Fat. I like that," said Stanley. "I haven't a square inch of fat on me. Feel that."

"It's rock—it's iron," mocked she.

"You'd be surprised," said Stanley, as though this were intensely interesting, "at the number of chaps at the club who have got a corporation. Young chaps, you know—men of my age." He began parting his bushy ginger hair, his blue eyes fixed and round in the glass, his knees bent, because the dressing-table was always—confound it—a bit too low for him. "Little Wally Bell, for instance," and he straightened, describing upon himself an enormous curve with the hairbrush. "I must say I've a perfect horror . . ."

"My dear, don't worry. You'll never be fat. You are far too energetic."

"Yes, yes, I suppose that's true," said he, comforted for the hundredth time, and taking a pearl penknife out of his pocket he began to pare his nails.

"Breakfast, Stanley." Beryl was at the door. "Oh, Linda, mother says you are not to get up yet." She popped her head in at the door. She had a big piece of syringa stuck through her hair.

"Everything we left on the veranda last night is simply sopping this morning. You should see poor dear mother wringing out the tables and the chairs. However, there is no harm done—" this with the faintest glance at Stanley.

"Have you told Pat to have the buggy round in time? It's a good six and a half miles to the office."

"I can imagine what this early start for the office will

be like," thought Linda. "It will be very high pressure indeed."

"Pat, Pat." She heard the servant girl calling. But Pat was evidently hard to find; the silly voice went baa—baaing through the garden.

Linda did not rest again until the final slam of the front door told her that Stanley was really gone.

Later she heard her children playing in the garden. Lottie's stolid, compact little voice cried: "Ke—zia. Isa—bel." She was always getting lost or losing people only to find them again, to her great surprise, round the next tree or the next corner. "Oh, there you are after all." They had been turned out after breakfast and told not to come back to the house until they were called. Isabel wheeled a neat pramload of prim dolls and Lottie was allowed for a great treat to walk beside her holding the doll's parasol over the face of the wax one.

"Where are you going to, Kezia?" asked Isabel, who longed to find some light and menial duty that Kezia might perform and so be roped in under her government.

"Oh, just away," said Kezia . . .

Then she did not hear them any more. What a glare there was in the room. She hated blinds pulled up to the top at any time, but in the morning it was intolerable. She turned over to the wall and idly, with one finger, she traced a poppy on the wall-paper with a leaf and a stem and a fat bursting bud. In the quiet, and under her tracing finger, the poppy seemed to come alive. She could feel the sticky, silky petals, the stem, hairy like a gooseberry skin, the rough leaf and the tight glazed bud. Things had a habit of coming alive like that. Not only large substantial things like furniture but curtains and the patterns of stuffs and the fringes of quilts and cushions. How often she had seen the tassel fringe of her quilt change into a funny procession of dancers with priests attending . . . For there were some tassels that did not dance at all but walked stately, bent forward as if praying or chanting. How often the medicine bottles had turned into a row of little men with brown top-hats on; and the washstand jug had a way of sitting in the basin like a fat bird in a round nest.

"I dreamed about birds last night," thought Linda. What was it? She had forgotten. But the strangest part of this coming alive of things was what they did. They listened, they seemed to swell out with some mysterious important content, and when they were full she felt that they smiled. But it was not for her, only, their sly secret smile; they were members of a secret society and they smiled among themselves. Sometimes, when she had fallen asleep in the daytime, she woke and could not lift a finger, could not even turn her eyes to left or right because *they* were there; sometimes when she went out of a room and left it empty, she knew as she clicked the door to that *they* were filling it. And there were times in the evenings when she was upstairs, perhaps, and everybody else was down, when she could hardly escape from them. Then she could not hurry, she could not hum a tune; if she tried to say ever so carelessly—"Bother that old thimble"—*they* were not deceived. *They* knew how frightened she was; they saw how she turned her head away as she passed the mirror. What Linda always felt was that *they* wanted something of her, and she knew that if she gave herself up and was quiet, more than quiet, silent, motionless, something would really happen.

"It's very quiet now," she thought. She opened her eyes wide, and she heard the silence spinning its soft endless web. How lightly she breathed; she scarcely had to breathe at all.

Yes, everything had come alive down to the minutest, tiniest particle, and she did not feel her bed, she floated, held up in the air. Only she seemed to be listening with her wide open watchful eyes, waiting for someone to come who just did not come, watching for something to happen that just did not happen.

VI

In the kitchen at the long deal table under the two windows old Mrs. Fairfield was washing the breakfast dishes. The kitchen window looked out on to a big grass patch that led down to the vegetable garden and the rhubarb beds. On one side the grass patch was bordered by the scullery and washhouse and over this whitewashed lean-to there grew a knotted vine. She had noticed yesterday that a few tiny corkscrew tendrils had come right through some cracks in the scullery ceiling and all the windows of the lean-to had a thick frill of ruffled green.

"I am very fond of a grape vine," declared Mrs. Fairfield, "but I do not think that the grapes will ripen here. It takes Australian sun." And she remembered how Beryl when she was a baby had been picking some white grapes from the vine on the back veranda of their Tasmanian house and she had been stung on the leg by a huge red ant. She saw Beryl in a little plaid dress with red ribbon tie-ups on the shoulders screaming so dreadfully that half the street rushed in. And how the child's leg had swelled! "T—t—t—t!" Mrs. Fairfield caught her breath remembering. "Poor child, how terrifying it was." And she set her lips tight and went over to the stove for some more hot water. The water frothed up in the big soapy bowl with pink and blue bubbles on top of the foam. Old Mrs. Fairfield's arms were bare to the elbow and stained a bright pink. She wore a grey foulard dress patterned with large purple pansies, a white linen apron and a high cap shaped like a jelly mould of white muslin. At her throat there was a silver crescent moon with five little owls seated on it, and round her neck she wore a watch-guard made of black beads.

It was hard to believe that she had not been in that kitchen for years; she was so much a part of it. She put the crocks away with a sure, precise touch, moving leisurely and ample from the stove to the dresser, looking into the pantry and the larder as though there were not an unfamiliar corner. When she had finished, everything in the kitchen had become part of a series of patterns. She stood in the middle of the room wiping her hands on a check cloth; a smile beamed on her lips; she thought it looked very nice, very satisfactory.

"Mother! Mother! Are you there?" called Beryl.

"Yes, dear. Do you want me?"

"No. I'm coming," and Beryl rushed in, very flushed, dragging with her two big pictures.

"Mother, whatever can I do with these awful hideous Chinese paintings that Chung Wah gave Stanley when he went bankrupt? It's absurd to say that they are valuable, because they were hanging in Chung Wah's fruit shop for months before. I can't make out why Stanley wants them kept. I'm sure he thinks them just as hideous as we do, but it's because of the frames," she said spitefully. "I suppose he thinks the frames might fetch something some day or other."

"Why don't you hang them in the passage?" suggested Mrs. Fairfield; "they would not be much seen there."

"I can't. There is no room. I've hung all the photographs of his office there before and after building, and the signed photos of his business friends, and that awful enlargement of Isabel lying on the mat in her singlet." Her angry glance swept the placid kitchen. "I know what I'll do. I'll hang them here. I will tell Stanley they got a little damp in the moving so I have put them in here for the time being."

She dragged a chair forward, jumped on it, took a hammer and a big nail out of her pinafore pocket and banged away.

"There! That is enough! Hand me the picture, mother."

"One moment, child." Her mother was wiping over the carved ebony frame.

"Oh, mother, really you need not dust them. It would take years to dust all those little holes." And she frowned at the top of her mother's head and bit her lip with impatience. Mother's deliberate way of doing things was simply maddening. It was old age, she supposed, loftily.

At last the two pictures were hung side by side. She jumped off the chair, stowing away the little hammer.

"They don't look so bad there, do they?" said she. "And at any rate nobody need gaze at them except Pat and the servant girl—have I got a spider's web on my face, mother? I've been poking into that cupboard under the stairs and now something keeps tickling my nose."

But before Mrs. Fairfield had time to look Beryl had turned away. Someone tapped on the window: Linda was there, nodding and smiling. They heard the latch of the scullery door lift and she came in. She had no hat on; her hair stood upon her head in curling rings and she was wrapped up in an old cashmere shawl.

"I'm so hungry," said Linda: "where can I get something to eat, mother? This is the first time I've been in the kitchen. It says 'mother' all over; everything is in pairs."

"I will make you some tea," said Mrs. Fairfield, spreading a clean napkin over a corner of the table, "and Beryl can have a cup with you."

"Beryl, do you want half my gingerbread?" Linda waved the knife at her. "Beryl, do you like the house now that we are here?"

"Oh yes, I like the house immensely and the garden is beautiful, but it feels very far away from everything to me. I can't imagine people coming out from town to see us in that dreadful jolting bus, and I am sure there is not anyone here to come and call. Of course it does not matter to you because—"

"But there's the buggy," said Linda. "Pat can drive you into town whenever you like."

That was a consolation, certainly, but there was something at the back of Beryl's mind, something she did not even put into words for herself.

"Oh, well, at any rate it won't kill us," she said dryly, putting down her empty cup and standing up and stretching. "I am going to hang curtains." And she ran away singing:

"How many thousand birds I see
That sing aloud from every tree . . ."

". . . birds I see That sing aloud from every tree . . ." But when she reached the dining-room she stopped singing, her face changed; it became gloomy and sullen.

"One may as well rot here as anywhere else," she muttered savagely, digging the stiff brass safety-pins into the red serge curtains.

The two left in the kitchen were quiet for a little. Linda leaned her cheek on her fingers and watched her mother. She thought her mother looked wonderfully beautiful with her back to the leafy window. There was something comforting in the sight of her that Linda felt she could never do without. She needed the sweet smell of her flesh, and the soft feel of her cheeks and her arms and shoulders still softer. She loved the way her hair curled, silver at her forehead, lighter at her neck, and bright brown still in the big coil under the muslin cap. Exquisite were her mother's hands, and the two rings she wore seemed to melt into her creamy skin. And she was always so fresh, so delicious. The old woman could bear nothing but linen next to her body and she bathed in cold water winter and summer.

"Isn't there anything for me to do?" asked Linda.

"No, darling. I wish you would go into the garden and give an eye to your children; but that I know you will not do."

"Of course I will, but you know Isabel is much more grown up than any of us."

"Yes, but Kezia is not," said Mrs. Fairfield.

"Oh, Kezia has been tossed by a bull hours ago," said Linda, winding herself up in her shawl again.

But no, Kezia had seen a bull through a hole in a knot of wood in the paling that separated the tennis lawn from the paddock. But she had not liked the bull frightfully, so she had walked away back through the orchard, up the grassy slope, along the path by the lace-bark tree and so into the spread tangled garden. She did not believe that she would ever not get lost in this garden. Twice she had found her way back to the big iron gates they had driven through the night before, and then had turned to walk up the drive that led to the house, but there were so many little paths on either side. On one side they all led into a tangle of tall dark trees and strange bushes with flat velvet leaves and feathery cream flowers that buzzed with flies when you shook them—this was the frightening side, and no garden at all. The little paths here were wet and clayey with tree roots spanned across them like the marks of big fowls' feet.

But on the other side of the drive there was a high box border and the paths had box edges and all of them led into a deeper and deeper tangle of flowers. The camellias were in bloom, white and crimson and pink and white striped with flashing leaves. You could not see a leaf on the syringa bushes for the white clusters. The roses were in flower—gentlemen's button-hole roses, little white ones, but far too full of insects to hold under anyone's nose, pink monthly roses with a ring of fallen petals round the bushes, cabbage roses on thick stalks, moss roses, always in bud, pink smooth beauties opening curl on curl, red ones so dark they seemed to turn back as they fell, and a certain exquisite cream kind with a slender red stem and bright scarlet leaves.

There were clumps of fairy bells, and all kinds of geraniums, and there were little trees of verbena and bluish lavender bushes and a bed of pelargoniums with velvet eyes and leaves like moths' wings. There was a bed of nothing but mignonette and another of nothing but pansies—borders of double and single daisies and all kinds of little tufty plants she had never seen before.

The red-hot pokers were taller than she; the Japanese sunflowers grew in a tiny jungle. She sat down on one of the box borders. By pressing hard at first it made a nice seat. But how dusty it was inside! Kezia bent down to look and sneezed and rubbed her nose.

And then she found herself at the top of the rolling grassy slope that led down to the orchard . . . She looked down at the slope a moment; then she lay down on her back, gave a squeak and rolled over and over into the thick flowery orchard grass. As she lay waiting for things to stop spinning, she decided to go up to the house and ask the servant girl for an empty matchbox. She wanted to make a surprise for the grandmother . . . First she would put a leaf inside with a big violet lying on it, then she would put a very small white picotee, perhaps, on each side of the violet, and then she would sprinkle some lavender on the top, but not to cover their heads.

She often made these surprises for the grandmother, and they were always most successful.

"Do you want a match, my granny?"

"Why, yes, child, I believe a match is just what I'm looking for."

The grandmother slowly opened the box and came upon the picture inside.

"Good gracious, child! How you astonished me!"

"I can make her one every day here," she thought, scrambling up the grass on her slippery shoes.

But on her way back to the house she came to that island that lay in the middle of the drive, dividing the drive into two arms that met in front of the house. The island was made of grass banked up high. Nothing grew on the top except one huge plant with thick, grey-green, thorny leaves, and out of the middle there sprang up a tall stout stem. Some of the leaves of the plant were so old that they curled up in the air no longer; they turned back, they were split and broken; some of them lay flat and withered on the ground.

Whatever could it be? She had never seen anything like it before. She stood and stared. And then she saw her mother coming down the path.

"Mother, what is it?" asked Kezia.

Linda looked up at the fat swelling plant with its cruel leaves and fleshy stem. High above them, as though becalmed in the air, and yet holding so fast to the earth it grew from, it might have had claws instead of roots. The curving leaves seemed to be hiding something; the blind stem cut into the air as if no wind could ever shake it.

"That is an aloe, Kezia," said her mother.

"Does it ever have any flowers?"

"Yes, Kezia," and Linda smiled down at her, and half shut her eyes. "Once every hundred years."

VII

On his way home from the office Stanley Burnell stopped the buggy at the Bodega, got out and bought a large bottle of oysters. At the Chinaman's shop next door he bought a pineapple in the pink of condition, and noticing a basket of fresh black cherries he told John to put him in a pound of those as well. The oysters and the pine he stowed away in the box under the front seat, but the cherries he kept in his hand.

Pat, the handy-man, leapt off the box and tucked him up again in the brown rug.

"Lift yer feet, Mr. Burnell, while I give yer a fold under," said he.

"Right! Right! First-rate!" said Stanley. "You can make straight for home now."

Pat gave the grey mare a touch and the buggy sprang forward.

"I believe this man is a first-rate chap," thought Stanley. He liked the look of him sitting up there in his neat brown coat and brown bowler. He liked the way Pat had tucked him in, and he liked his eyes. There was nothing servile about him—and if there was one thing he hated more than another it was servility. And he looked as if he was pleased with his job—happy and contented already.

The grey mare went very well; Burnell was impatient to be out of the town. He wanted to be home. Ah, it was splendid to live in the country—to get right out of that hole of a town once the office was closed; and this drive in the fresh warm air, knowing all the while that his own house was at the other end, with its garden and paddocks, its three tip-top cows and enough fowls and ducks to keep them in poultry, was splendid too.

As they left the town finally and bowled away up the deserted road his heart beat hard for joy. He rooted in the bag and began to eat the cherries, three or four at a time, chucking the stones over the side of the buggy. They were delicious, so plump and cold, without a spot or a bruise on them.

Look at those two, now—black one side and white the other—perfect! A perfect little pair of Siamese twins. And he stuck them in his button-hole . . . By Jove, he wouldn't mind giving that chap up there a handful—but no, better not. Better wait until he had been with him a bit longer.

He began to plan what he would do with his Saturday afternoons and his Sundays. He wouldn't go to the club for lunch on Saturday. No, cut away from the office as soon as possible and get them to give him a couple of slices of cold meat and half a lettuce when he got home. And then he'd get a few chaps out from town to play tennis in the afternoon. Not too many—three at most. Beryl was a good player, too . . . He stretched out his right arm and slowly bent it, feeling the muscle . . . A bath, a good rub-down, a cigar on the veranda after dinner . . .

On Sunday morning they would go to church—children and all. Which reminded him that he must hire a pew, in the sun if possible and well forward so as to be out of the draught from the door. In fancy he heard himself intoning extremely well: "When thou did overcome the *Sharpness* of Death Thou didst open the *Kingdom* of Heaven to *all* Believers." And he saw the neat brass-edged card on the corner of the pew—Mr. Stanley Burnell and family . . . The rest of the day he'd loaf about with Linda . . . Now they were walking about the garden; she was on his arm, and he was explaining to her at length what he intended doing at the office the week following. He heard her saying: "My dear, I think that is most wise . . ." Talking things over with Linda was a wonderful help even though they were apt to drift away from the point.

Hang it all! They weren't getting along very fast. Pat had put the brake on again. Ugh! What a brute of a thing it was. He could feel it in the pit of his stomach.

A sort of panic overtook Burnell whenever he approached near home. Before he was well inside the gate he would shout to anyone within sight: "Is everything all right?" And then he did not believe it was until he heard Linda say: "Hullo! Are you home again?" That was the worst of living in the country—it took the deuce of a long time to get back . . . But now they weren't far off. They were on the top of the last hill; it was a gentle slope all the way now and not more than half a mile.

Pat trailed the whip over the mare's back and he coaxed her: "Goop now. Goop now."

It wanted a few minutes to sunset. Everything stood motionless bathed in bright, metallic light and from the paddocks on either side there streamed the milky scent of ripe grass. The iron gates were open. They dashed through and up the drive and round the island, stopping at the exact middle of the veranda.

"Did she satisfy yer, sir?" said Pat, getting off the box and grinning at his master.

"Very well indeed, Pat," said Stanley.

Linda came out of the glass door; her voice rang in the shadowy quiet. "Hullo! Are you home again?"

At the sound of her his heart beat so hard that he could hardly stop himself dashing up the steps and catching her in his arms.

"Yes, I'm home again. Is everything all right?"

Pat began to lead the buggy round to the side gate that opened into the courtyard.

"Here, half a moment," said Burnell. "Hand me those two parcels." And he said to Linda, "I've brought you back a bottle of oysters and a pineapple," as though he had brought her back all the harvest of the earth.

They went into the hall; Linda carried the oysters in one hand and the pineapple in the other. Burnell shut the glass door, threw his hat down, put his arms round her and strained her to him, kissing the top of her head, her ears, her lips, her eyes.

"Oh, dear! Oh, dear!" said she. "Wait a moment. Let me put down these silly things," and she put the bottle of oysters and the pine on a little carved chair. "What have you got in your button-hole—cherries?" She took them out and hung them over his ear.

"Don't do that, darling. They are for you."

So she took them off his ear again. "You don't mind if I save them. They'd spoil my appetite for dinner. Come and see your children. They are having tea."

The lamp was lighted on the nursery table. Mrs. Fairfield was cutting and spreading bread and butter. The three little girls sat up to table wearing large bibs embroidered with their names. They wiped their mouths as their father came in ready to be kissed. The windows were open; a jar of wild flowers stood on the mantelpiece, and the lamp made a big soft bubble of light on the ceiling.

"You seem pretty snug, mother," said Burnell, blinking at the light. Isabel and Lottie sat one on either side of the table, Kezia at the bottom—the place at the top was empty.

"That's where my boy ought to sit," thought Stanley. He tightened his arm round Linda's shoulder. By God, he was a perfect fool to feel as happy as this!

"We are, Stanley. We are very snug," said Mrs. Fairfield, cutting Kezia's bread into fingers.

"Like it better than town—eh, children?" asked Burnell.

"Oh, yes," said the three little girls, and Isabel added as an after-thought: "Thank you very much indeed, father dear."

"Come upstairs," said Linda. "I'll bring your slippers."

But the stairs were too narrow for them to go up arm

in arm. It was quite dark in the room. He heard her ring tapping on the marble mantelpiece as she felt for the matches.

"I've got some, darling. I'll light the candles."

But instead he came up behind her and again he put his arms round her and pressed her head into his shoulder.

"I'm so confoundedly happy," he said.

"Are you?" She turned and put her hands on his breast and looked up at him.

"I don't know what has come over me," he protested.

It was quite dark outside now and heavy dew was falling. When Linda shut the window the cold dew touched her finger tips. Far away a dog barked. "I believe there is going to be a moon," she said.

At the words, and with the cold wet dew on her fingers, she felt as though the moon had risen—that she was being strangely discovered in a flood of cold light. She shivered; she came away from the window and sat down upon the box ottoman beside Stanley.

In the dining-room, by the flicker of a wood fire, Beryl sat on a hassock playing the guitar. She had bathed and changed all her clothes. Now she wore a white muslin dress with black spots on it and in her hair she had pinned a black silk rose.

> Nature has gone to her rest, love,
>   See, we are alone.
> Give me your hand to press, love,
>   Lightly within my own.

She played and sang half to herself, for she was watching herself playing and singing. The firelight gleamed on her shoes, on the ruddy belly of the guitar, and on her white fingers . . .

"If I were outside the window and looked in and saw myself I really would be rather struck," thought she. Still more softly she played the accompaniment—not singing now but listening.

". . . The first time that I ever saw you, little girl—oh, you had no idea that you were not alone—you were sitting with your little feet upon a hassock, playing the guitar. God, I can never forget . . ." Beryl flung up her head and began to sing again:

"Even the moon is aweary . . ."

But there came a loud bang at the door. The servant girl's crimson face popped through.

"Please, Miss Beryl, I've got to come and lay."

"Certainly, Alice," said Beryl, in a voice of ice. She put the guitar in a corner. Alice lunged in with a heavy black iron tray.

"Well, I have had a job with that oving," said she. "I can't get nothing to brown."

"Really!" said Beryl.

But no, she could not stand that fool of a girl. She ran into the dark drawing-room and began walking up and down . . . Oh, she was restless, restless. There was a mirror over the mantel. She leaned her arms along and looked at her pale shadow in it. How beautiful she looked, but there was nobody to see, nobody.

"Why must you suffer so?" said the face in the mirror. "You were not made for suffering . . . Smile!"

Beryl smiled, and really her smile *was* so adorable that she smiled again—but this time because she could not help it.

VIII

"Good morning, Mrs. Jones."

"Oh, good morning, Mrs. Smith. I'm so glad to see you. Have you brought your children?"

"Yes, I've brought both my twins. I have had another baby since I saw you last, but she came so suddenly that I haven't had time to make her any clothes yet. So I left her . . . How is your husband?"

"Oh, he is very well, thank you. At least he had an awful cold but Queen Victoria—she's my godmother, you know—sent him a case of pine-apples and that cured it im—mediately. Is that your new servant?"

"Yes, her name's Gwen. I've only had her two days. Oh, Gwen, this is my friend, Mrs. Smith."

"Good morning, Mrs. Smith. Dinner won't be ready for about ten minutes."

"I don't think you ought to introduce me to the servant. I think I ought to just begin talking to her."

"Well, she's more of a lady-help than a servant and you do introduce lady-helps, I know, because Mrs. Samuel Josephs had one."

"Oh, well, it doesn't matter," said the servant carelessly, beating up a chocolate custard with half a broken clothes peg. The dinner was baking beautifully on a concrete step. She began to lay the cloth on a pink garden seat. In front of each person she put two geranium leaf plates, a pine needle fork and a twig knife. There were three daisy heads on a laurel leaf for poached eggs, some slices of fuchsia petal cold beef, some lovely little rissoles made of earth and water and dandelion seeds, and the chocolate custard which she had decided to serve in the pawa shell she had cooked it in.

"You needn't trouble about my children," said Mrs. Smith graciously. "If you'll just take this bottle and fill it at the tap—I mean at the dairy."

"Oh, all right," said Gwen, and she whispered to Mrs. Jones: "Shall I go and ask Alice for a little bit of real milk?"

But someone called from the front of the house and the luncheon party melted away, leaving the charming table, leaving the rissoles and the poached eggs to the ants and to an old snail who pushed his quivering horns over the edge of the garden seat and began to nibble a geranium plate.

"Come round to the front, children. Pip and Rags have come."

The Trout boys were the cousins Kezia had mentioned to the storeman. They lived about a mile away in a house called Monkey Tree Cottage. Pip was tall for his age, with lank black hair and a white face, but Rags was very small and so thin that when he was undressed his shoulder blades stuck out like two little wings. They had a mongrel dog with pale blue eyes and a long tail turned up at the end who followed them everywhere; he was called Snooker. They spent half their time combing and brushing Snooker and dosing him with various awful mixtures concocted by Pip, and kept secretly by him in a broken jug covered with an old kettle lid. Even faithful little Rags was not allowed to know the full secret of these mixtures . . . Take some carbolic tooth powder and a pinch of sulphur powdered up fine, and perhaps a bit of starch to stiffen up Snooker's coat . . . But that was not all; Rags privately thought that the rest was gunpowder . . . And he never was allowed to help with the mixing because of the danger . . . "Why, if a spot of this flew in your eye, you would be blinded for life," Pip would say, stirring the mixture with an iron spoon. "And there's always the chance—just the chance, mind you—of it exploding if you whack it hard enough . . . Two spoons of this in a kerosene tin will be enough to kill thousands of fleas." But Snooker spent all his spare time biting and snuffling, and he stank abominably.

"It's because he is such a grand fighting dog," Pip would say. "All fighting dogs smell."

The Trout boys had often spent the day with the Burnells in town, but now that they lived in this fine house and boncer garden they were inclined to be very friendly. Besides, both of them liked playing with girls—Pip, because he could fox them so, and because Lottie was so easily frightened, and Rags for a shameful reason. He adored dolls. How he would look at a doll as it lay asleep, speaking in a whisper and smiling timidly, and what a treat it was to him to be allowed to hold one . . .

"Curve your arms round her. Don't keep them stiff like that. You'll drop her," Isabel would say sternly.

Now they were standing on the veranda and holding back Snooker, who wanted to go into the house but wasn't allowed to because Aunt Linda hated decent dogs.

"We came over in the bus with mum," they said, "and we're going to spend the afternoon with you. We brought over a batch of our gingerbread for Aunt Linda. Our Minnie made it. It's all over nuts."

"I skinned the almonds," said Pip. "I just stuck my hand into a saucepan of boiling water and grabbed them out and gave them a kind of pinch and the nuts flew out of the skins, some of them as high as the ceiling. Didn't they, Rags?"

Rags nodded. "When they make cakes at our place," said Pip, "we always stay in the kitchen, Rags and me, and I get the bowl and he gets the spoon and the egg-beater. Sponge cake's best. It's all frothy stuff, then."

He ran down the veranda steps to the lawn, planted his hands on the grass, bent forward, and just did not stand on his head.

"That lawn's all bumpy," he said. "You have to have a flat place for standing on your head. I can walk round the monkey tree on my head at our place. Can't I, Rags?"

"Nearly," said Rags faintly.

"Stand on your head on the veranda. That's quite flat," said Kezia.

"No, smarty," said Pip. "You have to do it on something soft. Because if you give a jerk and fall over, something in your neck goes click, and it breaks off. Dad told me."

"Oh, do let's play something," said Kezia.

"Very well," said Isabel quickly, "we'll play hospitals. I will be the nurse and Pip can be the doctor and you and Lottie and Rags can be the sick people."

Lottie didn't want to play that, because last time Pip had squeezed something down her throat and it hurt awfully.

"Pooh," scoffed Pip. "It was only the juice out of a bit of mandarin peel."

"Well, let's play ladies," said Isabel. "Pip can be the father and you can be all our dear little children."

"I hate playing ladies," said Kezia. "You always make us go to church hand in hand and come home and go to bed."

Suddenly Pip took a filthy handkerchief out of his pocket. "Snooker! Here, sir," he called. But Snooker, as usual, tried to sneak away, his tail between his legs. Pip leapt on top of him, and pressed him between his knees.

"Keep his head firm, Rags," he said, and he tied the handkerchief round Snooker's head with a funny knot sticking up at the top.

"Whatever is that for?" asked Lottie.

"It's to train his ears to grow more close to his head— see?" said Pip. "All fighting dogs have ears that lie back. But Snooker's ears are a bit too soft."

"I know," said Kezia. "They are always turning inside out. I hate that."

Snooker lay down, made one feeble effort with his paw to get the handkerchief off, but finding he could not, trailed after the children, shivering with misery.

IX

Pat came swinging along; in his hand he held a little tomahawk that winked in the sun.

"Come with me," he said to the children, "and I'll show you how the kings of Ireland chop the head off a duck."

They drew back—they didn't believe him, and besides, the Trout boys had never seen Pat before.

"Come on now," he coaxed, smiling and holding out his hand to Kezia.

"Is it a real duck's head? One from the paddock?"

"It is," said Pat. She put her hand in his hard dry one, and he stuck the tomahawk in his belt and held out the other to Rags. He loved little children.

"I'd better keep hold of Snooker's head if there's

going to be any blood about," said Pip, "because the sight of blood makes him awfully wild." He ran ahead dragging Snooker by the handkerchief.

"Do you think we ought to go?" whispered Isabel. "We haven't asked or anything. Have we?"

At the bottom of the orchard a gate was set in the paling fence. On the other side a steep bank led down to a bridge that spanned the creek, and once up the bank on the other side you were on the fringe of the paddocks. A little old stable in the first paddock had been turned into a fowl-house. The fowls had strayed far away across the paddock down to a dumping ground in a hollow, but the ducks kept close to that part of the creek that flowed under the bridge.

Tall bushes overhung the stream with red leaves and yellow flowers and clusters of blackberries. At some places the stream was wide and shallow, but at others it tumbled into deep little pools with foam at the edges and quivering bubbles. It was in these pools that the big white ducks had made themselves at home, swimming and guzzling along the weedy banks.

Up and down they swam, preening their dazzling breasts, and other ducks with the same dazzling breasts and yellow bills swam upside down with them.

"There is the little Irish navy," said Pat, "and look at the old admiral there with the green neck and the grand little flagstaff on his tail."

He pulled a handful of grain from his pocket and began to walk towards the fowl-house, lazy, his straw hat with the broken crown pulled over his eyes.

"Lid. Lid—lid—lid—lid—" he called.

"Qua. Qua—qua—qua—qua—" answered the ducks, making for land, and flapping and scrambling up the bank they streamed after him in a long waddling line.

He coaxed them, pretending to throw the grain, shaking it in his hands and calling to them until they swept round him in a white ring.

From far away the fowls heard the clamour and they too came running across the paddock, their heads thrust forward, their wings spread, turning in their feet in the silly way fowls run and scolding as they came.

Then Pat scattered the grain and the greedy ducks began to gobble. Quickly he stooped, seized two, one under each arm, and strode across to the children. Their darting heads and round eyes frightened the children—all except Pip.

"Come on, sillies," he cried, "they can't bite. They haven't any teeth. They've only got those two little holes in their beaks for breathing through."

"Will you hold one while I finish with the other?" asked Pat. Pip let go of Snooker. "Won't I? Won't I? Give us one. I don't mind how much he kicks."

He nearly sobbed with delight when Pat gave the white lump into his arms.

There was an old stump beside the door of the fowl-house. Pat grabbed the duck by the legs, laid it flat across the stump, and almost at the same moment down came the little tomahawk and the duck's head flew off the stump. Up the blood spurted over the white feathers and over his hand.

When the children saw the blood they were frightened no longer. They crowded round him and began to scream. Even Isabel leaped about crying: "The blood! The blood!" Pip forgot all about his duck. He simply threw it away from him and shouted, "I saw it. I saw it," and jumped round the wood block.

Rags, with cheeks as white as paper, ran up to the little head, put out a finger as if he wanted to touch it, shrank back again and then again put out a finger. He was shivering all over.

Even Lottie, frightened little Lottie, began to laugh and pointed at the duck and shrieked: "Look, Kezia, look."

"Watch it!" shouted Pat. He put down the body and it began to waddle—with only a long spurt of blood where the head had been; it began to pad away without a sound towards the steep bank that led to the stream . . . That was the crowning wonder.

"Do you see that? Do you see that?" yelled Pip. He ran among the little girls tugging at their pinafores.

"It's like a little engine. It's like a funny little railway engine," squealed Isabel.

But Kezia suddenly rushed at Pat and flung her arms round his legs and butted her head as hard as she could against his knees.

"Put head back! Put head back!" she screamed.

When he stooped to move her she would not let go or take her head away. She held on as hard as she could and sobbed: "Head back! Head back!" until it sounded like a loud strange hiccup.

"It's stopped. It's tumbled over. It's dead," said Pip.

Pat dragged Kezia up into his arms. Her sun-bonnet had fallen back, but she would not let him look at her face. No, she pressed her face into a bone in his shoulder and clasped her arms round his neck.

The children stopped screaming as suddenly as they had begun. They stood round the dead duck. Rags was not frightened of the head any more. He knelt down and stroked it now.

"I don't think the head is quite dead yet," he said. "Do you think it would keep alive if I gave it something to drink?"

But Pip got very cross: "Bah! You baby." He whistled to Snooker and went off.

When Isabel went up to Lottie, Lottie snatched away.

"What are you always touching me for, Isabel?"

"There now," said Pat to Kezia. "There's the grand little girl."

She put up her hands and touched his ears. She felt something. Slowly she raised her quivering face and looked. Pat wore little round gold ear-rings. She never knew that men wore ear-rings. She was very much surprised.

"Do they come on and off?" she asked huskily.

X

Up in the house, in the warm tidy kitchen, Alice, the servant girl, was getting the afternoon tea. She was "dressed." She had on a black stuff dress that smelt under the arms, a white apron like a large sheet of paper, and a lace bow pinned on to her hair with two jetty pins. Also her comfortable carpet slippers were changed for a pair of black leather ones that pinched her corn on her little toe something dreadful . . .

It was warm in the kitchen. A blow-fly buzzed, a fan of whity steam came out of the kettle, and the lid kept up a rattling jig as the water bubbled. The clock ticked in the warm air, slow and deliberate, like the click of an old woman's knitting needle, and sometimes—for no reason at all, for there wasn't any breeze—the blind swung out and back, tapping the window.

Alice was making water-cress sandwiches. She had a lump of butter on the table, a barracouta loaf, and the cresses tumbled in a white cloth.

But propped against the butter dish there was a dirty, greasy little book, half unstitched, with curled edges, and while she mashed the butter she read:

"To dream of black-beetles drawing a hearse is bad. Signifies death of one you hold near or dear, either father, husband, brother, son, or intended. If beetles crawl backwards as you watch them it means death from fire or from great height such as flight of stairs, scaffolding, etc.

"Spiders. To dream of spiders creeping over you is good. Signifies large sum of money in near future. Should party be in family way an easy confinement may be expected. But care should be taken in sixth month to avoid eating of probable present of shellfish . . ."

How many thousand birds I see.

Oh, life. There was Miss Beryl. Alice dropped the knife and slipped the *Dream Book* under the butter dish. But she hadn't time to hide it quite, for Beryl ran into the kitchen and up to the table, and the first thing her eye lighted on were those greasy edges. Alice saw Miss Beryl's meaning little smile and the way she raised her eyebrows and screwed up her eyes as though she were not quite sure what that could be. She decided to answer if Miss Beryl should ask her: "Nothing as belongs to you, Miss." But she knew Miss Beryl would not ask her.

Alice was a mild creature in reality, but she had the most marvellous retorts ready for questions that she knew would never be put to her. The composing of them and the turning of them over and over in her mind comforted her just as much as if they'd been expressed. Really, they kept her alive in places where she'd been that chivvied she'd been afraid to go to bed at night with a box of matches on the chair in case she bit the tops off in her sleep, as you might say.

"Oh, Alice," said Miss Beryl. "There's one extra to tea, so heat a plate of yesterday's scones, please. And put on the Victoria sandwich as well as the coffee cake. And don't forget to put little doyleys under the plates—will you? You did yesterday, you know, and the tea looked so ugly and common. And, Alice, don't put that dreadful old pink and green cosy on the afternoon teapot again. That is only, for the mornings. Really, I think it ought to be kept for the kitchen—it's so shabby, and quite smelly. Put on the Japanese one. You quite understand, don't you?"

Miss Beryl had finished.

"That sing aloud from every tree . . ."

she sang as she left the kitchen, very pleased with her firm handling of Alice.

Oh, Alice was wild. She wasn't one to mind being told, but there was something in the way Miss Beryl had of speaking to her that she couldn't stand. Oh, that she couldn't. It made her curl up inside, as you might say, and she fair trembled. But what Alice really hated Miss Beryl for was that she made her feel low. She talked to Alice in a special voice as though she wasn't quite all there; and she never lost her temper with her—never. Even when Alice dropped anything or forgot anything important Miss Beryl seemed to have expected it to happen.

"If you please, Mrs. Burnell," said an imaginary Alice, as she buttered the scones, "I'd rather not take my orders from Miss Beryl. I may be only a common servant girl as doesn't know how to play the guitar, but . . ."

This last thrust pleased her so much that she quite recovered her temper.

"The only thing to do," she heard, as she opened the diningroom door, "is to cut the sleeves out entirely and just have a broad band of black velvet over the shoulders instead . . ."

XI

The white duck did not look as if it had ever had a head when Alice placed it in front of Stanley Burnell that night. It lay, in beautifully basted resignation, on a blue dish—its legs tied together with a piece of string and a wreath of little balls of stuffing round it.

It was hard to say which of the two, Alice or the duck, looked the better basted; they were both such a rich colour and they both had the same air of gloss and strain. But Alice was fiery red and the duck a Spanish mahogany.

Burnell ran his eye along the edge of the carving knife. He prided himself very much upon his carving, upon making a first-class job of it. He hated seeing a woman carve; they were always too slow and they never seemed to care what the meat looked like afterwards. Now he did; he took a real pride in cutting delicate shaves of cold beef, little wads of mutton, just the right thickness, and in dividing a chicken or a duck with nice precision . . .

"Is this the first of the home products?" he asked, knowing perfectly well that it was.

"Yes, the butcher did not come. We have found out that he only calls twice a week."

But there was no need to apologise. It was a superb bird. It wasn't meat at all, but a kind of very superior jelly "My father would say," said Burnell, "this must have been one of those birds whose mother played to it in infancy upon the German flute. And the sweet strains of the dulcet instrument acted with such effect upon the infant mind . . . Have some more, Beryl? You and I are the only ones in this house with a real feeling for food. I'm perfectly willing to state, in a court of law, if necessary, that I love good food."

Tea was served in the drawing-room, and Beryl, who for some reason had been very charming to Stanley ever since he came home, suggested a game of crib. They sat at a little table near one of the open windows. Mrs. Fairfield disappeared, and Linda lay in a rocking-chair, her arms above her head, rocking to and fro.

"You don't want the light—do you, Linda?" said Beryl. She moved the tall lamp so that she sat under its soft light.

How remote they looked, those two, from where Linda sat and rocked. The green table, the polished cards, Stanley's big hands and Beryl's tiny ones, all seemed to be part of one mysterious movement. Stanley himself, big and solid, in his dark suit, took his ease, and Beryl tossed her bright head and pouted. Round her throat she wore an unfamiliar velvet ribbon. It changed her, somehow—altered the shape of her face—but it was charming, Linda decided. The room smelled of lilies; there were two big jars of arums in the fire-place.

"Fifteen two—fifteen four—and a pair is six and a run of three is nine," said Stanley, so deliberately, he might have been counting sheep.

"I've nothing but two pairs," said Beryl, exaggerating her woe because she knew how he loved winning.

The cribbage pegs were like two little people going up the road together, turning round the sharp corner, and coming down the road again. They were pursuing each other. They did not so much want to get ahead as to keep near enough to talk—to keep near, perhaps that was all.

But no, there was always one who was impatient and hopped away as the other came up, and would not listen. Perhaps the white peg was frightened of the red one, or perhaps he was cruel and would not give the red one a chance to speak . . .

In the front of her dress Beryl wore a bunch of pansies, and once when the little pegs were side by side, she bent over and the pansies dropped out and covered them.

"What a shame," said she, picking up the pansies. "Just as they had a chance to fly into each other's arms."

"Farewell, my girl," laughed Stanley, and away the red peg hopped.

The drawing-room was long and narrow with glass doors that gave on to the veranda. It had a cream paper with a pattern of gilt roses, and the furniture, which had belonged to old Mrs. Fairfield, was dark and plain. A little piano stood against the wall with yellow pleated silk let into the carved front. Above it hung an oil painting by Beryl of a large cluster of surprised-looking clematis. Each flower was the size of a small saucer, with a centre like an astonished eye fringed in black. But the room was not finished yet. Stanley had set his heart on a Chesterfield and two decent chairs. Linda liked it best as it was . . .

Two big moths flew in through the window and round and round the circle of lamplight.

"Fly away before it is too late. Fly out again."

Round and round they flew; they seemed to bring the

silence and the moonlight in with them on their silent wings . . .

"I've two kings," said Stanley. "Any good?"

"Quite good," said Beryl.

Linda stopped rocking and got up. Stanley looked across. "Anything the matter, darling?"

"No, nothing I'm going to find mother."

She went out of the room and standing at the foot of the stairs she called, but her mother's voice answered her from the veranda.

The moon that Lottie and Kezia had seen from the storeman's wagon was full, and the house, the garden, the old woman and Linda—all were bathed in dazzling light.

"I have been looking at the aloe," said Mrs. Fairfield. "I believe it is going to flower this year. Look at the top there. Are those buds, or is it only an effect of light?"

As they stood on the steps, the high grassy bank on which the aloe rested rose up like a wave, and the aloe seemed to ride upon it like a ship with the oars lifted. Bright moonlight hung upon the lifted oars like water, and on the green wave glittered the dew.

"Do you feel it, too," said Linda, and she spoke to her mother with the special voice that women use at night to each other as though they spoke in their sleep or from some hollow cave—"Don't you feel that it is coming towards us?"

She dreamed that she was caught up out of the cold water into the ship with the lifted oars and the budding mast. Now the oars fell striking quickly, quickly. They rowed far away over the top of the garden trees, the paddocks and the dark bush beyond. Ah, she heard herself cry: "Faster! Faster!" to those who were rowing.

How much more real this dream was than that they

should go back to the house where the sleeping children lay and where Stanley and Beryl played cribbage.

"I believe those are buds," said she. "Let us go down into the garden, mother. I like that aloe. I like it more than anything here. And I am sure I shall remember it long after I've forgotten all the other things."

She put her hand on her mother's arm and they walked down the steps, round the island and on to the main drive that led to the front gates.

Looking at it from below she could see the long sharp thorns that edged the aloe leaves, and at the sight of them her heart grew hard . . . She particularly liked the long sharp thorns . . . Nobody would dare to come near the ship or to follow after.

"Not even my Newfoundland dog," thought she, "that I'm so fond of in the daytime."

For she really was fond of him; she loved and admired and respected him tremendously. Oh, better than anyone else in the world. She knew him through and through. He was the soul of truth and decency, and for all his practical experience he was awfully simple, easily pleased and easily hurt . . .

If only he wouldn't jump at her so, and bark so loudly, and watch her with such eager, loving eyes. He was too strong for her; she had always hated things that rush at her, from a child. There were times when he was frightening—really frightening. When she just had not screamed at the top of her voice: "You are killing me." And at those times she had longed to say the most coarse, hateful things . . .

"You know I'm very delicate. You know as well as I do that my heart is affected, and the doctor has told you I may die any moment. I have had three great lumps of children already . . ."

Yes, yes, it was true. Linda snatched her hand from mother's arm. For all her love and respect and admiration she hated him. And how tender he always was after times like those, how submissive, how thoughtful. He would do anything for her; he longed to serve her . . . Linda heard herself saying in a weak voice:

"Stanley, would you light a candle?"

And she heard his joyful voice answer: "Of course I will, my darling." And he leapt out of bed as though he were going to leap at the moon for her.

It had never been so plain to her as it was at this moment. There were all her feelings for him, sharp and defined, one as true as the other. And there was this other, this hatred, just as real as the rest. She could have done her feelings up in little packets and given them to Stanley. She longed to hand him that last one, for a surprise. She could see his eyes as he opened that . . .

She hugged her folded arms and began to laugh silently. How absurd life was—it was laughable, simply laughable. And why this mania of hers to keep alive at all? For it really was a mania, she thought, mocking and laughing.

"What am I guarding myself for so preciously? I shall go on having children and Stanley will go on making money and the children and the gardens will grow bigger and bigger, with whole fleets of aloes in them for me to choose from."

She had been walking with her head bent, looking at nothing. Now she looked up and about her. They were standing by the red and white camellia trees. Beautiful were the rich dark leaves spangled with light and the round flowers that perch among them like red and white birds. Linda pulled a piece of verbena and crumpled it, and held her hands to her mother.

"Delicious," said the old woman. "Are you cold, child? Are you trembling? Yes, your hands are cold. We had better go back to the house."

"What have you been thinking about?" said Linda. "Tell me."

"I haven't really been thinking of anything. I wondered as we passed the orchard what the fruit trees were like and whether we should be able to make much jam this autumn. There are splendid healthy currant bushes in the vegetable garden. I noticed them to-day. I should like to see those pantry shelves thoroughly well stocked with our own jam . . ."

XII

"MY DARLING NAN,

Don't think me a piggy wig because I haven't written before. I haven't had a moment, dear, and even now I feel so exhausted that I can hardly hold a pen.

Well, the dreadful deed is done. We have actually left the giddy whirl of town, and I can't see how we shall ever go back again, for my brother-in-law has bought this house 'lock, stock and barrel,' to use his own words.

In a way, of course, it is an awful relief, for he has been threatening to take a place in the country ever since I've lived with them—and I must say the house and garden are awfully nice—a million times better than that awful cubby-hole in town.

But buried, my dear. Buried isn't the word.

We have got neighbours, but they are only farmers— big louts of boys who seem to be milking all day, and two dreadful females with rabbit teeth who brought us some scones when we were moving and said they would be pleased to help. But my sister who lives a mile away doesn't know a soul here, so I am sure we never shall. It's pretty certain nobody will ever come out from town to see us, because though there is a bus it's an awful old rattling thing with black leather sides that any decent person would rather die than ride in for six miles.

Such is life. It's a sad ending for poor little B. I'll get to be a most awful frump in a year or two and come and see you in a mackintosh and a sailor hat tied on with a white china silk motor veil. So pretty.

Stanley says that now we are settled—for after the most awful week of my life we really are settled—he is going to bring out a couple of men from the club on Saturday afternoons for tennis. In fact, two are promised as a great treat to-day. But, my dear, if you could see Stanley's men from the club . . . rather fattish, the type who look frightfully indecent without waistcoats—always with toes that turn in rather—so conspicuous when you are walking about a court in white shoes. And they are pulling up their trousers every minute—don't you know—and whacking at imaginary things with their rackets.

I used to play with them at the club last summer, and I am sure you will know the type when I tell you that after I'd been there about three times they all called me Miss Beryl. It's a weary world. Of course mother simply loves the place, but then I suppose when I am mother's age I shall be content to sit in the sun and shell peas into a basin. But I'm not—not—not.

What Linda thinks about the whole affair, per usual, I haven't the slightest idea. Mysterious as ever . . .

My dear, you know that white satin dress of mine. I have taken the sleeves out entirely, put bands of black velvet across the shoulders and two big red poppies off my dear sister's *chapeau*. It is a great success, though when I shall wear it I do not know."

Beryl sat writing this letter at a little table in her room. In a way, of course, it was all perfectly true, but in another way it was all the greatest rubbish and she didn't believe a word of it. No, that wasn't true. She felt all those things, but she didn't really feel them like that.

It was her other self who had written that letter. It not only bored, it rather disgusted her real self.

"Flippant and silly," said her real self. Yet she knew that she'd send it and she'd always write that kind of twaddle to Nan Pym. In fact, it was a very mild example of the kind of letter she generally wrote.

Beryl leaned her elbows on the table and read it through again. The voice of the letter seemed to come up to her from the page. It was faint already, like a voice heard over the telephone, high, gushing, with something bitter in the sound. Oh, she detested it to-day.

"You've always got so much animation," said Nan Pym. "That's why men are so keen on you." And she had added, rather mournfully, for men were not at all keen on Nan, who was a solid kind of girl, with fat hips and a high colour—"I can't understand how you can keep it up. But it is your nature, I suppose."

What rot. What nonsense. It wasn't her nature at all. Good heavens, if she had ever been her real self with Nan Pym, Nannie would have jumped out of the window with surprise . . . My dear, you know that white satin of mine . . . Beryl slammed the letter-case to.

She jumped up and half unconsciously, half consciously she drifted over to the looking-glass.

There stood a slim girl in white—a white serge skirt,

a white silk blouse, and a leather belt drawn in very tightly at her tiny waist.

Her face was heart-shaped, wide at the brows and with a pointed chin—but not too pointed. Her eyes, her eyes were perhaps her best feature; they were such a strange uncommon colour—greeny blue with little gold points in them.

She had fine black eyebrows and long lashes—so long, that when they lay on her cheeks you positively caught the light in them, someone or other had told her.

Her mouth was rather large. Too large? No, not really. Her underlip protruded a little; she had a way of sucking it in that somebody else had told her was awfully fascinating.

Her nose was her least satisfactory feature. Not that it was really ugly. But it was not half as fine as Linda's. Linda really had a perfect little nose. Hers spread rather—not badly. And in all probability she exaggerated the spreadiness of it just because it was her nose, and she was so awfully critical of herself. She pinched it with a thumb and first finger and made a little face . . .

Lovely, lovely hair. And such a mass of it. It had the colour of fresh fallen leaves, brown and red with a glint of yellow. When she did it in a long plait she felt it on her backbone like a long snake. She loved to feel the weight of it dragging her head back, and she loved to feel it loose, covering her bare arms. "Yes, my dear, there is no doubt about it, you really are a lovely little thing."

At the words her bosom lifted; she took a long breath of delight, half closing her eyes.

But even as she looked the smile faded from her lips and eyes. Oh, God, there she was, back again, playing the same old game. False—false as ever. False as when she'd written to Nan Pym. False even when she was alone with herself, now.

What had that creature in the glass to do with her, and why was she staring? She dropped down to one side of her bed and buried her face in her arms.

"Oh," she cried, "I am so miserable—so frightfully miserable. I know that I'm silly and spiteful and vain; I'm always acting a part. I'm never my real self for a moment." And plainly, plainly, she saw her false self running up and down the stairs, laughing a special trilling laugh if they had visitors, standing under the lamp if a man came to dinner, so that he should see the light on her hair, pouting and pretending to be a little girl when she was asked to play the guitar. Why? She even kept it up for Stanley's benefit. Only last night when he was reading the paper her false self had stood beside him and leaned against his shoulder on purpose. Hadn't she put her hand over his, pointing out something so that he should see how white her hand was beside his brown one.

How despicable! Despicable! Her heart was cold with rage. "It's marvellous how you keep it up," said she to the false self. But then it was only because she was so miserable—so miserable. If she had been happy and leading her own life, her false life would cease to be. She saw the real Beryl—a shadow . . . a shadow. Faint and unsubstantial she shone. What was there of her except the radiance? And for what tiny moments she was really she. Beryl could almost remember every one of them. At those times she had felt: "Life is rich and mysterious and good, and I am rich and mysterious and good, too." Shall I ever be that Beryl for ever? Shall I? How can I? And was there ever a time when I did not have a false self? . . . But just as she had got that far she heard the sound of little steps running along the passage; the door handle rattled. Kezia came in.

"Aunt Beryl, mother says will you please come down? Father is home with a man and lunch is ready."

Botheration! How she had crumpled her skirt, kneeling in that idiotic way.

"Very well, Kezia." She went over to the dressing-table and powdered her nose.

Kezia crossed too, and unscrewed a little pot of cream and sniffed it. Under her arm she carried a very dirty calico cat.

When Aunt Beryl ran out of the room she sat the cat up on the dressing-table and stuck the top of the cream jar over its ear.

"Now look at yourself," said she sternly.

The calico cat was so overcome by the sight that it toppled over backwards and bumped and bumped on to the floor. And the top of the cream jar flew through the air and rolled like a penny in a round on the linoleum— and did not break.

But for Kezia it had broken the moment it flew through the air, and she picked it up, hot all over, and put it back on the dressing-table.

Then she tiptoed away, far too quickly and airily . . .

MACMILLAN COLLECTOR'S LIBRARY

Own the world's great works of literature in one beautiful collectible library

Designed and curated to appeal to book lovers everywhere, Macmillan Collector's Library editions are small enough to travel with you and striking enough to take pride of place on your bookshelf. These much-loved literary classics also make the perfect gift.

Beautifully produced with gilt edges, a ribbon marker, bespoke illustrated cover and real cloth binding, every Macmillan Collector's Library hardback adheres to the same high production values.

Discover something new or cherish your favourite stories with this elegant collection.

Macmillan Collector's Library: own, collect, and treasure